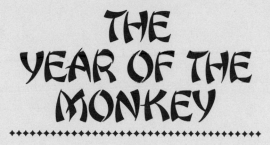

THE
YEAR OF THE
MONKEY

THE YEAR OF THE MONKEY

♦♦

A BONNIE INDERMILL MYSTERY

CAROLE BERRY

ST. MARTIN'S PRESS • NEW YORK

Grateful acknowledgment is made for permission to reprint from *Farewell, My Lovely* by Raymond Chandler. Copyright © 1940 by Raymond Chandler. Reprinted by permission of Alfred A. Knopf Inc.

Design by Glen M. Edelstein

Library of Congress Cataloging-in-Publication Data

Berry, Carole.
    The year of the monkey.

    I. Title.
PS3552.E743Y43   1988   813'.54   88-1866
ISBN 0-312-01850-9

First Edition

10 9 8 7 6 5 4 3 2 1

To Ben and Alan

The Interview
◆◆◆◆◆◆◆◆◆◆◆◆◆◆◆◆◆

The manager of personnel, Creative Financial Ventures, had a happy face. His chipmunk cheeks were dimpled. His several hundred teeth were straight and pearly white, made for a smile. Cheerful brown curls circled his forehead.

All the same, when he looked down and again scrutinized my resume, where the typo in my birthdate announced that I was nine years old and screamed that I'd written the thing the night before and never proofed it, I thought I detected a passing grimace. His jolly eyes shifted slightly, to follow the trail of coffee I'd spilled across his desk, over its side, down his pants leg, and into his shoe.

I began gathering my briefcase and purse, straightening my jacket, and preparing to stand.

He looked up, smile back in place. "So, Miss Indermill, how soon can you start?"

I should have known then that it wasn't going to be much of a job. There was no way I could have known it was going to last a whopping nine weeks.

It was their ad in the Sunday *Times* that attracted me.

Are you a motivated self-starter with a head for details? Are you trapped in a dead-end job? Become part of the technical revolution. Join our hands-on training program. You'll soon be part of the fastest-growing sales-leaseback organization on Wall Street. If you are selected, you will receive a competitive salary during training. . . .

Those vague, open-ended qualifiers were what did it: motivated self-starter, head for details. None of that nonsense about three years' experience. The competitive salary bit had me a little worried. A loose translation is usually something like, "You can compete with the best of them, in Bulgaria." To my surprise I was offered almost enough money to get by on in New York City, which is saying something.

When you really get down to it, though, what I especially liked was the fact that I was offered the job. When you've been unemployed for six months and your resume, even without typos, is mostly a bad work of fiction, and the man you'd intended as your principal reference isn't in prison only because a team of psychiatrists found him unfit to stand trial for murder, you can't be too fussy.

After my interview, as I waited by the lavish reception area for an elevator, I read the list of names engraved in brass on the company's mahogany door:

Offshore Tax Operatives
Grand Bahamas Group, Ltd.
Lesser Antilles Associates
Curaçao Capital Corp.
Hong Kong Holdings

Under this impressive lineup, a workman was busy attaching some new letters:

Leasing Enterprises

If you looked closely, you could just make out the outline of glue where those same letters had been attached once before. In the world of tax shelters, it's easy come, easy go.

PART 1

◆◆◆◆◆◆◆◆◆◆◆◆

The
Career Path

CHAPTER 1

◆◆◆◆◆◆◆◆◆◆◆◆◆◆

I started on December 7. Pearl Harbor Day.

On that first morning a well-dressed secretary led me through inch-thick carpets past walls hung with modern lithographs to the training center. She asked if I wouldn't like coffee or tea. How did I want my coffee? And maybe a bagel? It looked as if I'd found my way to employee heaven.

The training center was decorated with dark green carpet and upholstery. Light poured through a wall of windows with a spectacular twenty-fifth-floor view of downtown Manhattan and the River, so that the atmosphere was simultaneously hushed and exhilarating. If the Wall Street location Creative Financial's ad promised was an exaggeration—the office occupied the two top floors of a newish building just south of Chinatown, near City Hall—the canyons of Wall Street were an easy walk away. It all looked good to me.

On the inside wall of the training room hung a series of big maps, military-looking things with colorful pushpins in them. At the far end of the room there was a projector and some sound equipment. A blackboard on an easel was set up at the front, and above it was a movie screen that could be raised and lowered. Roomy, wood-grained workstations with computer terminals on them were placed in two semicircles farther back in the room. From the looks of it, no expense had been spared.

There were two other junior people starting C.F.'s eight-week probationary training program with me. One, a short young woman in a gray suit and black bow-tie, gave me a firm handshake. Her name was Helen Pilgrim, and she was one of those people who look exactly like their names. The other trainee was a slender, good-looking Chinese fellow who appeared to be about thirty, Edwin Fong.

"Fast Eddie, they call me."

He looked at my outstretched hand as if I had something nasty in it. "Lay five on me," he said, extending his own superfly version of a handshake. I grabbed for his curved fingers.

"All *right*," complete with a hipster drawl, followed. I gritted my teeth, waiting for the "outta sight" that sure enough came next.

"That looks like a nice setup." He nodded toward the audiovisual equipment. "Let's take a look." He was at the back of the room before I knew it. "Come on, you guys."

"I don't think they'd appreciate that," Helen said. She sat down at one of the workstations, pulled a notepad and pencil from her briefcase, and began writing. Eddie was already leaning over one of the big machines, wide-eyed as a five-year-old in a toy store.

I almost followed him, but stopped myself. Too often in the past, when faced with the choice of hanging back with the angels, like Helen, or rushing ahead with the devils, like Eddie, I'd gone with the devils. This time things were going to be different. I sat down at the workstation next to Helen and swung my chair to face hers.

"Have you worked with computers before?"

"Of course," she said, not looking up from her tablet.

I waited for her to go on, but after a second, when I saw

that Helen wasn't interested in idle chatter, I started looking through the brochure the personnel department had given me.

"Welcome Aboard!" it began enthusiastically. "Here at Creative Financial Ventures, our employees come first." The pamphlet went on about up-to-the-minute working conditions and the generous benefits package, and ended with "Remember, your job satisfaction is our goal."

Job satisfaction? I reread that sentence. For me, job satisfaction has always been one of those amorphous concepts, like faith healing and reincarnation. I'll believe it when I see it.

Behind me there was a muffled click as the door from the hallway opened, a soft whoosh as it closed quietly.

Think slick, and you'll know what the man who walked into the training room looked like. Pointed charcoal-colored shoes, razor-creased pants, a gold belt buckle as big as my fist, a shirt with swirls woven into the fabric, an ad-agency mustache and black hair so shiny you could almost see your reflection in it. He flashed me a great big smirking smile, nodded briefly at Helen, who had pulled herself to attention the minute he showed up, then smiled back at me. I was prepared to like anything and everything about this job. I smiled back.

"I thought there were three of you." Then he glanced toward the rear of the room. "Excuse me," he called to Eddie. "Are you ready to begin?"

Eddie was back in an instant. "That's some system, man." He slid into a chair.

"My name is Perry Dumont, AVP, TP."

My two classmates nodded knowingly. I didn't like starting out as the dumb one, but I hated starting out in the dark about what this man did. When I asked, he explained that he was assistant vice president, technical planning.

"I'll begin by telling you something about Creative Financial. The firm was started six years ago by three principals, one with experience in corporate tax planning, one with a marketing background, and a third with extensive computer know-how.

"What C.F. does is structure diversified tax-advantaged investment vehicles for business and private entities. For example, we are a licensed broker for investments in offshore tax havens that enjoy treaties with the U.S." He nodded toward the wall of maps. "In that capacity we set up and maintain accounts for our clients, wiring deposits as they desire.

"You three, however, won't be concerned with those accounts. Since you will all be working in our newly revitalized leasing department, I will concentrate there. Are any of you familiar with the leaseback concept?"

"I've taken several courses on the subject," Helen said.

Fast Eddie did her one better. Only he wasn't Fast Eddie anymore. He was Edwin. Without so much as a trace of slang he explained that he'd learned about sales-leaseback while earning his MBA from Columbia. He also said that his last job had been with a small manufacturing company that was on the other end of a sales-leaseback operation. Dumont looked suitably impressed.

"Very good. And how about you, Bonnie?"

My first day of training and I was already behind. I had a vague idea what he was talking about only because after I'd gotten the job, I had gone to the library and tried reading an article about it. I say "tried" because the subject had been boring in the extreme and I hadn't been able to get through it.

"Well," I said, "there are a couple points I'm not too clear on. Maybe if you could just touch on it?"

Thankfully he didn't ask me which points I needed clarified. Instead he walked to the blackboard in the corner and began drawing a diagram on it, talking as he did.

"Actually our leasing program revolves around a simple idea. Corporations have long maintained two sets of books, one for reporting profits to shareholders and one for reporting to the IRS."

"Legally?" I regretted my outburst instantly. Eddie grinned and Helen looked at me as if I were a half-wit.

"Naturally," Dumont said. "On capital equipment they take straight-line depreciations when they report to their shareholders, while for IRS purposes, they take accelerated depreciation. Obviously the differences between these two figures are often substantial.

Eddie chuckled. Helen nodded seriously.

"Oh, right," I said, as if this had simply slipped my mind.

"Now, under the new tax law, alternative minimum tax—or AMT—rules call for a twenty percent tax on half the difference between the figures in those two sets of books."

Dumont went on to explain how, by leasing equipment rather than buying it, a company could close the gap between those two figures for tax-paying purposes. For my purposes, he might as well have been speaking Greek, but I figured it would sink in, sooner or later.

He told us that a year before, the new tax rules had all but closed down C.F.'s leaseback operation, until a sharp-eyed tax lawyer discovered the AMT loophole. "Now," he assured us, "leasing is going to take off again."

"Creative Financial functions as a leasing brokerage. By leasing to our clients industrial and office equipment, which we purchase at their request, they gain tax savings, and we gain income."

Again the nods from Helen and Eddie. Who was I to argue? I nodded.

"All three of you passed our math test with flying colors, but am I correct that none of you have had extensive experience on the computer?"

"Actually, I had two years on the VAX-11. I've studied Cobol and Basic, know 'C' . . ." Edwin again, off and running. ". . . did a summer internship with Chase Bank, and . . ."

Helen slumped back in her chair, muttering "hot shot" under her breath.

When Eddie finally finished, Perry turned to Helen. She told him her bachelor's degree was a double major, finance and computer science.

"Interesting," he said.

Then, once again, it was my turn. I already had a nagging feeling that I was in way over my head, but I wasn't about to look like the dummy for the third time in ten minutes. I gave him a variation of what I'd put on my resume.

"In my last position I was responsible for the changeover from manual to computerized accounts payable and receivable, and also for upgrading secretarial equipment from electric typewriters to personal computers, and for implementing a training program for that equipment."

That wasn't quite true, but it wasn't an out-and-out lie either. The thing is, if I'd lasted long enough at my last job—for that matter, if my last employer had lasted long enough—it might have come true. It hadn't, but since my ex-employer, a law firm, had dissolved its partnership, it wasn't likely I was going to be found out. My immediate problem was, was I going to be able to do this job? My confidence was shrinking by the second.

Perry had been happy with the other two; he was thrilled with me.

"Well, Bonnie, that is fascinating. I've always said that you can't beat hands-on experience. Not that theory isn't important, but there's nothing quite like getting in there with your hands." While he spoke, he rubbed his hands together and leered. It wasn't my imagination. "Hands on" took on new meaning when Dumont said it to me. Thankfully he was wearing a big gaudy wedding band.

We spent what was left of the morning becoming acquainted with our terminals, to use Dumont's words. There was a whole new language here, of "booting the system" and "storing and retrieving files." With me asking questions every other minute, our progress was snaillike. Eventually Helen started making a muffled grunt every time I opened my mouth. I ignored her. Eddie, on my other side, was impossible to ignore.

He seemed to be stuck in a phase that teenage boys go through, when every tabletop is a bongo drum, when a pencil is something to tap with, when feet, and for that matter, the entire body, cannot remain still for more than fifteen seconds. In one hand he tossed his rabbit's-foot key chain, with the other he beat on the tabletop. He was either a slow maturer or a nervous wreck.

By the time Dumont announced that we should break for lunch, I was tired of Helen's scowls and Eddie's fidgeting and would have been happy going off alone for a slice of pizza, but at happy, congenial Creative Financial, perish the thought anyone should eat alone.

The employee cafeteria was a noisy, bustling affair, occupying part of the top floor. C.F.'s logo, "Eyes on Your Financial Security," with its socketless eyeball careening through space, was painted over the doorway, as well as stamped on the dishes, flatware, and napkins.

The executive section of the cafeteria on a platform by the picture windows was separated from the area where the rest of us ate by a row of live, exotic plants. Otherwise the executives stood in the same lines we stood in and ate the same food we ate.

We all went through the hot-lunch line. Eddie and I were first and got to a table ahead of the others. I wasn't even in my chair before he leaned across his tray and said, in a low voice, "You don't know what you're doing, do you?"

"What?"

"With the financial stuff, and the computer. I've got ten bucks that say you don't know a tax shelter from a bus shelter."

Was it that obvious? I collapsed into the seat. "Of course I do."

"Don't sweat it," he whispered. "There's nothing but a bunch of scams going on here. The whole operation will probably be busted by the IRS before our eight-week probation is over."

That announcement must have made me look as if I were going into shock. Eddie's grin faded and his eyes widened.

"Relax, Bonnie. I'm kidding you."

When Helen and Dumont joined us a second later, I was still on edge. Eddie had caught on to me so easily. I waited nervously for him to say something to the others, but when a few minutes passed without any more of his pronouncements, I pushed my fears to the back of my mind and started eating.

For cafeteria food my pot roast wasn't bad. There was something disconcerting about that eyeball staring up from my plate, but the price was certainly right. I was trying to arrange my mashed potatoes over the eyeball when Eddie looked past my shoulder and smiled.

"Man, that guy's a long way from the mother ship. Space cadet!"

Perry, who was next to me, turned around at the same time I did.

The man we were staring at was probably in his early fifties. He was tall and slender and wore an impeccable pinstripe navy suit. All the components were there for a distinguished look, but for some reason they didn't come together. The man's feet shuffled and he swayed as he maneuvered the tables, holding his tray. He had a kind of glassy-eyed, unhealthy look about him. In the happy, healthy C.F. crowd he stood out like a very sore thumb.

"That's Ashley Gartner, your chief executive officer," Perry said.

Helen gave Eddie a pious look. For her, making a nasty crack about a CEO was probably the equivalent of a seminarian slandering the pope.

Ashley Gartner had two companions. Both of them were worthy of comment. One of them was another man, which was about all he had in common with Gartner. He was short, balding, and bug-eyed. His trousers were tugged up over his little potbelly, so that they ended at about his ankles and made him look like Tenniel's drawings of Lewis Carroll's Tweedledee and Tweedledum. In his movement, too, he was nothing like Gartner. His steps were quick and determined, his bulging eyes looked as if they didn't miss a trick.

10

It was his other luncheon partner, though, who held my attention. She obviously had Eddie's. "Wow," he said. "Dragon Lady lives."

She was reed-slender, with a heart-shaped face and shiny black hair that fell straight past her shoulders to the middle of her back. Her suit was a gorgeous tweed, her shoes looked like a couple hundred dollars' worth. She was absolutely stunning.

"Mr. Gartner's companions are Amanda Paradise, his administrative assistant, and Morton 'Can Do' Fike, director of marketing. Mr. Fike, like Mr. Gartner, is one of C.F.'s owners."

"'Can Do'?" I repeated.

"Mr. Fike is known as a very aggressive manager," Perry explained.

I don't think Eddie had even noticed Fike. "Paradise," he said slowly, as if he was testing the word. "I'll just bet she is. Miss Paradise can assist me anytime she wants."

"I wouldn't count on that," said Perry. "You three will be assigned a secretary, but it won't be Miss Paradise. Her time is occupied with . . . administrative duties."

My first run-in with my new CEO occurred as we were leaving the cafeteria. Unfortunately, run-in just about sums up what happened.

I had carried my tray to the cleanup line and put it on a conveyor belt to be carried to the kitchen. To leave the cafeteria from there it was necessary to walk up a short ramp with rails on either side. My companions were ahead of me. I was halfway up the ramp when Mr. Gartner approached from the upper level of the cafeteria, balancing his tray precariously. In fact he was balancing himself pretty precariously. He came down the ramp fast, more stumbling than walking. He was swaying drunkenly, his tray waving in front of him, a glass perched on its edge.

Someone once told me that only about eight percent of the things we worry about actually happen. I can assure you this is not true. Almost everything I worry about happens. Even when Mr. Gartner was still a good six feet away from me, I knew we were going to collide.

I scooted as close to the railing as I could get, but he staggered on as if drawn by a magnet. At the last possible moment he looked at me with those glazed eyes, then looked to the side. Here was his chance to turn and avoid me, but he lurched and stumbled forward, jamming his tray into my stomach and forcing me back into the railing. I had this fleeting, terrible vision of the two of us crashing through the railing and falling onto the floor below, him on top, his trash-laden tray sandwiched between us. Then a hand reached out from behind him, grabbing his arm and stopping his progress before the worst happened. So that I only had to contend with the next worst. Before his tray clattered to the floor between us, it tipped up, onto me.

"Jesus," he said, looking at the lumps of cottage cheese and splattering of cantaloupe juice across the front of my new suit. A napkin materialized from somewhere, and the Paradise woman helped me scrape off the worst of it while my CEO kept repeating "Jesus" in this out-of-it voice.

Looking back on it now, I'm sure that no more than ten seconds passed between first lurch and cleanup, and that only the people seated closest to the cafeteria entrance, and those on the ramp behind me, saw what had happened, but right then I felt like the entire company had just watched their chief executive officer overturn his lunch on me.

"Oh, what a mess," Amanda Paradise said, eyes narrowing as she studied my damp lapel. The fact that she looked perfect, even up close, made me feel even messier than I was.

Morton Fike, who had grabbed Gartner at the last minute, stepped around the CEO. "You'll give us the cleaning bill, of course."

"Jesus." That was the CEO again.

"It's not that bad, really," I said. It wasn't. They were

12

making things worse. I shoved past the three of them and hurried to the top of the ramp on shaky knees. Dumont, Eddie, and Helen were waiting for me.

"Do you think if I dumped something down my front, she'd help me scrape it off?" Eddie joked.

Perry ushered Eddie and Helen back into the training room, then took me aside. He leaned toward me, focusing his watery gray eyes on about the third button of my silk blouse. "I'm so sorry that happened, Bonnie. Mr. Gartner has been under a lot of pressure lately. If you'd like to go home and change, I'll be glad to take you. My car's right downstairs in the garage."

Why was everyone making such a big deal out of this? "No," I said. "It's perfectly all right." And it was. The wet spot had dried, leaving only a faint stain and an occasional whiff of cantaloupe to remind me of my first meeting with my new CEO.

"If you're sure," Dumont said. "Otherwise . . ." He left his sentence dangling. I walked back into the room, determined to get on with my training. When Dumont returned to his spot in front of the class, his wedding band had disappeared from his hand. He was too gross to be believed. Not too gross to be ignored, though.

You see, I had made a decision before starting my new job. I was going to build a respectable, responsible, and lucrative career for myself at C.F., and I was going to ignore anything that threatened to sidetrack that career. There was going to be a new Bonnie Indermill, and she was going to live by the following commandments:

I will not gossip about, or with, my coworkers.
I will not drink with my coworkers.
I will not call in sick.
I will not be late.
I will not sneak out early.
I will never sleep with a coworker.
If a coworker should die mysteriously—which had been the

13

beginning of the end at my previous job—I will not become involved.

Was I ever kidding myself!

CHAPTER 2
◆◆◆◆◆◆◆◆◆◆◆◆◆◆◆

I suppose Perry Dumont deserves some credit. Oily as he was, and he was plenty oily, he wasn't a bad teacher. By the end of the first week I was reasonably comfortable moving around in the simpler programs, making notations about our clients' leases and payments. When I took a moment to think about it, I knew I hadn't learned much. I understood the basics of leasing, and how some of C.F.'s other tax shelters worked, but that was about it. Still, I was feeling pretty confident. My two classmates weren't worried that we were working without job descriptions. Why should I be?

While I'm on the subject of my classmates, what a pair! At one end of the spectrum there was Helen, a ferocious drudge. At twenty-three, she was eager to grind her way up the corporate ladder. She wrote down Perry's every word. Every chart he drew on the blackboard was painstakingly copied into her lined tablet. During lunch, while Eddie and I and anyone else who happened to join us were happily chatting, Helen would spread her notes over the table and make an annoyed face and groan if anyone interrupted her studies. God knows, she probably read her notes over in bed at night. She was that type.

Eddie was something else again. He took no notes. Half the time he didn't appear to be listening. He'd lean back, eyes half-closed, flipping that rabbit's-foot key chain, fingers beating to a soundless drummer. Then he would come out with such complex questions and thoughtful comments that it seemed he could easily have taught the class. At first this had me baffled. What was Eddie doing in a low-level training job like mine? As the week progressed, though, and I saw more of Eddie, I began to understand what his problem was.

Eddie gambled compulsively, mainly on the horses. Scarcely a lunch hour went by that he didn't run to the Off-Track Betting windows across the street. Every break included phone calls to bookies: "Can you get me a line on that one, Louie?" "Hey, Joe, who have you got in the fifth?" What his gambling had to do with his low-level job I didn't know, but I had a feeling the two were related.

The only hint I got that he was bothered by this was the day I saw him tip a bottle in a brown paper bag to his mouth and take a drink. Helen saw it too.

"Is that what I think it is, Eddie?" she said, huffy as anything.

"I don't know, Helen. What do you think it is?"

"Liquor. That's disgusting!"

"Wrong, Helen." Eddie pulled a blue bottle from the bag. "It's vitamin M. Maalox. The only disgusting thing here is your tiny little mind."

Needless to say, these two loathed each other. At first I tried being neutral, but after a few days, well, it was a new job and I was lonesome there. Eddie was just so much more likable than Helen. Not to mention so much more helpful. And I needed all the help I could get.

Late Friday afternoon, after Dumont had pronounced the three of us a "brilliant class," which, in my case, was stretching the truth, he set out to show us to our workstations. We walked down the plush corridors that were beginning to seem like home to me, toward an area of the building where a construction crew was working.

"You three are lucky," Dumont said. "Everything you're going to be working with is brand-new. New desks, new terminals. And of course you're doubly lucky because my office is at one end of our area, and here, at the other end . . ." He paused in front of a closed door and knocked.

A female voice with a truck-driver pitch answered, "Open!"

"This is Charlotte Smoot." Dumont ushered us through the door. "Charlotte is one of our three principals, as well as our technical manager. There is nothing about C.F. that she doesn't know."

The woman behind the desk had straight, earlobe-length mouse-brown hair, a round face devoid of makeup other than a smear of brownish lipstick, and broad shoulders encased in a man-tailored gray suit. Her blue oxford-cloth shirt was buttoned to the throat, and a navy bow tie was firmly in place under a jaw that looked as if it knew how to assert itself.

Almost subconsciously my hand flew to my collar. That morning I'd had so much trouble getting my tie into a presentable bow that I'd finally ditched it. Now I was the only person in that room without one. I felt underdressed, uncorporate.

"Welcome aboard," Charlotte Smoot said, sounding like the C.F. pamphlet. She carefully placed a small figurine she had been handling back into a colorful gift-wrapped box. Rising, she stepped from behind her desk.

The nicest word for Charlotte Smoot's appearance is "imposing." She appeared to be in her early thirties, but she was an "old" early thirties. She was tall and large-boned and, with a good haircut and well-cut clothes, could have looked both businesslike and feminine. But at our first meeting "feminine" was not the look Charlotte was aiming for.

As she walked around her desk, hand stretched toward me, all I could think was, "She looks just like a man." She didn't, really. There was a formidable bosom straining at the buttoned suit jacket, and considerable hips were tugging on the straight gray skirt. The legs above the low-heeled black pumps were muscular, but not masculine.

"I'm pleased to have you with us."

I took her extended hand. No nonsense there either. One firm shake and she moved on to Helen. Charlotte Smoot must have looked like the gold at the end of the rainbow to Helen. She gushed something fawning about the importance of a technical manager and all but genuflected. Her comment, however, might as well have been directed at that little statue on Charlotte's desk. Charlotte had already moved on to Eddie.

It turned out that they had met before.

"And Edwin." She gripped his one hand in her two. "I didn't expect to see you until Monday. I hope Perry has been treating you right."

"Perry's been great."

"That's good to hear. I'm glad you were able to start so soon, and in time for our Christmas party. Did Perry tell you about it?"

"He mentioned it."

Mentioned it? Perry had spent most of one of our afternoons in training talking about it. It sounded like a real bash.

"I hope you plan to attend," Charlotte said. "The company goes all out. This year it's at a disco. The Grapevine."

This was very peculiar. She was still holding Eddie's hand. She hadn't taken her eyes off him.

"In that case I can't wait."

"Oh," Charlotte added suddenly. "You are someone who will appreciate this. Look! I just got her. An early Christmas gift." Finally releasing Eddie's hand, she lifted the figure from the box. As she held it toward him, I noticed the card tucked among the wrinkled wrapping paper. "In appreciation of your continued efforts. H.W." Such a formal note for such a nice present. It had to be from a client.

The figure was of a crowned Oriental woman seated cross-legged on a pedestal. She was carved of wood and wore loose

17

robes lacquered in green and gold and a gold crown. In her left hand she held a red lotus blossom.

"She's Padmapani, the goddess. Ming dynasty. I have a few pieces. This one is from the Tibetan Buddhist tradition, of course."

"Right," Eddie said, with a halfhearted nod at the goddess. A second later he tugged his collar. I had figured Eddie as somebody who was impervious to embarrassment, but his tan coloring was reddening under Charlotte's special attentions.

Charlotte ran a blunted finger down the statue's side. Her expression grew dreamy. "Isn't she delicate? And mysterious? Just look at that expression. I'm so fond of the Oriental sensibility."

"Have you been to the Orient?" Helen asked, eager to break in on this duet.

"No. Here." She held the statue out to Eddie. "Hold her. You can almost feel the centuries ticking by."

Eddie hesitated. From what I had seen, there was nothing delicate or mysterious about his sensibilities. Finally he took the statue in one hand and kind of hefted it up. It was very small, no more than seven or eight inches. "Yeah! Real nice."

"I knew you'd appreciate her." Charlotte reached out her hand to retrieve the statue.

If I'd known Eddie better, what happened next wouldn't have surprised me, but this was early in our friendship. He held the statue toward Charlotte. Her fingers were almost around it. And somewhere in that split second between the time that he let go and she grasped, the statue dropped like a stone between them.

"Oh!" A simultaneous, collective gasp came from everyone in the office.

Then, with the quick, confident moves of a natural athlete, Eddie scooped up the statue with his other hand before it hit the floor.

"Ah!" That was our simultaneous sigh of relief.

Smiling wickedly, he handed the goddess back to Charlotte.

Looking back on the episode now, that brief moment when Eddie first played a little rough with Charlotte Smoot's emotions may have marked the awakening of a part of Charlotte that had long been denied. The flirtatious part.

Sure, the incident smacked of immaturity. It was the kind of faking-out seventh-grade boys do to seventh-grade girls in the school yard, on a slightly less sophisticated level than spinning rubber, and about as attractive to most adults. But Eddie's childish macho display did something to Charlotte. Perhaps her heart beat a little faster. Maybe he was the only man who had ever paid her that, or any, kind of attention.

As she took the statue back, her fingers lingered on his for an extra second. Her lips parted slightly, and when she next spoke, her voice was whispery.

"If you have any problems at all, feel free to knock on my door, anytime." Though her quick glance at me and Helen assured us she meant all of us, her eyes came back to rest on Eddie.

"Absolutely," Helen barked.

We were on the way out of her office when Charlotte said, "Oh, Perry. Would you mind stopping back in here when you're though there? There's something I've got to go over with you." The pitch of her voice was a little bit stronger now. Dumont left us with no fanfare at our cubicles to rush back to Charlotte's office.

"Where did you meet Miss Smoot?" Helen asked Eddie the second Perry was out of sight.

"She interviewed me. She got a look at my resume and she was so impressed she decided she should talk to me."

Helen sniffed. "I'll bet she's not impressed anymore, after what you just did."

"Bull! She ate it up." Turning purposely away from Helen, he began looking over our workstations.

Like the rest of our area, the cubicles were in the process of being completed; the carpeting, a deep, plush turquoise, was in, as were the built-in walnut-grained computer desks. However, the walls hadn't been papered and we had mismatched chairs to sit in.

Our areas were surprisingly roomy, about eight by ten, with four-foot walls around three sides of them. Two of them faced the windows; the third, which backed up to these, was on the corridor.

Helen immediately glommed on to one of the window cubicles, spreading her mountains of paper all over it. Eddie rushed for the other window nook. After he claimed it, he gave me a brief, guilty glance. I was determined that I was going to be above this type of crap.

"That's all right," I said. "I have a top-floor corner apartment with a river view. After a while it gets so boring." With a show of disdain I took the inner cubicle. The key was still in the center drawer of my new desk, and next to me there was to two-drawer file cabinet with a key.

I began distributing my few belongings through my many empty drawers. When I had finished that, I flipped on my terminal and logged into the payment-schedule program. It felt terrific. Not that I had anything to do in the program, but I felt so professional. In retrospect it all seems ridiculous, but that Friday afternoon I thought I was finally, at thirty-six years of age, slipping into my perfect professional niche. It made me feel warm all over.

"Anybody for Thunder Road tonight?"

I looked up from my monitor into an Alpine lakeful of blue eyes. My new job was looking better by the second.

"What's Thunder Road," Eddie asked.

"A bar on Broadway. Some of us go there on Friday nights."

"Count me in," said Eddie.

"I can't," Helen said, a voice from behind a wall. "I have some work I have to finish."

"And how about you?" The stranger smiled at me. He had a slight accent, sort of Northern European. He was tall, with longish blond hair. He looked like an advertisement for a ski-Europe poster.

I flipped off my screen. "Just let me get my coat." As I walked out of the office, I called good-night to Helen. She didn't look up. Her eyes were glued to her monitor screen.

Thunder Road was well named. It occupied the bottom floor of a small, run-down building on a heavily traveled section of Broadway over the BMT subway line. Between the trucks rumbling by outside the bar, and the trains roaring underneath it, it sounded, and occasionally felt, as if we were sitting in the middle of an earthquake. To make matters worse, every now and then someone would jack up the jukebox to full blast, so that the patrons literally had to shout to be heard.

My blue-eyed friend was Derek Thorensen. He was from Denmark and had been working part-time in C.F.'s graphics department for about three years. Or as he put it, he *was* C.F.'s graphics department.

"What do you do the rest of the time?"

"I'm a starving artist."

I might have known. Every since puberty I've been attracted to marginally respectable men. At sixteen it was the Marlon Brando types with motorcycles and bad reputations. Twenty years later, show me a good accountant in a three-piece pin-striped suit and a bad playwright in patched jeans, and I'll go with the playwright every time.

Derek shoved his way through the crowd to the bar and emerged seconds later with a couple mugs of beer. I started to hand him some money. He shook his head.

"This week I'm rich; next time we'll see."

That "next time" was encouraging. My new job seemed to offer everything. Unfortunately, before we even found a place to sit, the gorgeous Amanda Paradise walked into the bar with Perry Dumont.

"Oh, Derek! I'm glad you're here," she said. "I've just got to talk to you." He glanced at me over his shoulder as she commandeered him. Then the two of them grabbed stools at the far end of the bar and put their heads together. Amanda didn't look like Derek's type, nor he hers, but they sure had a lot to say to each other.

Eddie, Dumont, and I joined some other C.F. employees at a big round table. Dumont was right next to me, but it

21

wasn't as bad as it could have been. Between the raucous gossip and joking going on at the table, the intermittent rumblings of the building, and blasts from the jukebox, his few attempts to engage me in private conversation fell, literally, on deaf ears.

A little later, after Amanda had gone, Derek came over and joined us. It was a doubly lucky moment for me. Someone had pulled the plug on the jukebox, and Dumont had just left the table. Derek slid into his chair.

"She always wants to talk about colors, that Amanda. So, Bonnie, are you enjoying your new job?"

"I love it."

Derek blinked, surprised by my enthusiasm. The funny thing was, I meant it. I had a pleasant, even plush place to work, it appeared that I was going to be able to handle anything I was given to do, and even the worst of my coworkers were more bearable than most of the people I'd worked with at my last job. "And," I added, smiling at him, "it doesn't seem like I'm going to be overworked, either."

Here he laughed. "No. Nobody at C.F. is going to be overworked." At that point several other people at the table joined our conversation. "Right," said a ponytailed woman. "Once I finish the *Times* crossword puzzle, I hardly know what to do with the rest of my day." Someone from accounting, a fellow in a plaid shirt, laughed in agreement. "I'm thinking of trying to get some free-lance tax returns to do at the office."

"Well, maybe your department's slow right now. They just hired us," I said, nodding toward Eddie, "and another junior person. They must know there's going to be work. After all, they are the fastest-growing company of their type."

"Where did you hear that?" Derek asked.

"It was in their ad."

"Ah! Their ad. Then it has to be true." He smiled at me. "I'm sorry, Bonnie. But let me ask you one question: If they're the fastest growing, why were there four senior peo-

22

ple and two junior in your area two years ago, where today there is one senior"—he nodded at Dumont, who, having returned to find his seat taken had wandered back to the bar—"and three junior?"

"Maybe it's good business," I replied defensively. "Most of the work isn't terribly complex, and management must have decided to cut their expenses, particularly when it looked as if leasing wasn't going to be a viable shelter."

From across the table Eddie laughed. "She bought it all. Every word of our orientation."

"Cut their losses is more like it," someone else said.

Some part of me wanted to close my ears to anything that threatened to unravel the job-satisfaction cocoon I'd spun. It wasn't easy, though, to ignore a lot of the things I heard around the table that evening. The most alarming rumor, for me, was the one about a potential merger with a major bank, and a concurrent reorganization.

A merger and reorganization, in themselves, didn't bother me. What did was the idea of company upheaval. Things like that are always hardest on new, untrained employees. When the belt-tightening starts, we're the ones who go.

"It's all talk. Been in the works forever," the fellow with · the plaid shirt said.

"But I hear Gartner's pushing for it now." That was the girl with the ponytail. "He wants to take it easier, but he doesn't want Fike in command. I hear he and Fike hate each other. Hey, Derek! Didn't you draw up the reorganization chart? How did it look to you?"

Derek shrugged. "Basically unworkable."

"Why is that?" I asked.

He thought for a second. "My guess is that with the personalities and egos involved, and what Gartner proposes for some of them, he'd have a small war on his hands. But I've already said too much."

The talk drifted to Mr. Gartner himself. He had founded the company, with immediate success, but was now considered on his way out. "A star whose light is fading" was

23

somebody's comment. There was a mishmash of rumors involving his health, drugs, and alcohol. I didn't say anything about the collision I'd had with him on my first day. Not that I don't enjoy gossip as much as anyone, but when someone's already being crucified, it seems unsporting to put in extra nails.

The rumors about Mr. Gartner and the company were nothing compared to the ones about Amanda Paradise. For a few minutes the table was rife with speculation about what Amanda did to earn the money for the expensive clothes she wore.

"On her back," a plain-looking man said.

"You'll never know," someone else joked.

The consensus was that Amanda, though rather stupid, knew her way around the bureaucratic maze. She was unpopular in the extreme, and when Eddie repeated his name for her, Dragon Lady, it instantly caught on.

The wildest bit of gossip by far came from the girl with the ponytail. "Did any of you hear that Gartner had accused Amanda of trying to poison him?"

"I heard she supplied him with uppers," a girl with freckles said.

"I've heard that too," ponytail said. "But this was something else. He thought she slipped something into his coffee."

"You're kidding? When was this?" I asked.

"Last week. Somebody at the copy machine outside her office heard him accuse her—"

"Wait a minute," Derek said, holding out his hand. "This is too much! I'm sure if Amanda intended to poison her boss, which she does not, she could come up with something more subtle than pouring kerosene into his coffee."

"I don't know," the ponytailed girl said. "She's pretty dumb."

"I rather like her," Derek said. "I find her—"

"Wholesome," the girl with freckles interjected sarcastically. A laugh went around the table.

Derek shook his head. "I was going to say pleasant. Uncomplicated and fun."

"Say, speaking of fun," the plaid-shirted fellow said, "is everyone going to the Christmas party?"

A burst of excited yes's answered that.

From what I heard for the next few minutes it sounded wild. I wouldn't have missed it for anything.

"You're going to go?" Derek asked me.

I nodded. "Yes. I love to dance. How about you?"

He hesitated. "I'm not sure. I was planning on getting an early start the next morning. There's a ski cabin in Vermont I might take a share in. But maybe a later start wouldn't be so bad."

It was a few minutes before eight and the crowd had begun to thin when Derek, who had been lost in his own thoughts for a while, leaned toward me.

"Which way are you walking, Bonnie?"

He was truly physically appealing. Those deep blue eyes seemed to have a permanent boyish smile in them, and his square chin had a dimple right in its center. The old Bonnie, the one I had been until starting this job, would have smiled warmly and said, "To the subway, I guess," and left the next move to him. The new career-woman Bonnie wasn't going to let loose her feminine wiles quite so readily.

"I'm getting a taxi."

"Don't you live uptown?" Dumont asked. He went on without waiting for my answer. "I'm going that way. We can share a cab."

Derek stood up. "In that case I'll say good-night."

A minute later as I watched him leave, I could have kicked myself. Particularly since that left the smirking Dumont holding my coat, and me in a quandary. I didn't want to encourage Dumont, but I didn't want to insult him either. He was my boss.

It was Eddie who saved me. He must have noticed my pained expression.

25

"Bonnie, I thought you wanted to have dinner at that place in Chinatown I was telling you about."

"Oh, that's right." I grabbed my coat from Perry, thanked him profusely for his offer, and followed Eddie out the door. I wasn't looking forward to the subway home, but almost anything was better than grappling with Perry in the back of a cab.

"Thanks," I said.

"Anytime. Perry's really hot for you, isn't he?"

"Just my luck."

Eddie grinned. "Too bad about the Viking."

"Like I said, just my luck."

"Don't sweat it, Bonnie. I can tell by the way he looks at you he'll be back. And if he's not, well, you know how it is with those big blond Wasp types."

"Tell you the truth, I can't remember. How is it?"

"Strong like bull; dumb like ox."

Eddie and I walked up to Walker Street and turned right, heading east. He had told me that he shared an apartment with an aunt and uncle and their children somewhere on the western fringe of Chinatown not far from the office, so I thought I was taking him out of his way.

"You don't have to walk me to the train," I said. "It's not late."

"I don't mind. I'm sort of . . . em . . . taking alternate routes these days."

"Why?"

"It's good for my health."

"What do you mean?"

He didn't answer. We were soon at the edge of Chinatown. After years of midtown offices I was enthralled by my new work area. The shops were tiny, some of them no more than holes in the wall, with dusty windows displaying a fantastic array of foods, dishes, Chinese magazines. It was twenty minutes removed from the Italian and French boutiques of Madison Avenue, but a world away.

Every few feet I stopped in front of another set of windows. Eddie, a bundle of nervous energy as usual, kept hurrying me along. A window full of brightly painted tea tins in a corner shop stopped me. With the colorful street and Christmas lights blinking around us, the display was a kaleidoscope of color.

"Let's go in here. I'd like to pick up some tea."

Eddie moaned impatiently. "Bonnie, half of these places are nothing but laundries." Standing on his toes, he peered in the shop window. "If this place sells tea, I'm Confucius. Come on. Someday I'll take you to a real tea store."

I hurried to catch up. "What do you mean, 'laundries'?"

"Fronts," he said, "for illegal income."

We were approaching the center of Chinatown when Eddie said out of nowhere, "Shit!"

"What's wrong?"

Again there was no answer. Then he surprised me. "Hey, Bonnie. Let me borrow your muffler."

It was warm for December; the evening was particularly clear, making the Christmas decorations lighting the buildings around us seem out of step with the weather. My coat swung open, my gloves stayed in my pocket. My wool scarf was draped around my neck. Pulling it off, I handed it to Eddie. He turned up his coat collar and wrapped the scarf so high around his head that almost nothing of him was visible.

"You must be coming down with something," I said.

"Yeah. Far down."

As we walked, Eddie kept turning his head and watching in back of us, always keeping most of his face buried in the folds of my scarf. I didn't know what to make of it. Eddie always seemed jittery to me.

"Damn!" he said suddenly under his breath. "Wouldn't you know it."

"What's the matter with you?"

"Don't turn around. I'll explain when we get to the subway."

27

On Canal Street we ran into heavy pedestrian traffic. All along the sidewalk vendors displayed their Christmas merchandise—bright wool scarfs and hats, earmuffs, and glittery glass pins. We were dodging people on our way to the subway when without warning Eddie took my arm and pulled me after him into a small grocery store. The old Chinese man behind the counter looked up expectantly, then almost as quickly looked away. Eddie walked into a corner and peered back out the window into the street.

"What's up?" The words were hardly out of my mouth before a young Chinese man with a leather jacket and a red scarf around his neck pushed the grocery door open and stared into the store. His glance took us both in, then he was gone. An instant later the proprietor stepped out into the aisle, balancing a baseball bat in both hands.

"Get out or I call the police. I know your kind. I don't want trouble in here."

Eddie waved his hand at the man. "Okay, okay, pop. We're going." To me he said, "It's nothing." He took another look out the window. "Oh, hell! Bonnie," he said hurriedly, "how much money do you have on you?"

"I don't know. Forty-some dollars, I guess."

He grimaced. "Wow! You live high, don't you? Let me borrow it."

"What?"

With an exaggerated flourish and a tiny bow he held out his hand. "May I please borrow some money for a little while. Until Monday. Or tomorrow. I'll come up to your place and pay you back."

I opened my wallet under the old man's glare and handed Eddie almost all my cash. Forty-three dollars.

"Monday is all right," I said. "I can get to a cash machine in the morning."

"Thanks, Bonnie. You're a pal. I owe you one."

He drew his coat collar back up to his chin. "Let's move it."

Back on the street he walked quickly, keeping his head

down. Finally we turned the corner at Centre Street, and the subway station lay half a block ahead. I'd soon be rid of my escort, which was fine with me. He was making me as jittery as he was. As we turned into the station, I looked back and saw, once again, the red scarf flapping in the breeze. Only now there were three of them. Three leather-jacketed Chinese men with the same red scarfs flowing around their necks.

By this time Eddie had given up his pretense that everything was okay. A northbound train was pulling into the station. I put my token into the turnstile and pushed through to the platform.

"Bonnie," Eddie yelled from the other side of the turnstile, "give me a token, quick."

I was searching my pockets desperately when our three shadows raced down the stairs. Eddie put one arm on the turnstile and jumped the gate. As the train stopped in front of us, the token clerk came out of his booth and shouted at Eddie. We leapt through the first open door. Looking back, I saw that the three men had followed Eddie over the turnstile and were running for the train. A bell rang twice, signaling that the conductor was closing up. As the door slid shut, one of them stopped it with his arm. The doors shuddered open briefly, and all three pushed into the car.

There were about a dozen other people scattered around the car. Eddie and I sat down in the center, where it was most crowded. One of our pursuers walked past us and stood between us and the door to our right. The two others stood against the door we'd entered. They gave me a perfunctory look and from then on kept their eyes on Eddie.

I studied them furtively. All three were Orientals, dressed in jeans, sneakers, leather jackets, and of course, the scarfs. I had thought they were kids, but was wrong about at least one of them. He was older than his companions—around thirty. He was also the most frightening of the three. A deep scar slashed his face, from under his left eye, across his cheek and into his upper lip. His left eyelid drooped as if it were following the scar's path.

I was in the outer seat. Next to me Eddie stared out the window as the express subway roared north.

"Eddie, who are these guys?" I asked softly from the side of my mouth.

"Associates of mine," he said after a moment. "We frequent the same businessmen's association. Don't worry about it; you're not involved."

It didn't look that way to me. I felt like the proverbial sitting duck.

Longtime subway riders develop a sort of sixth sense about impending trouble. Across from us a black woman suddenly stood, hustled her two children up, and edged them to the far end of the car. A older man moved away in the other direction.

When the train stopped at Thirty-fourth Street, the three men tensed. They must have expected Eddie to make a move because one of the younger ones, a tall, baby-faced hoodlum sporting a Fu Manchu mustache, allowed his leather jacket to fall open. His hand slid up to his waist. There was the softest click, and I saw that he was holding a long, thin knife against his leg. With a sly look at Eddie he ran his thumb down the knife's edge and winced. Goose bumps rose over my entire body. If this went on much longer, I was going to panic and run for it.

At Times Square the train was delayed and the doors remained open. A uniformed transit cop, his jacket hiked up over his holstered gun, stepped briefly into our car and looked around. I started to stand, the word "help" forming on my lips. Eddie threw his arms around my shoulders and muffled my head into his chest. A second later the doors closed and the train started moving. When Eddie let go of me, I looked up to see that the cop had gone. The three thugs had not.

By then I was not only scared. I was furious. I had no intention of running interference for Eddie, whatever his problems were.

"Listen," I said. "I don't know what this is all about, but if you're planning to get out when I do, you're in big trouble. There's not much open this time of night in my neighborhood, and we have to walk past a big empty park on the way to my apartment. Frankly, I don't want your business associates to know where I live. Why don't we get out at Columbus Circle and call a cop?"

I guess that made up his mind for him. Not to call a cop. That wasn't Eddie's style. But as the train approached Columbus Circle, he stood up and pushed past me.

"I've got to have a chat with these guys, Bonnie. I'll see you Monday. Have a nice weekend," he added, a pretty ridiculous statement when you consider the situation he was in.

When the doors opened and Eddie stepped into the big Columbus Circle station, his three shadows were right behind him.

Eddie liked to pretend that life was one big joke, but these guys didn't seem to find it quite so funny. The last thing I saw as the train pulled out heading north was Eddie standing against the stairwell surrounded by his three so-called business associates. One of them had taken hold of my scarf, which was still around Eddie's neck. He was twisting it into a cord.

CHAPTER 3

◆◆◆◆◆◆◆◆◆◆◆◆◆◆

It was the middle of our second week and I was looking forward to several things. Among them were another meeting with Derek Thorensen, the Christmas party, and last but not least, some work. I had yet to figure out what I was supposed to be doing. What I had figured out was that the crew at Thunder Road was right. The crossword puzzle wasn't enough. I'd hit the bookstore the evening before and loaded up on detective novels. Tucking a couple of them into the back of my top drawer, I opened one and propped it more or less out of sight between my lap and the bottom of my desk. The cover, with its blood-splattered corpse and dripping knife, was promising.

"Damned weird," I heard Eddie say from his cubicle.

"What?" Slipping my book into the drawer, I pushed my chair back from my desk and rolled around our partition, ready at that point for anything, weird or not.

He had his eyes glued to his monitor. His fingertips edged nervously over the keyboard.

"Do you remember last week, Dumont said the offshore shelters were maintained separate from our leasing accounts?"

"Yes. Why?"

He looked over at me, then turned back to the monitor and tapped his fingers on his desktop.

"I guess it's nothing," he finally said. "Probably a typo, but take a look at this."

I leaned in close. He was working in a sophisticated financial management program, one of those number-crunching things I was afraid to touch. "W.B. Ent." with an address on the Bowery showed in small letters at the top of the screen. Under it came columns of figures and dates. I followed the bottom line across and saw what he was talking about. Whoever or whatever W.B. Ent. was, it had sent four payments, each of them just under ten thousand dollars, to a joint venture in the Netherlands Antilles a week before.

I shrugged. "It's been placed in the wrong file. That's all."

"Yeah, but that's not what I'm concerned about. It's this." He tapped the screen where the name and the Bowery address showed. "It's in Chinatown, and if I'm not mistaken, it's some offshoot of one of the old tongs. They run bus tours to Atlantic City out of the Bowery office."

"The tongs? I thought they were secret Chinese under-world associations. You mean they run bus tours to Atlantic City?"

"Times have changed, Bonnie. The funny thing is seeing these guys on our client list. The Chinese community generally takes care of itself."

Reaching past Eddie, I pushed the page-up button a few times until I found the first page of the account. The name given there was Ward Broadcasting, a big client that leased a lot of equipment from C.F.

"Ward Broadcasting, Eddie. W.B. Ent. must stand for Ward Broadcasting something—Entertainment or Enterprises. Somebody put their offshore investment figure into their leasing account by mistake."

"What would Ward Broadcasting be doing with an office on the Bowery?"

"Saving money on rent, Eddie. Lots of big companies keep space in low-rent areas."

"I still say it's a tong."

"Right, Eddie. We have secret societies for clients. And half the stores in Chinatown are laundering money. And C.F. is going to be busted by the IRS any day. You see scams everywhere you look."

He shrugged. "You're probably right, but maybe I'll go check it out tonight."

"Don't get beaten up in the process."

"Aw, Bonnie, I told you everything was cool. I owed somebody a few bucks. That's all. It happens all the time."

"Not to me. And speaking of a few bucks. . . ?"

"Tomorrow, for sure. You can count on it."

"I'll bet." I was beginning to realize that counting on Eddie for anything but a quick laugh was a mistake. I had just about given up on my forty-three dollars, and on getting any kind of sensible explanation out of Eddie about Friday's run-in with his business associates. Monday morning he had brushed off my concerns like so much nonsense.

The powers at Creative Financial, however, did not share my opinion of Eddie's reliability. Or at least one of the powers. Charlotte Smoot couldn't look at Eddie without getting this starving-wolf-eyeing-the-woolly-lamb expression on her face.

During the first few days of that week Charlotte's lilting, "Oh, Edwin. I'd like to meet with you a few minutes, when you're free," became a familiar sound. Her trips into his cubicle carrying stacks of paper grew too numerous to count. And—here is the most amazing thing—her appearance began to change. On Monday there was an open top button on the oxford-cloth shirt and a splash of pink lipstick. Tuesday the mouse-brown hair had a curl to it and a reddish glow. Now it was Wednesday. At Charlotte's "Good morning, Edwin" I looked up, wondering what further transformations she had managed the night before.

She was at the coat closet. When Eddie stuck his head around our wall, she slid a massive white fur coat of some kind off her shoulders. Eddie got up right away, stepped to the closet, and took it from her.

"Wow, Charlotte!" He ran his fingers through the fur, then carefully placed it over a hanger. "This is gorgeous."

Gorgeous? It looked as if the woman had skinned a polar bear.

"Just look at you," he drooled. "What an outfit! None of the guys are going to get a thing done today."

Charlotte was, indeed, a distraction. She was wearing a yellow chiffon blouse and paisley black and yellow skirt. The top several buttons of her blouse had been left open, to display several inches of strangely uninteresting cleavage. Her skirt barely cleared her knees. On her feet were spike-heeled, open-toed shoes. Her toenails had been painted crimson to match her new manicure.

"Good morning, Charlotte," Helen barked from her side of the wall.

Charlotte followed Eddie back into his cubicle, tossing an off-handed "Good morning" Helen's way as she passed my cubicle. She had showered in perfume that morning. Opium. It was enough to make you think about throwing a chair through the window.

"Charlotte," Eddie was saying with a quiet voice that gave a personal tone to his words. "The way you look in that outfit is too much for me." He took a deep, audible breath.

Was he ever laying it on thick! Any normal woman would have told him to cut the crap and get his useless fanny to work. Charlotte Smoot, however, was not a normal woman.

"Oh, it's nothing. I've been needing some new clothes. When you're settled, could you possibly spend some time with me?"

"Sure. Hey, Charlotte. You want to make it lunch? I know where to get the best dim sum around."

"Dim sum? Oh! Well . . . Why, yes! Lunch would be lovely. And dim sum. What a wonderful idea. I haven't had dim sum for years."

I took enough of a look from the corner of my eye to catch the flames of red rising from those yellow ruffles. They said more about Eddie's effect on Charlotte than I can. Honestly, the woman's ears even turned pink.

I couldn't see it. Here was this woman who, from all appearances, had a rigid control over her life, getting all fluttery over a guy with very little control over his. A guy from a vastly different racial heritage, at that. Charlotte was doing the kind of out-of-control thing I might have expected from—me!

When she fluttered off, I rolled into Eddie's cubicle. He already looked settled. Too settled to move. He had the morning *Post* opened to the racing section. He had his jacket off, his collar undone, his yellow "power" tie with the little blue dots loosened. His nicely polished wing tips were on the floor. His feet were on the desk.

I nodded toward Charlotte's office. "She thinks you're coming on to her. You better watch it. You're going to end up with a lot more woman than you know what to do with."

He grinned. "Just keeping my options open, Bonnie. A guy never knows what's going to happen in this world." As he spoke, his eyes widened. Half-rising, I followed his stare.

Here came Amanda Paradise, floating down from the executive corridor. That's the only word for it. Floating. Her feet didn't seem to touch the floor. She was wearing a powder-blue suede minidress and had to be worth a thousand dollars on the hoof. A young, olive-skinned man limped behind her, sheaves of cloth samples in his arms.

She stopped at my cubicle, ran her beautifully manicured fingers across a rough seam at its edge, and looked up at me. She had eyes the color of honey, shadowed by a long fringe of black lashes. Her skin was like unblemished porcelain, her teeth a dentist's dream. The woman was disconcertingly beautiful. Even without Mr. Gartner's lunch coating my blouse she made me feel messy.

"Did you notice this bump? The paper isn't going to set properly."

It was my cubicle so she had to be speaking to me. I stood and looked at the offending bump. It was hardly noticeable.

"I'll have it redone over the weekend," she assured me, as if I had complained.

"Oh, good."

"Anyway," she went on, "Mr. Gartner feels it makes the work atmosphere much more comfortable if workers have some input into their surroundings. He's very progressive. So . . ."

"Hector," she called, and the young man, who was well trained, dropped the samples on my desk and limped back until he was out of the way.

"Of course we've chosen shades that go with the carpeting and the paper we've picked, but you can pick from any of these fabrics for your new chair, and then I'll help you find a framed print that complements the entire scheme for the wall behind you."

She had a funny way of speaking, slowly enunciating each syllable as if she were reading a speech in a language she understood phonetically, but was uncomfortable with. That, coupled with what she had just said, made me wonder for a second if she wasn't putting me on. You have to understand, I came from a law firm where you needed three signatures on a requisition to buy paper clips, and here I was being asked to choose fabric for my own chair. I stared right at her. She looked straight back, her expression as uncomplicated as a child's. Looking away, I studied the samples. The fabric was all of the same type, but the colors—muted turquoises, bright ones, a rainbow of turquoise—swam before me.

I made a tentative decision. "The sea foam."

"The sea foam? You like that?"

I shrugged. Maybe the sea foam could only be complemented by a painting of Elvis Presley on black velvet. "What do you think?"

"Oh, I'm supposed to let the individual choose."

To tell you the truth, I didn't much care one way or the other, as long as it was comfortable. "Sea foam," I said decisively.

"Sea foam it is." She wrote something on her sample, then nodded to the waiting Hector. He quickly picked up the samples and followed Amanda to Helen's cubicle. Helen ordered the same color as the carpet. Leave it to her to blend in. I half expected her to ask for gray so her chair would match her endless supply of gray suits.

Then it was Eddie's turn.

"What's happening, man," he said to Hector. Hector mumbled something inaudible, then immediately stepped out of the cubicle. He was clearly in awe of Amanda.

She ignored the exchange between the two men. "These are your possibilities," she said to Eddie.

"Oh, come on. Don't I have any other possibilities?"

I couldn't bear missing the rest of this. I got out of my chair and started fiddling around in the supply cabinet on the wall behind us.

Amanda went on thumbing through the sample pages. I suspect she had been fed so many double entendres by men that they were meaningless to her.

"Don't you have anything in red? It's my lucky color."

"Red? Red wouldn't go."

"Then, you choose."

Eddie could be a real charmer. A strand of black hair fell

appealingly over his forehead. When he smiled, which was most of the time, he had big dimples in his cheeks. This wasn't entirely lost on Amanda. The corners of her mouth twitched. Picking up a lock of her hair, she ran it through her fingers, then she looked at Eddie through narrowed eyes, as if she was really considering him for the first time. "You really want me to do that?"

"I'd appreciate anything you do for me. Deeply and sincerely. You have no idea how appreciative I can be. Hey, you going to the Christmas party?"

It was at that unfortunate moment that Charlotte walked back around to Eddie's cubicle. I'm sure she hadn't noticed Amanda bent low over his desk until it was too late to withdraw. Charlotte would never have pitted herself purposely against someone who looked like Amanda.

"Edwin, is twelve-thirty all right for our dim . . ." Charlotte stopped mid-sentence. She was right beside me, and I caught her little gasp.

"Dim sum? I love dim sum," Amanda said. "That means 'a little bit of love,' you know."

"Yes, I know." Charlotte pulled her shoulders back. "I didn't realize you were busy, Edwin."

"No, no. Amanda is just helping me with colors," Eddie answered. "What do you think, Charlotte?"

Charlotte's steel-eyed glance fell toward the sample book, then rose again, first taking in Amanda's very long legs, and then her very short dress. "I suspect Amanda is much better at choosing colors than I am. I tend to concentrate on making money for C.F. rather than spending it."

This was getting good. By peering around Hector I had a clear view of Amanda's face. This may not have been any Rhodes Scholar whose brain was clicking into gear, but it took Amanda no more than two seconds to pick up on the fact that Charlotte was interested in Eddie. Amanda experienced about the fastest change of heart ever.

"I'd love to help you choose, Eddie." Her smile was the warmest I'd yet seen from her. Stretching past him, she leaned over his desk for the sample book. The skirt inched up her legs. "And of course, I always go to the Christmas party. Do you like to dance?"

"Depends on who I'm dancing with."

Amanda tossed her hair over one shoulder and looked at her competition. "You've never gone, have you, Charlotte?"

"I'll be there this year," the other woman retorted sharply. Softening her voice, she said to Eddie, "Is twelve-thirty all right for lunch?"

"Perfect."

"Fine. Just stop in my office when you're ready."

The second Charlotte was gone, Amanda nudged Hector, made another note for herself, then drifted away down the corridor, eyes alert for any smudges or bumps. Hector limped behind, respectful as a nineteenth-century Chinese wife.

Eddie leaned over the top of my cubicle. "Looks like I'm going to the Christmas party. I've got twenty bucks that says I make it with Dragon Lady."

I laughed out loud. "I've got twenty dollars that says you're going to have a big problem at that Christmas party and it's not going to have anything to do with Amanda."

"Oh, come on. Ten? Five? Don't we have any sports around here?"

Helen stood and glared over the wall. "Can you two keep it down. Some of us are trying to work."

"You're a barrel of laughs, Helen," Eddie shot back. He disappeared behind his half-wall.

I rolled my chair into his bay. "Who is Hector? The harem eunuch?"

"Just about. I met him the other day in the lottery line. He does odd jobs for the CEO. Hector's father is the superintendent in Gartner's building."

"Odd jobs is right," I said. "This is the only place I've ever been where the secretaries have slaves."

"Maybe, but I'll follow Dragon Lady around anywhere."

Eddie looked up from his racing form. "Hey, Bonnie. You look lucky today. Who do you like in the fifth at Aqueduct?"

I shrugged.

"Come on. Be a sport. You call it, I'll bet it. And if I win, you get double your forty-three dollars back." He held the form toward me.

"That would be nice." I looked down the list of names. "Double Happiness," I said. "That sounds good."

Eddie acted as if I'd said something profound. "Oh, man! You're all right! Do you know what Double Happiness is?"

"No. What is it?" I expected to hear some pearl of Buddhist enlightenment. I should have known better.

"Chinese beer. It is good." He made some check marks on his paper then picked up his phone.

"Louie, my man. Fast Eddie here. Can you put one hundred dollars on Double Happiness in the fifth?" A pause, then, "Yeah, yeah. For sure. What kind of guy do you think I am? I've never skipped yet." Another pause. "Thanks, Louie. You're a real pal. I owe you one."

"A hundred dollars, Eddie?" I said after he'd hung up. "I'd rather just have my forty-three dollars out of that."

"Relax, Bonnie. By this afternoon you will have doubled your money. Doesn't eighty-six dollars sound better than forty-three dollars?"

"Sure," I countered. "But forty-three dollars sounds better than nothing."

"Nothing? Nothing? Bonnie, there is no way that this guy"—Eddie cocked both thumbs at his chest—"and his friends are going to end up with nothing. You stick with me, you'll need an armored car to get your money to the bank."

CHAPTER 4

◆◆◆◆◆◆◆◆◆◆◆◆◆◆

The eagerly awaited day of the Christmas party finally arrived, ushered in by falling temperatures, a slate-colored sky, and the threat of snow. Considering that the party was to begin right after work Thursday, I thought my red and white silk jacket dress was perfect. Without the jacket the dress had a scooped neckline and deep-cut armholes and was, in my opinion, smashing. But whether or not the jacket ever came off depended entirely on whether Derek Thorensen was at the party.

That Helen—she was some hot tamale! She got right into the spirit of things with one of those little Heidi outfits: you know, the red felt vest piped with black braid, a white embroidered blouse, and a red pleated skirt.

Eddie gave a wolf whistle when he saw her. "Lookin' good, Helen." A flush of red climbed her cheeks as she disappeared into her cubicle. He grinned over our mutual wall at me.

"Cute," I said, nodding at his red suspenders with red holly leaves.

"Thanks. You look okay yourself. If the Viking can resist you, there's something wrong with him."

"Good-bye, Eddie. I have work to do." I really did, about an hour's worth to fill my seven-hour day.

"Oh," he said. "I thought Helen was doing all our work for us."

41

"You're so childish, Eddie," she piped over her wall. "I thought Chinese parents were too intelligent to raise little morons."

Eddie must have been waiting for that one. "Hey, Helen. Did you two hear what happened when the little moron and the big moron climbed up the hill?"

Silence from Helen's cubicle.

"The big moron fell off but the little moron didn't, because he was a little more on."

I laughed, but I wasn't the one he was trying to get a rise out of. When there wasn't a peep from Helen, he banged on her wall.

"What did your parents raise you to be, Helen? Mother Superior?"

"An adult," she shot back.

Eddie was so quiet for a few seconds I thought Helen had finally gotten to him. I was logging into my terminal screen when he said, "Oh, man, would you check that out!"

Standing, I peeked over my partition. "Oh, no." I sat down again fast. A second later Perry Dumont oozed into my cubicle, raised both his arms to shoulder height, and shook his hips. "Cha-cha-cha," he said, ogling me.

He was wearing shiny black pants, tight to below the knees then flaring at the ankles, a black shirt laced with silver threads, a silver brocade tie, a red crushed-velvet jacket, and—I am not kidding you—pointy black patent loafers with flat red grosgrain bows on them. There was enough oil in his hair to lubricate an Oldsmobile.

The handwriting was on the proverbial wall about C.F.'s Christmas party. These things can bring out the worst in people, and with people whose best isn't so hot to begin with, like Perry, they can be deadly. He had made it obvious, in a variety of revolting ways, that he thought I was pretty hot stuff. I, with my concern for my new job always paramount, had tried to make it clear that I considered him a fine supervisor and a nice office acquaintance. I asked about his wife and children so often that most people would have thought me peculiar. With his kind you can't tell.

"Great threads, Perry," Eddie said. "You've got that *Gentleman's Quarterly* look down pat."

"Thank you, thank you. I like those suspenders. Helen— ah—you could be right out of the Swiss Alps." Then, too soon, his moist gaze dropped to take me in.

"And Bonnie—what's that you're wearing? A suit? To the party?" He leaned closer, perplexed. "Oh, I've got it. You're going to change. Right?"

"No, Perry. I'm afraid this is it."

"That's all right. On you, anything looks good. I hope you plan to save a dance for me." He cha-chaed out of my bay, across the hallway, and into his office, humming as he did an old Brazilian samba tune.

Eddie collapsed into his chair giggling. Then his phone rang and things were back to normal, with him whispering, cursing, hanging up the phone, slamming his drawers open and shut, and slugging at that Maalox bottle, and Helen standing up and glaring at him every half hour or so. I spent my morning with my face buried in one of my paperbacks.

Amanda wandered in a little after lunch, in full-length, neck-to-calf black mink. From the look of her hair she had spent the morning in the beauty parlor. It looked even shinier and straighter than usual. Her makeup was perfection. As she walked past me, I saw she was wearing spiked sandals with rhinestone straps, and glittery nylons. She stopped at the closet and slipped out of her mink, and I couldn't quite believe my eyes. Talk about hot stuff.

Amanda was wearing a drop-dead Oriental-styled red brocade dress. Her alabaster skin glowed over a high mandarin collar. The red brocade clung to her slender figure, except that the skirt was slit thigh-high up one side. I am talking a serious slit. There was enough skin showing on her leg to give her an "X" rating in most offices. When she raised her arms to chain her coat to the rack, the split rose higher still. There was a muffled groan behind me. Eddie, his chin resting on our partition, was about to expire from lust. His eyes followed Amanda all the way down the hall to the executive offices.

By two o'clock the first surreptitious bottles of brandy were being passed around. By four, champagne corks were popping in offices up and down the corridor. Nobody was trying to hide it. Voices were bold, faces flushed.

I hadn't seen Derek all day, but I wasn't concerned about it. The thing is, I love to dance, and I'll dance with almost anyone who's ambulatory. And I'm good at it. I'm not bragging. I do countless things badly, and very few well. I don't swim or ride well, or play tennis or any of those other ball-and-net games. Things like rock climbing or sky diving are out of the question. But I do dance. I was going to enjoy myself no matter who I ended up doing it with.

Eddie, Helen, and I had planned to walk to the Grapevine Club together, but at the last minute my slimy pursuer, Dumont, came up with this nonsense to keep me in the office. He poked his head over my partition—I was beginning to regret my mature impulse and wish I'd fought for a window seat—and asked if I couldn't help him check up on one of my accounts. It was only a few minutes after five, but already the veins in his nose were purple.

"That's all right, Bonnie," Eddie said. "Helen and I don't mind waiting."

"Speak for yourself," Miss Personality snapped from over her wall. "I have to catch the seven-forty for Weehawken, and if we hang around here, I might as well just forget the party."

"It's okay, Eddie," Dumont said. "I'll walk over with Bonnie and we'll meet you two there."

The minute Helen and Eddie were gone, Dumont rolled Eddie's chair into my cubicle.

"What account is it you wanted to see?" I asked.

He stared hard at my throat. "I get it. It's a jacket dress." He winked and raised a tentative hand toward my shoulder. "I'll bet it's silk." He was breathing all over me, and the combination of ruminated champagne, cheap hair oil, and the gallon of after-shave he was wearing was pulverizing. I started getting this awful trapped feeling.

44

"It's polyester," I said. "Now which account did you say?"
I stabbed at the page-down button on my computer and my
accounts rolled past. "If it's the AAA Auto—"

He was no more interested in AAA Auto Leasing than I
was. "Bonnie? What a lovely name. What's it short for?"

"It's not short for anything. You see"—I pointed to my
screen—"their payment didn't get here on time for last
month's accounts—"

"Come on, you can't fool me. It's Bonita, isn't it? It means
'beautiful girl' in *español*." He had leaned even closer, until it
looked as if the only way out of my cubicle was going to be
over the top of it. "Now, don't get the wrong idea," he said,
flipping off my screen. "I want you to know I have tremendous respect for you."

It might have been funny if it hadn't been so disgusting. I
turned away from my darkened monitor and stared at him.
As I did, his hand moved toward his lap. I didn't seriously
believe he'd try anything right there, with half the staff still
milling around, but for a second I had an awful feeling Perry
was planning to show me just how tremendous his respect
was. Then his hand slipped into his pocket and emerged
holding a small flask. As he unscrewed the cap, his increasingly unfocused eyes sought mine.

"Has anyone else ever called you Bonita?"

"Only my matador boyfriends."

That caught him off guard. He tilted back a little and I
saw my chance. Bracing my feet against my bottom drawer,
I shoved as hard as I could and sent his chair rolling into the
wall. When I was able to stand, I shoved past him and out of
the cubicle.

I was down the hall before he untangled himself from the
chairs. I heard his plaintive, "Wait for me, Bonnie. I'll walk
you over," as I dragged my coat from the closet and pulled it
on.

"I'll be right back, Perry," I called over my shoulder.
Yanking my hat over my ears, I took off in the direction
opposite the one I'd come from. There was a back exit off the

floor, the one Eddie and Hector used when they snuck out to place their bets. I'd never taken it, but it would save me from having to pass Dumont again.

An EXIT sign was suspended from the ceiling about three quarters of the way down the hall. The lights in the hall had already been turned off, and the sign's red neon shone like a welcoming beacon. Beyond it were three doors, one on either side and one at the end. In the dim light I couldn't easily read the small brass plates at their sides. I should have stopped to study them, but I was in a hurry to get out of there. I pushed through the door on the end. It opened in, with a muffled sound hardly audible even to me.

"You bastard! I could kill you!" Amanda's voice, low and constricted, preceded a zinger of a slap. It was immediately, hideously obvious that I had opened the extremely private back escape door from our CEO's inner office. For a second I was frozen by what I saw. Amanda the Dragon Lady stood across the room, her back to me. Facing her, but largely concealed from me by his position next to the wall behind a bookcase, was the man who had just been on the receiving end of her palm. His arm shot from behind the bookcase to grab her wrist. There was a soft "Oh!" He had seen me.

Amanda spun toward me, her dark hair swinging magnificently, shielding him like an exotic fan. All of us gasped. I jumped back into the hall, pulled the door shut, and crashed through the one next to it. This time I got it right.

I thundered down a flight of stairs, through another door, and ran for the elevator bank. The lower floor's layout was a little different from the one I worked on, and I found myself tearing around a maze. Many of the lights were already out, and by the time I reached the elevator bank I was totally unhinged. As I waited for the elevator, I tried to convince myself they hadn't seen my face. And it was possible they hadn't, with the hall behind me in darkness and Amanda and the man standing in the office light. God, if only I hadn't been wearing my bright red coat! With the red EXIT sign glowing behind me I probably stood out like a Christmas tree.

I waited an eternity before a light indicated one of the elevators was arriving. As I stepped in front of the door, my other problem came back to me. Perry Dumont! In my panic I'd forgotten all about him. For all I knew, he was on that elevator. When the doors slid open it appeared unoccupied, but when I stepped into it a man who had been standing in the corner by the controls moved toward me. I was so spooked I jumped about a foot.

"Just the woman I was looking for. What are you so nervous about?" Derek was looping his necktie. His overcoat was over his arm.

"It's nothing. I didn't think there was anyone on here, that's all. I thought you didn't work on Thursday," I added.

"I don't. I stopped on my way to the party to see if you had already gone. Dumont said you were going with him. What were you doing down on my floor?"

"I had to drop something off."

"Sometime you should let me show you around the graphics office. It's quite interesting."

"I'm sure."

I hadn't intended to sound curt, but it came out that way. Derek didn't give up easily though. As we stepped off the elevator and walked across the lobby floor, he asked how my job was going.

"It's fine."

"Still fine? You like dealing with numbers like that, all day?"

We pushed through the revolving doors and out into the street. The light snow that had begun around noon was getting heavier. Already several inches had accumulated. Derek looked down at my feet.

"Where are your boots?"

"Upstairs under my desk."

"Let's go back up for them. There's no rush. Your feet are going to be soaked."

I had no intention of going back upstairs with my red coat on. "No, no. I'm fine. And yes, working with numbers is fine."

He shook his head. He must have been finding me pretty dull going by them. "So many things are fine with you. It must be comforting to be so easily pleased."

I almost slipped on the coating of snow. He took my elbow.

"I'm not that easily pleased. It's just that right now, the job suits my career path." I hated the way I sounded, cranky and pious like Helen.

"How could I forget your career path. Your name, Indermill. It's German?"

"Swiss."

"The same root," he said. "*Unter Mühle*. Beneath, or surrounded by, the mill."

"That's me." I smiled at last. "Under the yoke."

We stopped to wait for a WALK light on a corner, and he stared at me. My hair had slipped from under my hat. I could see curls falling over my eyes. The damp weather was doing a job on my careful pageboy.

"Looking at you, I get the feeling that the yoke slips from time to time."

Even though the snow I could see that he was grinning. He was so cute. Inappropriate, but cute. I thought about telling him what I'd just seen, but I couldn't. I hardly knew him, and he and Amanda had looked pretty friendly that evening at Thunder Road. He could even have been the other half of the scene I'd just witnessed. Had he had time to get himself together and get on the same elevator I'd caught?

As we walked into the hotel, I looked carefully at his face, searching for signs of a handprint. The crisp cold of the walk over had turned his complexion ruddy, and I could see nothing.

"Actually," he said, "I hate office parties almost as much as I hate to dance."

"Then why are you here?"

He gave me a look I probably deserved. "Somebody told me it might be a good place to meet women."

*   *   *

"Whoops," Charlotte Smoot shrieked as her hip slammed into the small of my back, knocking me off balance. Catching a glimpse of my dance partner, Mr. Gartner, she raised a coy hand to her lips and hooted hysterically behind it. Her other hand had a firm grip on Eddie's. He, a graceful dancer and about as game as anyone could be, looked desperately unhappy.

Mr. Gartner smiled across the dance floor at them. He stiffened and took a deep breath, then he gripped my back harder. I braced myself for another of the spin-and-dip steps he favored. Seconds later my back was bent, my head dangling inches from the floor.

In my strange upside-down world I saw Amanda float with a man from accounting. She was truly Queen of the Prom. From the number of men who couldn't wait to dance with her, there was no telling what was going on in her love life. My partner, Mr. Gartner, headed my list of possible slap victims. His office, his assistant. It fit. But the longer I danced with him, the harder it was to picture him as any woman's idea of a bastard, much less the recipient of her slap. Sure, he was attractive, in a sort of stuffy way, but there was something about him that was not all right. His thoughts wandered. His sentences were full of non sequiturs. Once again the people around the table at Thunder Road had been right. Ashley Gartner was, indeed, a strange man.

The music quickened and he began tugging me upright. My head was swimming, but not enough to blur the sight of the object of my lust, Derek, cutting in on Amanda's partner.

"What a marvelous partner you are, Bonnie. I could dance with you all night." As Ashley Gartner spoke I strained to look past him. Sure enough, Amanda and Derek were dancing together. For a guy who hated to dance, who, in fact, I'd had to drag onto the floor, he was eager enough to dance with the Dragon Lady. Was it my imagination or was he holding her closer than he'd held me? He threw back his head and laughed at something she said, and a wave of jealousy washed over me.

A crash of drums finally announced the end of the record. Couples separated, wiping their brows. The temperature was beginning to rise and with it, I'm afraid, the pulsebeat of the dancers.

"Let's see if we can scare up something to eat," Mr. Gartner said.

That was a good idea. I'd had several drinks but nothing to eat except a couple tiny cheese puffs I'd managed to snatch off a passing tray. I was starting to feel a bit off center.

In an outer room separate from the dance floor, tables of food had been arranged. By now the tables looked as if Attila the Hun's troops had come through. A couple decimated chicken wings and a lone, icy cheese puff. Mr. Gartner smiled benignly. "I suppose we can always have some champagne."

If food was scarce, liquor was abundant. A deadly combination. Two bars had been arranged for C.F.'s people. The one in the ballroom was going great guns; the one here was dead. A bartender with tired eyes filled two glasses for us.

"This stuff never fails to go right to my head, but what the heck. Merry Christmas!" Mr. Gartner held his glass toward me. I raised mine and clicked it against his.

"Merry Christmas!"

"And to a prosperous new year," he added.

"I'll drink to that." I'd taken only a sip when Mr. Gartner lowered his eyebrows thoughtfully, then abruptly thrust his glass toward me.

"Smell this!"

When your CEO commands you to smell, you smell. I sniffed the rim of his glass, then looked at him.

"You don't smell something funny? Gasoline, kerosene?"

Kerosene? The same thing he had accused Amanda of putting in his coffee. Was I about to be accused of trying to poison him, too?

"No. It smells the same as mine." I had seen the waiter

50

pour our drinks from the same bottle. "Let's change glasses," I said, feeling pretty silly.

"No, no. It must be my imagination." Gartner raised his glass to his lips and downed half of it. His face, though not in the same league as Perry's, was growing rosy. Perspiration dotted his brow. Maybe it was alcohol or drugs, as rumors suggested. But why this poison paranoia?

He forgot the problem as quickly as it had arisen. Looking past the door at the dance floor, he nodded. "You don't know how much pleasure it gives me to see Charlotte relaxing."

I turned in time to see Charlotte Smoot gallop Eddie past.

"Charlotte has given C.F. a lot, and when my reorganization goes through, she's going to get the kind of support she needs. At the same time, there are those who . . ." Hesitating, he looked out across the floor. For a moment he seemed to slip into some private space, forgetting I was there. Then he finished his champagne in one swallow, sniffed the glass again, and shook his head.

"But enough of this business talk. This is a party, and I'm talking when I could be dancing with the prettiest girl here."

I half expected Mr. Gartner to leave me standing there and rush off after Amanda, but he led me back onto the floor.

The music was slower now, a ballad.

"You are a fine dancer, Bonnie. Have you taken lessons?"

I hadn't told anyone at C.F. that for years I'd tried to make it as a professional dancer. No one would ever have known it from my resume, that's for sure. But with the drinks and Mr. Gartner's being so friendly, I couldn't help it. I didn't admit that my resume was mostly a fabrication, and I wasn't about to tell him about dancing on the street in San Francisco for spare change, but I did tell him I'd taken some lessons and danced in a few off-Broadway productions.

You never know how employers are going to react to that news. Gartner stopped mid-step and looked at me, clearly happy about what he was seeing.

"But that's splendid! You're just the person I had in mind."

"I am?"

51

We completed a series of intricate turns before he went on. "You see, new research indicates that people with varied backgrounds, such as yours, do exceptionally well in business. An article I've been working on for the C.F. news-letter discusses that very subject. Maybe you'd like to take a look at it before it goes to press? I'd be interested in your opinion."

"I'd love to read it," I said as the music ended.

"If there's time," he added, "we could have a brief inter-view with you in the same issue."

As we walked off the dance floor, Mr. Gartner explained that he was flying to Florida the next morning.

"My wife's already there," he said. "When I get back, though, I'll give you an advance copy of the newsletter."

We wished each other a merry Christmas and Ashley Gartner left me at my table. Helen had been sitting there alone. I smiled at her, but she looked away. That was all right. My evening was going so well that nothing could ruin it. Even if my worst fears about Derek and Amanda were true, even if Eddie never gave me back my forty-three dol-lars, I had it made. The head of my company liked me. I was going to be in the newsletter. Luxuriating in my new-found upward mobility, I watched my fellow employees around me.

Charlotte Smoot was the loudest thing in the ballroom, and I'm not just talking about her intermittent peals of laugh-ter. Brunhild had gone Gidget and Gidget had gone berserk. Charlotte wriggled in a sheath of skin-tight electric-purple spandex. The low bodice exposed even more cleavage than her yellow blouse, and the skirt was positively obscene. Something had been done to her hair. It glowed like neon tubing under the flashing red bulbs on the big Christmas tree in the corner.

God help the poor misguided woman, I thought.

She had managed to hang on to Eddie and between dances held him prisoner in a corner. Morton Fike, the third owner of C.F., was with them. While I watched, Perry Dumont staggered up to their group. He put his arm around Charlotte's shoulder, and it must have distracted her for a second. A second later Eddie used that opportunity to slide between Charlotte and the wall. Charlotte knocked Perry's arm away, but too late. Her eyes followed Eddie as he made his escape. I could read his expression all the way across the floor—relief!

If you ask me, Charlotte was making a real ass of herself. Perhaps behind that buttoned-down businesswoman there had always existed a voluptuary, just waiting for her pin-striped shackles to loosen. In every respect she was a monument to bad taste and poor judgment. I couldn't help wondering what time her drinking had started. I turned to Helen.

"Was Charlotte already here when you and Eddie arrived?"

Helen glared across the table. "Eddie and I didn't arrive together."

That was odd. "I thought you left at the same time." I mentioned it only out of curiosity, but Helen's face twisted into such a little fit you'd have thought I was prying into her deepest secrets.

"Eddie forgot his gloves. He went back for them. I walked over alone. And incidentally, flirting with Mr. Gartner isn't going to get you anywhere. Everyone knows he's on his way out." With that, she compressed her lips into an angry line.

What a nasty little snot! I should have ignored her, but I couldn't resist: "Who have you been dancing with, Helen? Or hasn't anyone asked you?"

She turned away angrily.

I felt suddenly flushed. It was probably a combination of my brief anger and the sight of Derek making his way across the floor toward me.

How can I describe the effect that man had on me? It was one of those nonverbal experiences that make your toes tingle. Merely to say longish blond hair caught in a tiny ponytail, broad shoulders, blue eyes, doesn't half do it. He looked good enough to . . . well, good enough to slip off the jacket to my dress for. I hung it over the back of my chair. The dress wasn't all that low cut, but Helen took one look and drew back as if I'd just bared my breasts to the C.F. staff.

Derek, it turned out, had been trying to find something edible. In one hand he balanced three drinks and in the other a plate containing one chicken wing, a fried zucchini, and a few cold meatballs.

"I bribed a waiter. It's not much, but it's all they've got." He sat down next to me. Helen and I each took a drink, then we turned our backs on each other.

Derek pulled his chair closer. "Did I interrupt something?" His voice was low and his breath tickled my neck. I raised my face and found myself looking right into his eyes. It was an unexpectedly intimate moment for two people who hardly knew each other. I had to force myself to turn back to the floor.

"Not a thing." My heart wasn't in being bitchy. I leaned back so that my shoulder rested against Derek's chest.

My neat hairdo was totally undone by then. Derek slid his fingertip along my neck and under the mass of shoulder-length curls.

"Your hair is nice like this. Loose."

I've never been quite sure what the expression "smiled to herself" means, but I think I did it then. Eddie was wrong; Derek wasn't dumb at all. At least not in this area.

Eddie joined us a second later. He'd not only escaped Charlotte, he'd managed to snag a prize for himself, the beauteous Amanda. They scooted a couple chairs together, and she kind of tucked herself into his side, their backs to the floor.

"Don't you worry," she said in a little-girl voice. "I'll protect you from Big Bad Charlotte."

"You better, because here she comes," Derek said, nodding past them. It was true. Charlotte was weaving across the floor, a determined eye on our table.

I grinned. "Hey, Eddie. Hope you've got your running shoes with you, because you're going to need them."

Everybody laughed but Helen. She jumped up from the table. Her chair teetered and flipped backward onto the floor. "All of you are just . . . disgusting." Her words ended with a little hiccup. She stormed across the floor, passing Charlotte on her way. Eddie and Amanda were right behind her, but they veered off before they crossed Hurricane Charlotte's path. Charlotte stopped dead and stared at Eddie as the music began and he took Amanda in his arms. Then she turned toward the bar.

Eddie and Amanda were worth staring at. They were gorgeous together. That's the only word for it. Him—tall, thin, graceful as a panther; her—leggy and lithe, following him effortlessly, her mandarin-collared dress playing up her quasi-Oriental looks. They were by far the most exotic-looking couple on the floor, and for a moment I was lost in admiring their beauty. Then, in a flash of lucidity, I realized that if Eddie hadn't walked to the party with Helen, he could very well have been the man I'd seen with Amanda in the CEO's office. If he had been, though, she was no longer ready to kill him, and he was one of the fastest workers in history.

Derek draped his arm over my shoulder. It felt good, and I was fast learning that there were few things I could do to ruin my reputation at C.F. With this crowd, excess was impossible.

"Bonnie," Derek said, "I'm bored and I'm starving and I'd love to get out of here. What about you?"

Before I had a chance to answer, he withdrew his arm. "Oh, my! That looks like trouble over there."

He was staring at the bar, and it didn't take long to see that the trouble was with Charlotte. She, too, was mesmerized by Eddie and Amanda, but she wasn't enjoying their joint beauty. She smacked her empty glass down on the bar and picked up a full one. Finishing it in one long swallow, she began making her way across the floor toward the unsuspecting couple, moving like a tank through a field of daisies, knocking anything and anyone out of her path. Her eyes were fixed on one target, Amanda's swaying, shining black hair.

We weren't the only ones who had noticed. Helen and Dumont were staring from over by the Christmas tree. A few feet away, an obviously alarmed Ashley Gartner watched the big woman. Next to him, Morton Fike stared. Neither Dumont nor Gartner struck me as a man of action, and from the way Fike yawned it didn't look like "Can Do" intended to do a thing about the impending brawl on the dance floor. I couldn't imagine how Charlotte's progress was going to be stopped unless someone produced a tranquilizer gun and shot her like they would a charging rhino.

"Somebody's got to do something," Derek said. Jumping from his chair, he darted across the floor, grabbing Charlotte's arm just as it shot out toward Amanda's hair. Half pulling, half pushing, he dragged Charlotte to our table.

". . . hate that useless little witch." Charlotte's words slurred. She glared down at Derek's hands around her wrists. "Leggo. I wanna go home." Her lower lip started to quiver. Another second and she was going to be bawling.

"Bonnie, I'm going to put Charlotte in a cab. I'll be right back." Derek escorted Charlotte from the ballroom.

Through it all Eddie and Amanda remained oblivious to everything but each other. Her hands were around the back of his neck, her serpentine body coiled against his. Both his arms circled her waist. Though I still couldn't imagine this pair as compatible, there have been couples who looked a lot worse.

And one fine example of that—an odd couple—was Helen and Perry Dumont when they finally got on the dance floor. It took a lot of persuasion to get her out there, I'm sure. I saw her lift his flask to her lips a couple times before she risked it. She had one step—left foot down, bend the knees, right foot down, bend the knees. Her shoulders barely moved, her hips and her expression were rigid.

Dumont, as you can imagine, was demented. He dipped, he swirled, he leapt in the air, he dashed across the floor and spun back, his wide-bottomed pants circling his ankles like a bell. His face was red with exertion and shiny with sweat.

It took a long time for Derek to get back. When he did, he was wet and frazzled. "That was a lot of fun. The streets have turned into slush. It took forever to get a cab for her."

"How is Charlotte?"

"She sobered up once she got some air. Maybe we should get going?"

It no longer sounded like a question. I had had enough party by then, too. "All right. Let's go."

A lot of other people had already had the same idea. We ended up at the end of a knot of people in front of the coat check window. Eddie and Amanda were right in front of us, but at first they were so wrapped up in each other they didn't notice. When their turn at the window came, Amanda took me by surprise by turning and saying, right out of the blue:

"Look at that pretty red coat hanging there. Is that yours, Bonnie? Women with your coloring look so good in red." Her scarlet-tipped finger pointed across the counter at my telltale coat, which was one of the few remaining in the coat check.

I knew immediately why Amanda was interested in my red coat. "No," I answered. "I think it's Helen's." That was inspired, as was what I did next. I snapped my fingers. "Oh, Derek, I left my boots under the table. Let's go back and get them." He looked dumbfounded, but I didn't give him a chance to say anything. Taking his hand, I pulled him back to the dance floor.

They were playing a slow, party's-over-type song. Helen and Dumont the greaseball were one of the few couples left. His hair had passed the limits of the wet look. It hung in oily strings over his forehead. His leching hand was around Mother Superior's bottom. She looked as if she could barely stand up. I hoped they stayed away from the coat check until

57

Amanda was out of the building. Then I didn't care what happened to either of them.

"Okay, Bonnie." Derek had leaned up against a wall. "Do you mind telling me what that was all about? You cannot intend to leave without your coat."

I peeked around the doorframe. Amanda and Eddie were just leaving the club. Propping myself up next to Derek, I told him what I'd seen in the private conference room. As I spoke I started giggling. I couldn't help it. The whole situation was ridiculous. I even told him I'd suspected he might be the slap victim.

"Me?" he said, eyes wide. "I have never had the least interest in Amanda. What an idea!" Pretty soon he was laughing with me. Through tearing eyes we watched Perry Dumont lead Helen past us. His arm was around her waist. She was absolutely green.

Once outside, Derek and I found Mr. Gartner trying to flag a cab. There was none in sight. There was nothing in sight but snow. It wasn't sticking to the streets—the temperature was a little high for that—but there was enough of a slushy mess on the sidewalk to soak through the soles of my shoes.

I usually enjoy snow. New York City looks a lot better covered with it. It softens the hard edges of the buildings and mutes harsh traffic sounds. It obscures the trash. Or most of it. Helen and Dumont were all too visible. They were at the curb between two parked cars. He was holding her up as she bent double at the waist and gagged. I'll bet Weehawken was never like this.

A lone yellow cab finally pulled up at the club, its tires splattering the slush. "Do you mind sharing?" Derek asked Mr. Gartner.

"Not at all."

The three of us piled into the backseat.

"Where to?" the cabbie asked.

"I live in Washington Heights, so I guess I'm last," I said.

"Where do you live, Mr. Gartner?" That was Derek.

"Gramercy Park. Just look at this. Soaked!" Pulling out a handkerchief, Mr. Gartner scrubbed at his briefcase.

"We'll drop you first," Derek said. His hand closed over mine. I'm sure Mr. Gartner was unaware of the undercurrents on our side of that dark cab, but by the time we pulled up at his apartment building in the East Twenties, I had a pretty good idea I wouldn't be going to Washington Heights that night.

We said our good-nights and Mr. Gartner got out of the taxi. As we pulled away, I glanced back through the snow-dusted rear window. Mr. Gartner was walking to his steps, a gray figure against the white. Our cab was rounding the corner when I glimpsed a second figure, one with a shambling walk, approaching Mr. Gartner from the street. I was ready to say something when Mr. Gartner paused and put his hand on the stranger's shoulder. A neighbor, I thought. Everything was pretty fuzzy by then, and a second later things were even more fuzzy because Derek had pulled me toward him, and we were the only two people in that soft white world.

CHAPTER 5
◆◆◆◆◆◆◆◆◆◆◆◆◆◆

I am sorry to say that I called in sick the next morning. Not that I made my call from under the quilt on Derek's bed. That I don't regret in the least. It's the way we were found out by a squadron of policemen that I'm sorry about.

The click of a phone's dial woke me. When I opened my

eyes, light from the wall of arched windows in Derek's apartment temporarily blinded me. Derek was already speaking to one of the receptionists at work.

"Not very well," he said, his voice unnaturally low. "Put me down for a sick day." He saw that I was awake and winked at me. "Bronchitis," he said. "Can hardly talk. Thank you. I'm sure I'll be fine by Monday." He cradled the receiver and pushed the phone over to me.

I looked past his arm at the digital clock beside his bed. It was eight forty-five. If I dressed, caught a cab home, changed, and hurried back downtown, I could be at work by eleven, a respectable time for a postparty morning. That was, if I could find anything to wear. I'd have to press a blouse, and . . . Oh, I'd have to do something about my hair! It was sticking out in every direction.

Closing my eyes, I tried to will a rush of energy over my still-tired body, will my blood to pump faster, those deadened nerves to tingle to life. Nothing.

"Who should I call?"

"Try Dumont."

Perry's phone rang about ten times before the twenty-fifth-floor receptionist picked it up and mumbled a sleepy, "Creative Financial."

"Good morning. This is Bonnie Indermill. Could I speak to Perry Dumont please."

"He's not coming in," she said. "He threw his back out last night."

"Oh. Have you seen Eddie Fong around?"

"He won't be in either. He has the flu. So does Amanda Paradise. Helen Pilgrim is here. Do you want to speak to her?"

Helen! What a drudge! Throwing up in the gutter in the middle of the night with the biggest lecher in the office, and she makes it to work early the next day.

"No, thanks. How about Derek Thorensen? Is he in?" I thought I was really being cute there.

"Let me check with the receptionist on twenty-four." She

was back a second later. "Derek called in a few minutes ago. Bronchitis."

"Poor guy," I said, grinning at him. "You're going to have to add me to your sick list." Then it was time to pick my disease. Did I want to share one with someone, or did I want one of my own. Derek's arm was around my waist and he was whispering something in my ear. "Intestinal virus," I said quickly. That one was always good. We made the customary noises over the phone before we hung up.

"How would you feel about a Danish for breakfast?" Derek repeated.

That, and a long nap, took care of the next couple hours. We finally got up around eleven-thirty.

What an apartment Derek had! Not an apartment actually, but a tremendous loft. The night before, what with one thing and another, I hadn't gotten much of a look at it. It covered the entire top floor of an old five-floor warehouse on Beach Street in Tribeca. In the back, a space about twenty by forty and with a ceiling of skylights was sectioned off by waist-high shelving into a studio. One corner of the remaining area contained a big kitchen, and in another was a bathroom you could have held a dance in. The rest of the place was an area easily the size of a tennis court, broken up only by floor-to-ceiling columns.

A few pieces of modern furniture, the kind you see in design magazines, defined the rooms—living room, dining room, and bedroom. On the floor was a colorful collection of thick Scandinavian rugs. The walls were hung with modern paintings. As Derek prepared breakfast I wandered around, increasingly fascinated by what I saw. Against a windowless side wall was a big canvas of strong blacks, whites, and reds that reminded me of something I'd seen in the Museum of Modern Art. I bent close to a small painting, a somehow familiar sea of vivid rectangles, and was stunned to see Mark Rothko's signature.

"You like modern art?" Derek asked as he set two steaming coffee mugs on the smoked-glass dining table.

I couldn't help staring at him for a second. In his faded, paint-splattered cords he looked as if he didn't belong in his own apartment. There had to be a healthy trust fund supporting all this.

"You have quite a collection." I sat down across from him. "I'm impressed."

"Yes, it is something, isn't it." He had put a carton of yogurt and a basket of fruit on the table. Picking a pear from the basket, he sliced it expertly and divided it into our bowls. "Unfortunately," he continued, "it isn't mine."

"It isn't?" I spooned yogurt over my fruit and took a bite. "Needs sugar."

He shook his head. "Very unhealthy." As he walked back to the kitchen, he explained that he was a subtenant in the apartment.

"A wealthy friend of mine wanted someone he could trust to stay here. So I enjoy all of this"—he gestured at the space around him—"for a nominal rent."

"How wonderful for you. What kind of work do you do? Is any of yours hanging here?"

He put a ceramic sugar bowl on the table. "None of mine is of this quality. I'll show you my studio after breakfast."

Paying no attention to what I was doing, I lifted the lid from the sugar bowl and stuck in my spoon. It hit a surface that gave slightly and crackled, but yielded not so much as a grain of sugar. At the same time that I picked up the bowl to peer into it, Derek rolled his eyes.

"Oh-oh! There goes my reputation."

I pulled out the small plastic baggie of marijuana and dangled it in front of him. "It didn't have that far to go in the first place," I said with a giggle. I pushed the baggie back into the sugar bowl and was on my way to the kitchen to look for the real thing when the doorbell rang. "Are you expecting someone?"

"No." He walked over to the windows along the front of the loft and looked down into the street. "Oh, hell!" he said, slapping his forehead. "A policeman. Several policemen. Such a fuss for a few damned parking tickets."

Back in his kitchen he pushed the intercom button that released the street door. Seconds later the building's old metal stairway shook with the sound of running feet. We could hear them pause at each floor, then climb again, slower on each flight, but louder. Finally they—for it sounded like a dozen feet by then—reached the fifth floor. Derek opened his door wearing an expression of abject boredom, to be greeted by three uniformed cops with their hands on their guns and one tall, skinny man with a rumpled brown suit and a face that belonged on a hangman.

Before Derek could get a word out, the man in the brown suit snapped at one of the uniformed cops, "Watch the hall." Reaching into his vest, allowing us a good look at the pistol in his shoulder holster in the process, he pulled out a silver badge and a photo identification.

"Detective Vincent O'Hagan, Manhattan South, Homicide. You are Derek Thorensen?"

Derek nodded.

O'Hagan looked over at me. "And I take it this is Miss Bonnie Indermill?"

"Yes."

"I'd like to ask you two some questions if you don't mind." With that, O'Hagan and one of the uniformed cops walked into the apartment, leaving the one in the hall and another standing guard at the door.

"What's this all about?" Derek asked.

The skinny detective's head turned slowly, taking in the apartment. His eyes came to rest on the black, white, and red painting on the far wall. "That worth anything?"

"Yes, it is worth something. Look, don't you guys have anything better to do?"

O'Hagan shook his head. "Can't see it, myself. I look at a picture, I want to know what I'm looking at." He turned to me. I hadn't moved from the kitchen door. "You live up in Washington Heights," he said accusingly. But what was he accusing me of?

Derek, by now, was looking belligerent, his jaw jutting

out, his fists balled. "Enough of this nonsense. I'm calling my lawyer." He started toward the phone.

O'Hagan stepped in front of him. "Wait, wait, wait. Don't let's make a federal case out of this. A couple questions, then I'm gone. Out of your hair. What do you say we sit down? Relax?"

I was anything but relaxed. "You can't do this," I said.

O'Hagan made a dismissive gesture. "I'm doing it, Miss Indermill." He nodded toward a sofa, the one under the Rothko. I joined Derek on it. O'Hagan sat in a leather chaise that faced us. He tested the leather with his fingers and gave a grunt of appreciation. "Always wanted one of these." Looking at the Rothko, he shook his head sadly. "Can't see that, though."

"I'm sure you're not here to discuss art," Derek said.

O'Hagan looked back down at him. "Unfortunately, no. Last night at ten forty-five P.M. you two were seen leaving the Grapevine Club in the company of Ashley Gartner, the chief executive officer of Creative Financial Ventures. We have two witnesses who were in front of the club at the time the three of you got into a cab."

"What of it?" Derek said.

We both jumped as glass shattered on the other side of the room. The uniformed cop stooped to pick up the pieces of a glass he'd dropped.

"Careful!" Derek said, standing up abruptly. "I don't know what you storm troopers want, but I've had enough."

"The 'what of it,'" O'Hagan continued, "is that at six-twenty this morning Gartner's body was discovered in the bushes next to his front steps. We also have witnesses that say you"—here O'Hagan looked at me—"spent a lot of time with Gartner during the course of the party."

I was so totally unprepared for this that it took a couple seconds for it to sink in. When it finally did, a chill passed over my entire body. I started trembling violently. I don't know what O'Hagan was seeing in my expression, but his eyes dug into mine.

"Anything you'd like to say about that, Miss Indermill?"

"We just danced together," I stammered.

O'Hagan shook his head. "Just danced." His undertaker face was growing grimmer by the second. He looked across the room at Derek, who was sitting white-faced on the bed, his hand resting on the phone. "You by any chance get a hack number? Notice the driver's name?"

Derek and I shook our heads.

O'Hagan hesitated for a moment, then said, "You didn't happen to know the driver, by any chance?"

I realized immediately that O'Hagan was suggesting that Derek, the cabbie, and I had been involved with Mr. Gartner's death. My "No" came out in a frightened gasp.

"What I'm thinking is, much as I hate to interrupt this nice brunch"—O'Hagan nodded sourly at the dining table— "maybe you two ought to come down to the station."

"Hey, Sarge." The uniformed cop was standing over the table now. His hand dropped toward the open sugar bowl, and the panic that had been creeping up on me since this started took over. My heart battered the walls of my chest as the cop pulled the baggie from the sugar bowl. "Look what they've been using to sweeten their coffee."

Derek and I exchanged terrified looks. Glancing once more at the cop holding the baggie, Derek picked up his phone.

O'Hagan shook his head sadly. "That wouldn't be an illegal substance, would it? It may be time to call the narcs in on this." He looked across the room at Derek. "You better tell your lawyer to meet you at the precinct house."

The day was brilliant and mild, as days that follow an early snow sometimes are. The hard bright light pierced the grime-encrusted windows in the ancient precinct building. Under the window in O'Hagan's tiny office a radiator hissed feebly. It was lukewarm to the touch. The room itself was stifling. Or maybe that was just the way I was feeling.

Derek and I had been separated when we arrived at the precinct. I'd drawn O'Hagan. Who knows why? Maybe he was convinced I'd break more easily. Maybe it was because he couldn't stand Derek. That he made clear.

It came out, as O'Hagan questioned me, that Mr. Gartner had been struck over the head, perhaps several times, with a large clay flowerpot packed with soil and some half-dead ivy. "Hoisted that pot by the ivy and let it swing," he said with as much animation as I would ever see out of him.

I was forthcoming, probably to the point of tedium. I told O'Hagan everything I recalled about my conversation with Mr. Gartner, about his planned company reorganization, about the article Gartner wanted to share with me. I told him about Amanda in Gartner's private conference room. I even told him about Gartner's peculiar behavior at the party.

"He was smelling things?" O'Hagan asked, incredulous.

"He said the champagne smelled like kerosene. I understand that he once accused somebody at the office of putting kerosene in his coffee."

"Kerosene? You drank some of this champagne?"

"Yes. From the same bottle."

"Did you smell anything?"

I shook my head.

"What about the glasses?" he asked. "Could there have been something in his glass?"

"I don't see how." I explained that the glasses had been lined up randomly on the bar. "And anyway," I continued, "Mr. Gartner asked me to smell his champagne. I did, and I didn't smell anything."

"Who was the person at the office he accused of tampering with his coffee?"

"It was Amanda Paradise. But that's only gossip," I added.

O'Hagan had an unfortunate face, but I guess in his field it worked to his advantage. No matter how much I said, his incredulous sneer remained, so that I talked more and more, filling in details. Needless to say, what interested him most was the stranger I'd seen walking up to Mr. Gartner when our cab pulled away. Or had there really been a stranger? After a while, with O'Hagan's prodding, I started wondering myself if it hadn't been a shadow, some shifting snow, a figment of my imagination. On top of everything else going on, I kept having these awful stabs of guilt, not that I had done anything to cause Mr. Gartner's death, but that I was the one person who might have prevented it.

"You say this person may have limped," O'Hagan said.

"Limped, lumbered. Had a strange walk. But there was snow on the ground. Maybe his boots were too big."

"*His* boots," O'Hagan said laboriously. "A minute ago you said you couldn't tell if it was a male or female figure."

"His or her boots. Its boots. Maybe it was the abominable snowman."

O'Hagan sighed. "I gotta check on something."

As soon as he left the room, I took a couple deep breaths.

What was the matter with me, anyway? I didn't have anything to worry about. They would find the cabdriver. And when Derek's story matched mine, they would have to let us go. As for the marijuana, when I thought about it sensibly, I knew it was such a ridiculously small amount that it was probably only a misdemeanor, if that. By the time O'Hagan returned, I had talked myself into an edgy bad humor.

"Thorensen doesn't know anything about this 'abdominal snowman' of yours."

"*Abominable.* He probably didn't notice."

"Didn't notice," O'Hagan repeated. "And you didn't want to mention it."

"We got occupied with other things."

"Other things."

His habit of repeating everything I said was beginning to grate. "Yes, other things," I snapped.

"Like what?"

"You know what!"

He shook his head unhappily. The questions went on and on: "You mean to tell me you're in a cab for a half an hour and you don't see the cabbie's face? . . . You're telling me you've never been intimate with Thorensen before? . . . You're living in a neighborhood where every other person's dealing drugs, and here we find drugs in his place? What do you know about that? . . . How about the rumors that Gartner was into drugs? You know anything about that?"

Then abruptly he changed directions on me. "Do you happen to be acquainted with one Hector Rodriguez?"

"Hector? Sure. He works at C.F. His father is the super in the Gartners' building."

"This Rodriguez walks with a limp. Right? You think he could be your snowman?"

"No." Even as I said it, though, I realized that Mr. Gartner's mysterious midnight caller could easily have been Hector. "I mean, I don't know."

"What about the other people at C.F., Miss Indermill? Any of them with an active dislike of Gartner? Other than possibly this Miss Paradise?"

"How would I know? I haven't even been working there two weeks. It doesn't seem likely."

"Why do you say that?"

"He was nice, in a dingy way. It's hard to imagine anyone hating him."

O'Hagan almost smiled as he studied me. "Someone did."

My head was pounding when another plainclothes cop walked into the room and whispered something to O'Hagan. I looked down at my watch and was surprised to see that only forty-five minutes had passed since I'd walked into the precinct. When I looked at O'Hagan again, he was shaking his head. "Okay, Miss Indermill. That's about it for now. Thank you for your cooperation."

His habit had rubbed off on me. "Cooperation?" I repeated.

"Cooperation." He smiled that hangman's smile. "I never said you couldn't leave."

I was so worn down I could only gape. He asked me if I was planning to leave town for the holidays and I told him I'd be going to New Jersey the following Wednesday.

"New Jersey," he said sadly. He stood up and pulled my chair out for me. "As long as you're not planning on leaving the country. Just out of curiosity, Miss Indermill, maybe you could tell me one thing. Where does Thorensen get his money?"

"He doesn't have money. That apartment belongs to a friend of his."

"Ah. A friend of his." He nodded. "I guess that explains why a long-haired punk like him has a three-hundred-dollar-an-hour lawyer with a limo waiting to take the two of you home."

Derek and another man were waiting in the hall downstairs. Derek looked more angry than worried. The other man looked neither. He looked like a million dollars. I'm serious. From the top of his styled salt-and-pepper hair to his tweed overcoat to his buffed cordovan boots, he reeked success.

I've known a lot of lawyers, most of them one-hundred-percent polyester ambulance chasers, several of them just one step ahead of one or another legal ethics committee. This was an entirely different species. Derek introduced him to me, mentioning the firm he was with. I didn't recognize the name, but I recognized his type, and his type didn't come cheap. Where paint-splattered, part-time-working Derek had come up with him was a mystery. How he proposed to pay him was another one.

"It's illegal search and seizure," the lawyer said as we walked out to the waiting car. "You have nothing to be concerned about. You've just experienced New York's finest at their worst." He smiled at me, and I was immediately reassured by his confidence.

O'Hagan had been exaggerating. It wasn't a limo. It was only a great big expensive American car with a driver. We spread ourselves across the backseat, me between the two men.

"Do you want to be taken home?" the lawyer asked me.

Derek answered for me. "I'll drive her home."

"You still driving the Mercedes?"

"Yes. I know you're right," Derek said, getting back to the

subject, "but what I'm objecting to is their fascist tactics. In my country the police would never dare to behave like that."

The other man groaned. "I've seen those Viking movies. In your country they'd throw you in the peat bogs and forget you for a thousand years. Look, if you want, I'll take it further, but everything else considered . . ." He hesitated there, and for me that hesitation was curiously discomforting. There was something going on between these two men, the way they were talking around me. What was the "everything" Derek should be considering? After a few seconds the lawyer went on:

"Frankly, as your lawyer I'd advise you to drop it. But that's up to you. Think it over and let me know."

The big car glided quietly through Manhattan's wet streets, its interior like a womb, shielding me, taking care of me royally. Instead of helping, though, it contributed to my hellish emotional state. Certainly the violent death of a man I'd just met upset me. Being pulled in and questioned about it upset me even more. But there was something else going on—with Derek. I closed my eyes and rested against the back of the seat, trying to get myself together.

"How come I haven't seen you at the club lately?" the lawyer asked. "I miss our games."

"I've been getting ready for an exhibit. I'll send you an invitation."

The club? What club? What were these men talking about? As soon as the big car dropped us at Derek's loft, I brought up one of the many things that was churning around in my head.

"Where did you ever come up with that lawyer, anyway?"

Derek was unlocking the front door of his building. At my question, he shrugged. "He's a fine lawyer."

"I'm sure he is. But he looks like an expensive one."

"Last year when I had a little money to blow, I joined an athletic club. He and I discovered we were a good handball match. We usually try to play a couple times a week."

I had no reason not to believe Derek, but something about

that didn't ring true. It's hard enough to drag a low-rent lawyer away from his office. You'd have to wave thousand-dollar bills in front of a high-priced one to get him into a police station. It was difficult to imagine any lawyer willing to do so much to hang on to a handball partner.

"I'd still like to go after that bastard cop," Derek added, following me into the building.

"Your lawyer didn't think that was a good idea. Why is that?"

Derek looked at me thoughtfully. Then, taking my arm, he led me onto his stairwell. "I will tell you something, but you must not repeat it around the office."

I nodded. "Okay."

"I'm an illegal alien. I'm not permitted to work in this country. I'm trying to get a green card, but something like this—especially the marijuana—might screw things up."

What a mess! I rubbed my forehead as if I could wipe this latest shocker away. Derek picked up a lock of my hair. "I can see that's made you even more unhappy. It's not so bad. My lawyer's working on it now."

"But isn't it awful for you, never sure if you're going to be caught?"

Shrugging, he said, "I spend the night with a loving woman who I hope to be spending more nights with, I'm on my way to Vermont to look at a ski cabin, my rent is paid, and I have food in my refrigerator if I ever get a chance to eat it. Do I seem like someone living an awful life?"

"Not really." We started up the stairs together, arms around each other's waist.

Once in the loft Derek immediately headed for the phone. Keeping my coat on, I walked back into his studio.

"Do you mind if I look at your work?"

"No. Go ahead," he said absently as he began dialing.

A standing easel held an unfinished oil painting, a white stucco house by a very blue sea. On the terrace was an auburn-haired woman holding a book. Her face was out of sync with the rest of the painting. The background was lovely, quietly relaxing. The woman's face was apprehensive. Who was she, I wondered, and why did she look like that? What had Derek been thinking when he painted her? I looked over at him.

For some reason I wasn't ready to deal with, I was feeling an invisible barrier between us. Derek's acquaintance with the lawyer had brought home to me that I knew almost nothing about him. Not even the basic things. Had he been married? Divorced? Was his whole family in Denmark or did he have relatives here? Who were his friends? What kind of food did he like? Movies? Books? I didn't even know how old he was. Friendships that start in bed are tenuous enough as it is. This jarring interruption had come early in ours, perhaps too early.

Derek made a couple calls. First he called an airline and canceled the round-trip reservations he'd had for Christmas. Then, in the guttural German-like Danish, he called his family in Denmark. As he spoke to them I flipped through some mounted canvases stacked against a wall.

Though I am no judge of art, I was impressed by what I saw. There were vivid, semiabstract cityscapes, and some placid paintings of that same seaside house. They were good. At least to me. Affecting. They made me think about the mood of the place. Being who I am, they also made me wonder about the russet-haired woman. Was she a model? A friend? Or a lover? Why did she look unhappy? Maybe someday he'd tell me about her. I was prepared to listen.

I was not prepared for the last canvas I flipped over. In fact, I was violently unprepared when I discovered myself staring at one contorted female nude.

It was on canvas board and looked like a quick sketch. The model's back was to the artist, but her head twisted over her shoulder. With one hand she knotted her hair atop her head. With the other she supported herself on her hip as she stretched forward. The face belonged to Amanda Paradise.

Uncomplicated he had called her. And fun. Looking at this sketch, I'd have to agree. Uncomplicated by clothing and ready for a good time. Twelve hours earlier he had denied ever having anything to do with Amanda. Unless this drawing came from his imagination, which seemed unlikely, he had lied.

What a horrible morning this had turned into. I took another deep breath. This has nothing to do with me and Derek now, I told myself. Whatever Derek's age, he was old enough to have a past. I certainly had one. Flipping the canvas back to the wall, I walked out of the studio.

Derek had just hung up the phone.

"My father has a heart condition," he said. "I couldn't tell him what's going on here. I had to tell him I was working. What a bummer!"

Sitting next to him, I leaned my head against his chest. He put his arm around my waist. For a few minutes we drew comfort from each other that had nothing to do with sex.

"Do you ski?" he asked after a little while. "I'm driving to Vermont tonight to look at that house. Maybe you'd like to go?"

"I'd like to, but I can't. I have to do my Christmas shopping. I'm going to my brother's house after work on Wednesday."

"So we won't see each other until after Christmas?" That idea made him look even more dejected than he had.

"You could go home with me." I regretted those words the second they were out of my mouth. Some things shouldn't mix, and I had a feeling Derek and my family were two of them.

He was genuinely pleased. "Thank you. I'd like that very much. A real American Christmas."

My problems were piling up one on top of the other. I suddenly wanted to be alone. I pulled my coat tight around me. "I'm exhausted. I'm going to take off now."

"I'll drive you."

We picked Derek's car up at a private garage around the corner. It was exactly what his lawyer had said it was. A Mercedes. Deep burgundy, with a polished walnut dashboard and soft, glove-leather bucket seats.

We pulled into the street and Derek got out to close the

garage door, leaving me alone in the car. I'd never been in a Mercedes. In my wild youth I'd had friends with Corvettes, and a few years earlier a boyfriend had owned an old Porsche, but this was something else, another breed of car altogether, the kind of car rich people drive.

I looked out the side window at Derek. He was fighting with the garage door. His blue parka had a paint smear across the back. His boots were the army-navy store variety. His hat was the kind you buy on the street for two dollars. He was good-looking and smart and fun and considerate. He was a talented artist. He was a marvelous lover. Men like that were hard to come by. If he had at one time been involved with Amanda, so what? The past was just that. Past. I'd have to be a fool to hold that against him.

"Your friend's car?" I asked when Derek finally climbed in beside me.

He was rubbing his hands together to warm them.

"Yes, but mine to use while he's in Europe."

"You're very lucky to have that kind of friend."

He smiled at me briefly before he pulled into traffic. "I've been very lucky in many things."

CHAPTER 6
◆◆◆◆◆◆◆◆◆◆◆◆◆◆

My next week as a Creative Financial employee began and ended in the police station.

Sergeant O'Hagan called me at home early Monday morning and told me that the cabdriver had been located and that his trip sheet had confirmed our stories. That was the good news. The bad news was, Hector Rodriguez had been picked up and was being held for questioning.

"Would you mind stopping by the precinct and taking a look at Rodriguez?" O'Hagan asked.

"I told you I didn't see the person who walked up to Mr. Gartner," I said. "It wouldn't do any good for me to look at Hector."

"Just a few minutes of your time is all I'm asking, Miss Indermill. You've got to consider my position. I've got one man dead and this young fellow's future at stake. . . ."

Oh, spare me from O'Hagan the humanist. The way he put it though, as if I were trying to shirk my public-spirited duty, got to me.

An hour later there I was, feeling like the ultimate creep, watching through a one-way mirror as Hector limped across a room, catty-corner, moving toward me like I'd seen the stranger cross the street toward Mr. Gartner.

"I don't know," I told O'Hagan honestly.

"You don't know." He shook his head and picked up a microphone on a table beside him. "Let's see that one more time."

When I still couldn't identify Hector as Gartner's late-night caller, O'Hagan had him repeat his walk again, and then again. And every time Hector shuffled across that room, lumbering, moving closer to me, he looked worse. Not only more dejected, but more and more furtive, as if he had something awful to hide, until even I, who wanted to believe he was innocent, could almost feel his guilt. It seemed as if the terrible enormity of what he had done couldn't go on being contained in his insignificant frame and was radiating out of it.

Still, I was so certain he'd be released that it came as a surprise when O'Hagan said they'd be holding Hector for a while.

"We've got a suspect with two prior arrests for burglary," he explained. "A one-hundred-fifty-dollar-a-week messenger who had over three hundred dollars on him when we picked

75

him up Friday afternoon. We found his prints on the victim's front door and on his briefcase, which was inside the apartment, and on various other objects in Gartner's house."

O'Hagan's theory was that Hector had approached Mr. Gartner on the steps as our cab pulled away. He had asked Mr. Gartner for a loan. When Mr. Gartner refused and turned to unlock the building door, Hector, in a rage, picked up the clay flowerpot from the steps and hit Mr. Gartner with it. O'Hagan hypothesized that Hector took the cash from Mr. Gartner's wallet and shoved his body into the bushes. Then, picking up Gartner's attaché case, he carried it into the Gartner apartment where he searched the briefcase and the apartment for further cash.

I tried thinking this through in the cab on the way to the office. Hector's fingerprints on Gartner's door, and even those in the apartment itself, weren't surprising. As Gartner's super's son, Hector undoubtedly did odd jobs around the building. Even the money Hector had on him wasn't in itself incriminating. The most incriminating thing was his fingerprints on the leather attaché case. I may have been blurry about the stranger I'd seen approach Mr. Gartner, but I'd clearly seen Gartner wipe off his attaché case in the cab. With Hector, for his part, denying seeing Mr. Gartner that night, it looked as if those prints could be his downfall.

By the time I got to the office I was feeling pretty gloomy. Unfortunately the atmosphere in Technical Resources was anything but helpful. Maybe nothing short of a good cry and a couple hours of hashing this terrible thing over with some sympathetic friends could have helped. There was none of that going on at C.F. Oh, nobody pretended the murder hadn't happened, and certainly nobody acted happy about it. The customary "Isn't it awful"s abounded. It was apparent, though, that the people mouthing these sentiments weren't actually going to miss Mr. Gartner. For some reason the man had never connected on a personal basis with his staff. Most of the lower-level staff had found him relatively harmless, but aloof, not the kind of guy you'd ever have a beer with.

As for the upper-levels, the Morton Fikes and the Charlotte Smoots, I suspect that most of them thought Gartner had become pretty eccentric. And who could argue with that? I'd found him pretty eccentric myself. But to them his oddities weren't as harmless as they were to me. When you are a company man or woman, particularly one with a financial share of the company, eccentricity in management can be deadly.

That morning was the one and only time that I missed my previous job, the one at the law firm. There, one of the lawyers could have been depended on to deliver the last rites with a ceremony that stopped just short of throwing himself into the open grave. Grotesque as that was, there is something to be said for it. "Comforting" may be the wrong word. "Cleansing," perhaps.

Eddie gave me an unusually curt nod when I said good morning to him. He was in business mode that morning, eyes on his monitor, pencil in hand. Guilt, maybe, about what he had done to Charlotte, though I couldn't see guilt as an emotion Eddie was strong in. Fear was more likely. After his performance at the party, did Charlotte still have him marked for stardom?

A few minutes after I got to my cubicle, he stood up to get something out of the supply closet. As he passed me he leaned into my bay:

"I hear you put the cops on to Hector. Good move, Bonnie. A guy like Hector doesn't have enough trouble."

I was so stunned by that I couldn't even answer. By the time I recovered, Eddie was back at his desk. I didn't say anything to him. This was no time for a fight.

Across the partition Helen was keeping quiet. A good thing, too. She had seen Derek and me get into the cab with Mr. Gartner and was doubtless the main reason Derek and I had been questioned the next morning. I wasn't actively plotting revenge, but she wasn't going to find me doing her any favors in the future, either.

Her partner in crime, Dumont, had his coat in the closet, and a dim light shone from under his office door, but cha-

cha-cha himself was lying low. He may have been hiding from me, from Helen, from both of us, or from the world in general. I didn't much care, as long as he stayed away from me.

Charlotte Smoot showed up at C.F. shortly after I did, carrying a bulging briefcase and wearing the harried look of someone who had already gone to several meetings. As she hung her white fur coat in the closet, she looked into Eddie's cubicle. I got the feeling she wanted to say something to him, and it was all she could do to stop herself. For a moment her expression was a study in pure longing, but when she saw me watching her, a veil seemed to drop over her face. She nodded briefly and walked into her office as if this was just another Monday morning.

The Christmas party and its aftermath had done their work with a vengeance. No one was speaking to anyone.

Early in the afternoon I heard from O'Hagan again. "Miss Indermill. Are you able to talk now without anybody overhearing?"

"Hardly." Not with Eddie on one side of me and Helen on the other.

"Then could you please get to a private phone and call me back."

What did the man want from me now? I found an unused conference room, closed and locked the door, and returned his call.

"There's a new development I'd like to check out with you," he said. "Rodriguez has changed his story. He admits approaching Gartner now. Says he asked Gartner for a loan. What he's claiming is that Gartner agreed to loan him some money, but suggested they go inside out of the snow."

Hector had told O'Hagan that he followed Mr. Gartner into the apartment, carrying Gartner's attaché case for him. He said that after Mr. Gartner handed him two hundred dollars, he left.

That was a way to explain Hector's prints on Mr. Gartner's attaché case, as well as the money in Hector's wallet. Whether or not Hector's story was true was another matter. However, it was a matter that didn't have anything to do with me. My story was the same.

"And what do you need to check out with me?"

"Over the course of the evening, Miss Indermill, you didn't happen to hear Gartner mention that he might have been expecting any company at his apartment later that night?"

"No."

"How about the fact that he may have been planning to go out later?"

"No," I repeated. "As a matter of fact, he mentioned that he wanted to get a good night's sleep." If anything, Mr. Gartner had been too exhausted to entertain a late-night visitor, much less go out.

O'Hagan hesitated before he asked his next question. "What about Miss Paradise? Think hard. When you observed her in the office before the party, you didn't overhear anything other than what you told me earlier?"

"Only what I said. 'You bastard. I could kill you.'" I repeated. "And I can't swear it was Mr. Gartner she said it to."

"I understand that," O'Hagan said. "Later that night, when Miss Paradise was at your table, she didn't mention anything about having someplace to go later?"

"No. What's this all about, anyway?"

"Just checking out a few things."

"Do you believe Hector's story?"

O'Hagan's answer was a long time coming. Finally he said, "Miss Indermill, I make it a point never to believe anybody anymore. I'll be talking to you."

How confusing this was! O'Hagan's questions suggested that Mr. Gartner had had a late date, or possibly that Hector was saying Mr. Gartner had had a late date to save his own neck. If Hector was telling the truth, Amanda Paradise had to be a likely suspect. But only if she and Eddie had parted company after leaving the Grapevine. Eddie was capable of a lot of shady things, but not helping to murder his new CEO.

If Eddie and Amanda hadn't parted company and Hector was telling the truth, then who had Mr. Gartner's late-night caller been? Well, when I thought about it, it could have been anyone—a neighbor, a relative, a friend. I hardly knew the man, and I knew next to nothing about his personal life.

Anyway, I told myself, Hector was probably lying. And whatever he said, there was one thing I was certain of, and that was my story. It wasn't going to change. Apart from my role as a witness who hadn't actually seen anything, I wasn't involved.

I returned to my desk and was sitting there, half lost in my own thoughts, when Eddie's phone rang. After only one week of sitting next to him I had learned to shut out his phone calls. There were so many, and so much whispering and mumbling and slugging on that Maalox bottle that he had to be supporting half the bookies in Manhattan and running from the other half. This time, though, I heard a sharp, "Certainly Charlotte. I'll be right there."

Aha! I hadn't figured Charlotte for a woman who would give up without a fight.

The moment his conversation with Charlotte ended, Eddie dialed another number. "Damn! Hey, Bonnie," he said. "I need a favor."

I don't forget that easily. I ignored him.

"Please, Bonnie. I apologize. It was a crummy thing to say. I'm a jerk. I admit it. I'm on my knees, begging you. Help!"

I poked my head around our partition. Eddie was not on his knees. With one hand he was slipping on his suit jacket. With the other he was stabbing at the buttons on his phone. The receiver was balanced on his shoulder.

"What's the matter? Sounds like you're about to get a reprieve."

"I'm supposed to be meeting Amanda for coffee break and Charlotte wants to see me ASAP. Amanda's phone is busy." He stood up. "Bonnie, I need you to do something for me."

I shrugged. "Maybe."

"Run around to Amanda's office and catch her before she leaves for the cafeteria. Otherwise she'll think I've stood her up."

Oh, brother! He really had it bad. "Sure."

"Thanks. You're a pal. I owe you one." He took off toward Charlotte's office, adjusting his tie on the way.

I have to admit it wasn't a purely magnanimous gesture on my part. I was more than a little curious about Amanda. There was her friendship with Derek, which evidence suggested was a lot more involved than he admitted. There was, of course, her slapping scene, presumably with the now-dead Ashley Gartner. There was her implausible relationship with Eddie. And now there were O'Hagan's strange questions. This woman I'd scarcely spoken to had begun occupying a big space in my thoughts. I wanted to know more about her.

Amanda's office was along the executive corridor. Her door was open, but she was nowhere in sight. I went to her desk intending to leave a note, "Eddie will be a couple minutes late," or something like that, but before I'd even picked up a pen, I noticed the light on her phone was lit. Someone was speaking on one of the extensions.

On the other side of her French provincial desk was the door that led to Mr. Gartner's suite. I put my ear to it, and sure enough I could just make out the sound of Amanda's voice. I decided to give her a couple seconds.

Amanda, unlike her dead boss, left a strong impression. The furniture, the pictures on the wall, even her faint perfume remained, so elegant, so personally "Amanda." No other woman would be able to occupy that office and fit it the way Amanda did. No other woman would be able to dance with Eddie and make him look as good as she had, either. Let's face it—he was a decent dancer, but Fred Astaire he wasn't. As for her relationship with Mr. Gartner— well, those words of hers had certainly left their impression on me. A slap and "I could kill you" meant one thing in a burst of anger, another when the slapee is killed a few hours later.

When I realized what I was doing, I felt a shiver of dismay. Keep out of it, Bonnie, I reminded myself. It's not your business. The phone light was still on. I didn't have all day to sit around inventing plots. I had a drawer full of paperbacks with plots of their own waiting for me. I knocked and called, "Amanda?" A second later she opened the door.

She had been crying. Believe me, I know all the signs. Her eyes were watery, her nose pink. In spite of myself I felt a twinge of pity.

"I'm sorry to interrupt. Eddie asked me to tell you he's going to be a few minutes late."

That exquisite chin trembled, and her words came out with a little shudder. "That's all right. I was just straightening out Mr. Gartner's papers." She waved her hands at the room behind her, flustered. "I don't know what I'm supposed to do anymore. Everything is so confused. Mr. Fike made me cancel the order for your new chairs. And . . ." Her eyes filled with tears. "This horrible policeman keeps calling me. He wants to see me again this afternoon. What does he want?"

"Probably just a few questions," I said, walking past her into the room. "He keeps calling me too."

"I bet he's not asking you the same questions he's asking me. Bonnie," she said, scarcely able to talk now, "I wouldn't have hurt Mr. Gartner. He was . . . he was my . . ." She sobbed, unable to go on.

"I'm sorry. This must be awful for you." I moved toward Amanda, intending to offer some comfort, but she whispered, "I'll be right back." She rushed from the room, through her own office, and into the hall.

Now I really felt awful. Maybe I was misjudging Amanda. Not two minutes earlier I'd been on the verge of concocting some nonsense about how this clothes-happy seductress had murdered her boss, and here she was the only person in the office mourning Ashley Gartner.

Walking around Mr. Gartner's desk, I slid into his chair. Merely from habit I straightened the blotter, then reached to straighten a stack of files on the left of the desk. Honestly, I didn't intend to snoop around, but the first thing my eyes fell on was the top file labeled "Reorganization."

Was this the famous unworkable reorganization plan I'd heard about at Thunder Road? The plan Gartner had put together that Derek had suggested would cause a small war? Right here on top of his desk?

I took the folder in my hands, not daring at first to open it. It was none of my business, it had nothing to do with me, and with Mr. Gartner dead, it wasn't likely to happen anyway. I started to lay it back on top of the stack—

I couldn't help it. I leaned forward in the chair far enough to watch the door to Amanda's office. Then I opened the folder.

Lines and boxes, going this way and that, initials strewn through them. I turned the sheet around. On it was an out-of-kilter pyramid, penciled in colors. It was a lovely looking thing, something fit to be hung on a gallery wall. Derek did beautiful work. Not that it made any sense to me.

The chart detailed the anticipated setup when and if C.F. merged with the bank. Ashley Gartner, from what I could make out, had taken good care of himself. He was right up there on the top row with the bank's officers. Charlotte Smoot was doing all right too. She'd made the second row—which on this chart amounted to the top line of C.F. Her title was to have been Vice President and Director of Technical and Strategic Planning. Under her there was quite a staff. It wasn't until I was almost at the bottom of the chart that I encountered Morton Fike's name. Marketing had been demoted from a division to a support group—like personnel and payroll. From what I'd heard, "Can Do" Fike was a feisty little devil. He wouldn't have liked this chart one bit. "Small war" was probably an understatement.

I flipped quickly through the rest of the folder. It was full of scribbled notes, nothing that made much sense to me. But somebody—perhaps Derek or Mr. Gartner or Amanda—had made several extra copies of the chart. Without really considering why, I quickly slid one copy off the bottom of the stack, folded it, and slipped it into my suit pocket.

I'd become so engrossed in what I was doing that I didn't notice Amanda until she walked back into the office. Since I still had the folder in my hand, I said, "I'm a compulsive straightener," and laid it neatly on the stack.

"So am I." Amanda looked down at the file. She was more composed than she had been but still puffy-eyed. "I wonder what I'm supposed to do with that. Everybody who saw it said it was crazy." She shook her head. "Sometimes it was like he was losing his mind. He was grouchy and . . ."

I felt an awful strain in my throat, a pinching behind my eyes. I made a futile gesture, pushing the file across the desk. "Somebody's going to want it."

She dismissed it with a sigh. "It will end up in the trash can. I know. Everything he did lately was . . . odd. He wasn't very happy with me anymore. I know that."

I couldn't help what happened next. One lone tear sort of slid from the corner of my eye. "I'm so sorry, Amanda. I understand what you're going through."

She sniffled and once again her eyes brimmed. "That's impossible," she said weakly. "None of you have any idea how many problems I have."

I nodded, too close to a sob to talk. She started to say something, but her voice cracked. I quickly searched my pockets for a Kleenex, but before I found one everything I'd been holding back rose to the surface. Amanda and I burst into tears simultaneously, then stumbled to the sofa so in unison we might have rehearsed it.

"You don't know. You can't imagine what a mess my life is," she kept sobbing.

"I know. I understand," I wept back.

I have no idea how long we went on like that. I don't know about Amanda, but the way I was feeling I could have kept it up all day. It's just as well Eddie showed up when he did.

"I just got handed this big project! Hey, what the hell's the matter with you two?"

He had stopped in the doorway as if he was afraid to come in. Who can blame him? I can only imagine how I looked. Amanda, wouldn't you know, was one of those rare women who cry well. Instead of getting all red and soggy looking, she turned pink and vulnerable.

Eddie remained in the door. The only possible move for me was a retreat. Best to let Amanda try to make a new life for herself. I rose, but before I headed for the door, I leaned toward her.

"I do understand, Amanda," I whispered.

She looked up, sniffled, and blubbered her tearful refrain. "You don't know. You can't imagine."

Eddie whispered as I hurried past him. "That's the last time I'll ever ask you to do me a favor."

Maybe our tears had unnerved Fast Eddie, but they were the catharsis I'd been looking for. Never mind that I was totally misguided, wrong about almost everything. I felt a hundred times better, ready to face the world and my life again.

It's coloring things to say that Derek and I spent the next couple of days and nights together. The nights, yes. The days were workdays, and we could only see each other sporadically. But then, calling those few days at Creative Financial workdays stretches the truth, too.

The back stairwell, the one I'd used to escape Perry Dumont, became our meeting place, a perpendicular lover's lane. We cuddled on the cold concrete stairs as an icy wind from somewhere above whipped across the landing between the twenty-fourth and twenty-fifth floors. We managed to stop short of necking shamelessly not because either of us had any self-control, but because we were never alone for more than a couple minutes. Along with the new chairs and the reorganization, all semblance of discipline at C.F. had vanished.

From landings above and below us the scent of marijuana hung in the air. Laughter and the footfalls of employees sneaking out early and sneaking in late echoed up and down the stairwell. Tuesday afternoon at about three, what had to be the entire accounting department pushed by us wearing their coats and making no secret of the fact that their workday was over. A raucously out-of-tune Eddie sang as he scooted past a couple times on his way out to the OTB.

On one of my many trips back from Derek's stairwell landing, I ran into the World's Most Unattractive Couple. Helen was leaning against the concrete-block wall. Perry was bending over her. As I approached they were whispering furiously. Helen's lips clamped together when I passed. They pretended not to notice me. I pretended not to notice them. We repeated this performance Wednesday morning.

During this time I learned a lot about Derek. He was thirty-four. He had never been married but had had several long-lasting relationships. He told me, without my asking, that his last girlfriend had lived with him for two years and had only moved out in September. She was the russet-haired woman in the paintings who had grown angry at his refusal to take a respectable five-day-a-week job. I learned that he had several distant relatives living in the midwestern United States, that he liked spy novels and adventure stories, thought *Kon-Tiki* was the greatest book ever written, was always willing to go to a movie, would eat anything put in front of him but eggplant, and liked to ski in the winter and sail in the summer.

He told me that as an adolescent he'd been pretty wild.

"Such as?" I asked.

He grinned. "The usual."

I confessed that I'd been a little wild too. Just a little. I told him I had been married and divorced years before, that I sometimes still fantasized about making it as a dancer, but that I fantasized more about a poverty-stricken old age, that I read detective stories and loved the forties and fifties dance movies, that I would eat anything he put in front of me but fatty meat, and that I would love to learn to ski and sail.

He assured me, again and again, that he was in no danger of being deported.

That was a good thing, because by the time Wednesday afternoon rolled around, I wouldn't have wanted to lose him.

CHAPTER 7

◆◆◆◆◆◆◆◆◆◆◆◆◆

Christmas at my brother and sister-in-law's was not the disaster it could have been. I'd had serious misgivings ever since inviting Derek. He wasn't the first boyfriend I'd ever taken home for a holiday, but he was probably the most "exotic," the most foreign, the most counterculture one I'd turned up with in a long time.

My last one—Tony—was a New York City police lieutenant. He'd been at the same job for over twenty years. He had a good pension plan, a house in Queens, and got his hair cut every three weeks. They loved him. My mother was ready to rent the hall and order the three-tiered cake. My brother Raymond and my father, who usually keep their mouths shut about my male friends, were calling him "good buddy" within ten minutes after being introduced. Only Noreen, my sister-in-law, hadn't been so sure. Taking me into the bedroom for a girl-to-girl, she explained that I should think twice about him. "Eye-talian men tend to play around, Bonnie. It's part of their culture."

Before Tony there was Emory, a sometimes lawyer with a questionable pedigree, artistic pretensions, and a Louisiana accent as thick and almost as impenetrable as a plate of ice-cold grits. Talk about inappropriate! He treated our trip to New Jersey as if we were off to Machu Picchu. "Will I be able to get a decent wine there, or should I bring my own?" he had asked, quite seriously. I don't think Emory exchanged three words with my father and Raymond after their preliminary handshakes. Now and then I'd caught my father looking at Emory from the corner of his eye, as though he suspected Emory might steal the silver-plate knives and forks. Noreen and my mother, they were enchanted. Noreen—she was in one of her culinary phases at the time—pushed homemade tarts and turnovers at Emory, then watched, fingers folded under her chin, as he bit and chewed. She held her breath waiting for his compliments, which he, the consummate food snob, delayed as long as possible, then dropped carelessly. "Most interesting taste, Noreen. And the texture! My!" My sister-in-law gobbled these crumbs like a starving child and Emory rose, temporarily, in my estimation. It took a formidable ego to shake Noreen's confidence in her homemaking abilities. That time Mother herself took me into the bedroom. "That's a good catch there, Bonnie Jean."

I should explain about Raymond and Noreen. He's a mechanic, part owner of a service station, and the unfailing light of my mother's eyes. Raymond's career is perfection, his marriage is a model for couples everywhere, his children a never-ending joy, a constant source of cute little sayings and darling anecdotes. According to Mom, that is.

The way I see it, the entire scene is straight out of Dante, even by my loose standards. How many times have I sat, white-knuckled, clutching the sticky arms of one of the chairs in their aptly named rec room, as precious angel Tammy bit her brother, Raymond, Jr. How often have I gritted my teeth while Raymond, Jr., the little mischief, bit back. Through all this, Noreen gazes beatifically, maternal pride oozing from her pores. The only time I've ever been pulled into their madness was the time I couldn't find a sitter for my cat, Moses, and brought him with me for a long weekend. When I caught Raymond, Jr., trying to push Moses into the burning fireplace, I smacked his precocious bottom so hard it turned the entire split-level house into a war zone. It was months before Noreen and I spoke.

It had been months this time, too. Nine of them to be exact, since the previous April when events at my last job—like a murderer on the loose—made it impossible for me to show up at her carefully planned Easter dinner. There I had been, in the center of a life-threatening situation, and she'd written me a snotty letter about the havoc I'd caused with the place cards she had so carefully lettered in calligraphy class. It goes without saying that I didn't bother answering.

Our cold war had lasted through the summer and into autumn. During this time Noreen the brood mare brought yet another bundle of happiness into the world. Darling sweetness Farrah cried for most of the twenty-four hours Derek and I spent there. I ought to know; I shared her nursery. Derek got the rump-sprung pull-out couch in the living room. God forbid an unmarried couple should get close enough to each other to do any hanky-panky in that home.

Derek was a good sport through it all. He watched endless cartoons from the time we arrived on Thursday until well into Christmas Eve. After dinner they switched to more sophisticated programming—to be specific, wrestling. I know it's absurd to think you might be falling in love with a man because he can sit on a gunk-smeared sofa between your brother and your father, eyes glued to the sweaty mounds of flab groping each other on the screen, sucking an orange Slurpee through a loop-d-loop straw, but that's what was happening to me. Derek seemed to fit into my life so nicely. Once my father and Raymond recovered from the length of his hair and got a look at the car he was driving, it was smooth sailing for Derek.

The same wasn't true for me. I suppose the best that can be said is, I didn't make a scene. I could have. A real nice opportunity was handed to me.

I was bored, almost beyond endurance, when in the nursery poor little Farrah woke up and started screaming. "Noreen," Raymond called over his shoulder in a television besotted voice. "Baby's crying."

Baby cried on, louder. Raymond turned to me, a pleading

look on his face. Raymond thinks child care is sex-related. Men do tune-ups; women do diaper changes.

"Sure, Raymond," I said. "I'll get her."

Farrah was on her back, wet-faced and hysterical. I picked her up and instantly saw, or felt, one of the problems. Changing her helped a lot. Then I propped her on my shoulder and started singing and bouncing around the nursery. "Up on the house top, click, click, click. Down through the chimney with old Saint Nick . . ." A few halfhearted sobs and she relaxed, eyes wide open, fingers twisted hard in my hair.

I walked up the hall, bouncing Farrah on my shoulder, past the chaos of the rec room toward the kitchen, where Noreen and my mother were doing last-minute things to the Christmas Day goose. I was ready to walk in when my mother's voice stopped me.

". . . can't be making much money. An artist. He only works three days a week."

I didn't have to see the expression accompanying that fretful voice. There would be the bewildered eyes searching Noreen's bland, confident ones for support, the lips compressed into their "bearing my cross" lament. The shoulders would slump in disappointment.

Noreen raised her voice over the whir of her blender. "He can't be doing that badly if he's driving an '83 Mercedes. Raymond said his car's the top of the line. Worth over forty thousand dollars, used. You want to taste this, Mom? It may need more nutmeg."

"You know I don't touch alcohol, Noreen. I wish I had your faith," my mother continued. "A man his age wearing his hair that long. I almost died when I saw it. He could be a dope fiend for all we know. He looks like one. We may all be murdered in our beds."

"Now, Mom," Noreen said. "You should be thankful he's white. With Bonnie you can never be sure."

My mother tossed out the final salvo: "That girl always was boy crazy. She didn't get that from my side."

I lugged Farrah back into the rec room, shoveled some toys off a chair, and slid into it. I was still fuming when Noreen came in a few minutes later, carrying a big bowl of eggnog, a silver-plate ladle, and cups so tiny they might have come from her daughter's dollhouse.

"Mom's lying down for a while. Worn out. I thought we might all have some Christmas cheer." Giggling, she set the bowl on the coffee table and proceeded to serve minuscule portions of eggnog. I slugged down the cup she offered me. "The recipe is from the *New York Post*." She beamed as she waited for the compliments that were her due.

"Hits the spot," my father said.

"Delicious." That was Derek.

"Uh huh," Raymond managed.

"The *Post*?" I said. "From the amount of liquor in it, I would have guessed *The Christian Science Monitor*."

Raymond and my father cracked up. Derek grinned kind of sheepishly. Noreen glared.

"Out here, Bonnie, we don't drink the way you do in New York."

"Sorry, Noreen. I was kidding." I adjusted Farrah on my shoulder and held out my glass. Noreen refilled it, watching me carefully.

I sipped my second glass, playing with the baby's fingers, purposely ignoring my sister-in-law. That Noreen cannot bear.

"Oh, doesn't that look sweet," she finally said after a moment of casting around for something to say. "Look at Bonnie and Farrah, Raymond. Have you ever seen anything so darling?"

Raymond, who is impervious to scenes like this, glanced my way, grunted, and turned back to the screen. There was no stopping Noreen, though. "Just look, Derek. Bonnie only pretends to hate kids, you know. See how good she is with them. I don't know why she's never had any of her own. Why, you and she"—the walleyed bitch raised her hand to her lips as if the idea had just popped into her head—"could have such beautiful blond babies. Can't you imagine a house-ful of itsy-bitsy blond—"

"Or maybe itsy-bitsy black ones," I said absently.

It took Noreen's itsy-bitsy brain a few seconds to realize that I'd overheard her in the kitchen. "Oh," she gushed. "Why, I love all babies. Black ones, white ones."

Derek, who was proving to be a island of sanity in these choppy waters, suddenly asked:

"Anyone interested in going for a ride?"

Everyone but Noreen shouted, "Yeah!"

"But I was just about to make more eggnog."

"That's okay, Noreen," I said, handing her the baby. "We have a quart of whiskey in the car."

That's how I got through the evening, with the help of that Mercedes. I looked into the recesses of the engine as Raymond and Derek eagerly explained its workings. We took turns driving each other around the block, and each time we passed the split-level, there was Noreen, hands on her hips staring out the picture window framed by the blinking Christmas lights. She probably thought we were all as drunk as lords out there.

We ended up in one of the ports down at Raymond's ser-vice station, with me in the driver's seat alternately turning the engine on and off as the men tuned the car. Watching the three of them, I slipped into a daydream. After years as a free spirit, it's not always easy to imagine myself in a domes-tic situation, but Derek was fitting so easily into my life that suddenly china patterns and recipes didn't seem so far-fetched.

"Bonnie!" Derek tapped on the passenger window, break-ing into my fantasy. "Open the glove compartment and hand me the maintenance manual."

I rifled through the glove compartment and handed the manual out the window. Derek gave it to Raymond, who made some gesture to my father, and the three of them once again buried their heads under the hood.

I wasn't looking for anything in particular when I started

searching through the glove compartment. It's just that there it was, that open maw, that small bastion of masculine possessions, holding who knew what. A quick look at the three men assured me I wasn't going to be interrupted. I emptied the contents onto the seat next to me.

There were the usual things—maps, credit card receipts, pen and paper, and a thin, pigskin case. No women's phone numbers, no tubes of lipstick. Nothing to upset me.

Pushing everything back into the compartment except the pigskin case, I pried open the snap that closed it. There, behind a plastic window, was the car's registration card. When I held it to catch the light, I saw that the car was registered in Derek's name at the Beach Street address.

I puzzled over this for a second, then closed the case and pushed it back into the glove compartment on top of everything else. There was obviously a simple explanation. Enough snooping for me. Snooping brings nothing but trouble.

Outside the car the three men were smiling and nodding portentously. Whatever they had set out to do to the engine, they had done. A second later Derek opened the door and returned the maintenance manual.

"So you fixed it?" I asked.

"It was nothing at all. Your brother's a good mechanic."

I nodded. "Your friend must really appreciate the care you give his possessions."

Derek's glance slid to the open glove compartment where the pigskin case was in plain view. When he looked back at me, I thought there was a chill in those blue eyes.

"Actually," he said after a moment, "for right now the car is mine. My friend signed it over to me while he's traveling. It makes things less of a problem."

Maybe for him things were less of a problem. For me, what I'd found in that glove compartment brought back Sergeant O'Hagan's question: "Where does your friend get his money?" The fact that I was able to push these suspicions out of my mind almost immediately says something about my strength of character. I had none where Derek was concerned. I didn't want to know anything bad about him, didn't want anything interfering with the way I felt. I was blissfully happy and I intended to stay that way, even if it meant being blissfully ignorant.

We left as early as we politely could Christmas Day, after the presents had been opened and the goose devoured, along with several bottles of good French wine Derek had brought with him. I asked Noreen for her stuffing recipe, ensuring myself of her good will for the immediate future.

"You promised you weren't going to buy presents for my family," I said as we drove toward the turnpike.

Derek shrugged. "I only bought for the children. And you, of course."

I looked down at the watch on my wrist. It was a wonderful watch. I'd gotten Derek a sweater, a nice blue vee-neck to match his eyes, but my gift wasn't in the same class as this watch.

"After all," he continued, teasing, "a woman who is obsessed by her career path should be able to tell time."

"Hey, I love the watch, but I'm not all that obsessed."

He smiled. "From the first time we met and you fed me that career path nonsense, I knew you were trying to convince yourself as much as me that you loved your job."

"You may be right, but it's about time I found something I could do for a living. I'd like to think I won't spend my old age in a welfare hotel. My family doesn't have any money. I want some kind of security."

My feelings on that subject weren't exactly a perversion, but I was afraid that Derek, with his free and easy life, would think it was. He continued driving, impassive.

"It probably sounds . . . old-fashioned to you," I said, "with the way you live."

"What do you mean? I live very sensibly."

"Well, you're not afraid to be on the edge, living in sublets with part-time work. I admire that. But artists can improve or change, or make it as they get older. Dancers just get older. Their joints start to hurt. They get slow."

We were on the turnpike then, moving steadily with little traffic around us. Derek put his arm around my shoulder and rubbed my neck.

"You take things so seriously. I know. I know," he said, stopping my protest before it was out of my mouth. "You think you have to. One of these days you and I are going to have to have a talk about . . . things."

"What things?"

He shrugged. "Life. For now, though, you should think about what I'm saying. Creative Financial is not the first business I've been involved in, but it is by far the loosest and the least likely to provide a career path. The nature of the company puts it in a continual race with the IRS. If Congress does something about that AMT loophole, there goes your leasing department. If the tax treaty with one of the offshore havens isn't renewed, there goes another department." He flicked his fingers. "Poof!"

"Let's not even think about that."

"What you should do is enjoy the fact that you have an easy job in a company that has no product other than tax manipulation. Believe me, I would not be there if C.F. were the type of place where people pursued career paths. It's a playpen for adults."

"That's not entirely true. What about Charlotte Smoot? She certainly takes the place seriously. And she's done wonderfully."

"Charlotte is a part owner. It's not the same thing. And she's only achieved her one-woman empire by watching it all the time. I find her pitiful. Until her infatuation with Eddie started, I never realized the woman had any human emotions."

Here was my chance to bring up the subject of Amanda. Just mention her as part of the Eddie-Charlotte-Amanda triangle and sort of step sideways into the nude drawing of her I'd found in Derek's studio. "By the way," I could have said.

"I just happened to notice that lovely nude of Amanda. When . . . ?" I could have said it, but I didn't. It was like the car registration. I didn't want to know anything bad.

We hit heavy traffic on the approach to the George Washington Bridge, finally coming to a full stop in the toll line. Derek shifted into neutral, then slid his hand across my knee. "Shall we go directly to your place?"

"Let's."

The next two days were as close to perfection as anything I have ever experienced. The rest of the world only existed peripherally, a fleeting momentary distraction. Life was a cornucopia, an emotional, physical feast. Were we rushing things? Sure, but once you find yourself on that kind of a high, sensible is the last thing in the world you want to be. By Sunday I had an extra toothbrush, a hairdryer, and a pair of jeans at Derek's apartment. His bathrobe was draped over the hook on my bathroom door, his razor in my cabinet. I was almost deranged with happiness.

We had decided to spend the night at my place. Generally, that's my least favorite time of the week, when the fun is ending and it won't start again for five days. Being with Derek, knowing we'd be taking the A train to the same place the next morning, made it much better.

We were on the sofa, me sitting, Derek sprawled over it with his head in my lap, and Moses resting comfortably on Derek's chest. The evening was heading into night, and the first credits of *A Christmas Carol* were just rolling across my television screen when my doorbell rang.

"Are you expecting anybody?"

"No. Maybe it's O'Hagan," I joked, remembering the last time this had happened to us. I got up reluctantly and padded across the room in my bare feet, my robe dragging on the floor.

"Who is it?"

"It's Henry, Miss Indermill."

Henry is my building's super. He's good at his job and always around when I need him. However, he is also an insatiable gossip. He and my neighbors the Codwallader sisters have gotten a lot of mileage out of me. My lifestyle—my tap dancing, my hours, my boyfriends—is an ongoing wonder to this trio. Straightening my robe until it came up to my chin, I cracked the door.

Henry peered back at me through the crack, shrewd dark eyes settling on my housecoat.

"Thought I heard company in there. Hope I'm not interrupting anything."

I shook my head.

"Well, you may know that Eunice and Ethel Codwallader have been gone for a week. Visiting family."

"Oh?"

"They asked me to get their mail for them."

I nodded. This had to be going somewhere.

"Well, the postman put this in their box by mistake, first of the week, and I never noticed till today that it was addressed to you." He thrust a flat manila envelope through the door.

"Thank you, Henry."

I reached for the envelope just as Derek called from the living room. "Hurry up, Bonnie. You're going to miss the best part." I closed the door on Henry's widening eyes.

Back on the sofa I examined the envelope casually. It was one of the nine-by-eleven ones used to mail flat documents. It bore a New York City postmark. The handwritten return address in the East Twenties meant nothing to me, nor was the handwriting familiar. I peeled the flap back, one eye on the television, and pulled out a bundle of papers stapled at their top. Clipped over them was a note in that same unfamiliar handwriting.

Dear Bonnie:

I came across an extra copy of my article and am taking the liberty of dropping it in a mailbox tonight. If you have a chance to read it over the holidays, and have your comments ready when I return from Florida, we'll be able to include them in January's staff newsletter. Hope you and yours have a Merry Christmas.

Cordially,
Ashley Gartner

I gasped and dropped the package like a hot potato.

At ten P.M. I was back in O'Hagan's damp, dismal office, a miserable place to end an idyllic weekend. After seeing Mr. Gartner's signature, I'd had enough sense to handle the letter and envelope by their edges. As soon as O'Hagan saw them, he sent them to be fingerprinted and looked at by handwriting experts. But not before making a sketch of the postmark. Now he sat across from me, studying it.

"New York, New York, 10010," he read. "A.M., eighteen December 1987." Looking up, he shook his head sadly. I guess he had every reason to be unhappy. This new evidence supported Hector Rodriguez's story that he had left Ashley Gartner alive and well.

O'Hagan sighed. "That's life." Slapping his hands flat on the desk, he pushed himself up. "It's late, Miss Indermill. I'll get one of the boys to run you home."

"Thank you, but someone's waiting to drive me."

He stared at me for a moment. "Would that someone be Derek Thorensen?"

"That's right."

"Sit back down for a second, Miss Indermill." He looked so concerned. For some reason this unnerved me. "You seem like a nice woman. You worry about Rodriguez, about things like truth. I'd hate to see you worrying so much about other people you forgot to take care of yourself."

"I take care of myself."

His eyebrows rose. Clearly he didn't think I was taking care of myself. "I feel like I've got this duty to tell you something about the kind of guy you're hanging around with," he said.

"I know everything about Derek I want to know."

"Then I'm going to tell you something you don't want to know. Right away I didn't like the guy, so I had one of my boys run a background check on him. Strictly legal," he added. "This was before we located your cabbie. My man uncovered a few inconsistencies in Thorensen's background you may be interested in."

"I'm not." Rising, I started toward the door.

"I'd like to tell you this, for your own sake."

Whenever someone tells me he's doing something for my own sake, I can be sure it's something that's going to leave me feeling rotten. I had this hollow, nervous feeling in the pit of my stomach. I didn't want to listen, but I knew I had to.

"That loft Thorensen lives in, the two thousand square feet in one of the hottest neighborhoods in town that a friend was kind enough to rent him, cheap?"

I nodded, afraid of what was coming.

"It's a co-op. Little over three years ago, Thorensen paid two hundred and thirty thousand dollars for it. He put fifty percent down. That's one hundred and fifteen thousand dollars."

"I can divide."

O'Hagan stood up and walked to his door.

"You might also be interested in knowing that he's on Interpol's records. In '72 Thorensen and a cousin were arrested trying to smuggle hashish out of Turkey. The only thing that kept them out of a Turkish jail was his uncle's diplomatic status."

I couldn't bear listening anymore. Jerking the door open, I walked past him and down the steps to the central corridor where Derek was waiting. I could feel O'Hagan's eyes on my back the entire way, and I was determined not to break down. My resolve held until Derek and I walked out of the precinct.

"How did it go?" he asked, reaching for my hand.

"It went fine." I moved several feet from him. On the other side of the street was a city bus stop. A block away was a bus, waiting at a light. I headed for the stop. Derek followed me.

"Then what's wrong? You're upset. What did that guy say?" At the other side of the street he took my elbow. I yanked my arm away, stepped on the curb, and began rummaging in my purse for a token, all the time refusing to look at Derek.

"You bet I'm upset," I said, "but it has nothing to do with O'Hagan." Finally I glared at him. "You've been lying to me. You lied about your apartment. You lied about your car. You probably lied about all that expensive art, didn't you? And about Amanda."

The bus stopped in front of us and its doors opened. Under the streetlight Derek's skin was pale. He rubbed his temple.

"Bonnie! Wait! If you would give me a chance to explain. I had planned to talk to you about . . ."

I climbed onto the bus. He put his foot on the bottom step. I was already stuffing my token in the box.

"You coming or not?" the bus driver asked him.

Derek looked frantically at the street, then back at me. "Please come with me. I can't leave my car there."

"Why not?" I snapped. "If anything happens to it, you can get your friend to loan you another one."

He stepped back into the street. As the bus lumbered away from the curb, I stumbled down the aisle to a window seat. When I looked out the window, Derek was slumped against the bus shelter wall. He looked miserable. Within seconds my eyes filled with tears. My hand reached toward the buzzer. I'd get out at the next corner and listen to whatever he had to say. Then we were rolling past his Mercedes, and I remembered that chill in his blue eyes a few nights earlier in Raymond's garage. I forced my hand away from the signal.

CHAPTER 8

◆◆◆◆◆◆◆◆◆◆◆◆◆

Tuesday morning Eddie peered over our wall. "Good morning, Bonnie. You're looking better. I ran into somebody last night who said to tell you hello." After that teaser his head sank from view.

I wheeled my chair around our partition. Good old Fast Eddie. His desk was covered with the multicolored racing forms he bought on the street. His collar was unbuttoned, his tie loose. He had tilted his chair back and stretched his feet across the window ledge.

"Eddie," I said, smiling for the first time in a while, "you're a credit to Creative Financial."

"I try."

Forcing myself to sound more offhanded than I felt, I asked, "Who said to tell me hello last night?"

There were the beginnings of a grin, but when he took a longer look at me, his expression turned serious.

"I'm sorry, Bonnie. It wasn't the Viking. It was Hector."

My spirits drooped. "Hector? What did he want?"

"He wanted to thank you for going to O'Hagan and getting him out."

"What else would he expect me to do? Withhold evidence and let him rot in jail?"

Eddie shrugged. "I don't know. Sometimes guys like Hector don't get a lot of breaks." He leaned forward suddenly, then said in a lower voice, "He told me he heard a woman in Gartner's apartment that night after the party."

I was right! O'Hagan had been fishing around for information about a late-night visitor.

"That's probably why O'Hagan's been giving Amanda
such a hard time," Eddie said.

"That's probably why he gave me such a hard time, too.
Fortunately I had an alibi." And it looked as if Amanda
didn't. O'Hagan wouldn't still be questioning her if Eddie
had provided an alibi, would he?"

"How does Hector claim to know about this woman," I
asked. "Was he watching Mr. Gartner's apartment?"

"No. His family lives in the superintendent's apartment
downstairs from the Gartners'. Hector said that in his living
room he can hear from upstairs."

"So who was it?"

"He doesn't know. It wasn't that clear, and he'd been nap-
ping anyway. Don't mention this to anybody. O'Hagan told
him to keep it quiet."

"Eddie, if I wanted to keep something quiet, you're the
last person on earth I'd tell."

"Aw. Is that why you won't tell me what happened with
you and Derek? You two looked pretty tight on that back
stairway last week."

"I don't want to talk about my problems anymore, Eddie.
I'd rather ignore them for a while."

The day before I had confided in Eddie, to a point. I had
to come up with something to explain my red, puffy eyelids
and the fact that I was incapable of coherent conversation.
I'd told him about our breakup, but not why. Derek's lies
were his own business. I'd told Eddie about my phone ringing all night long on Sunday, too, but I didn't tell him how
many times I almost picked it up. I had no intention of telling him how, last night, I'd broken down and tried Derek's
number. And if I tried explaining how many times I'd let
Derek's phone ring before giving up, I'd risk bursting into
tears once again.

"Don't want to talk about it," he repeated thoughtfully.
"I'll tell you what. Let's sneak out the back stairs and head

102

over to Thunder Road. We'll get smashed, and I'll tell you something I don't want to talk about, and then you can tell me something you don't want to talk about, and by the time we leave, we'll both feel better."

"Do I get to choose what you're going to tell me about?" I asked, half serious. "I'll tell you all my sordid details if you'll tell me what you and Amanda did after you left the Christmas party. Did you take a cab back to her place with her, or what?"

My question surprised him. To be honest, it surprised me too. I don't usually suggest to men I work with that I'm interested in hearing about their sex lives. But that's exactly what I meant where Amanda and Eddie and the night of the Christmas party were concerned.

"Amanda is not that kind of girl," he said finally, the implication being that I was.

"You could have fooled me."

Eddie swung around to face his desk. "Better get back to this work. Charlotte's given me a lot to do."

"Bull. Come on, Eddie. You can trust me. Did you go home with Amanda? Did you go out for something to eat? Did you get separate cabs?"

"Aw, Bonnie. What's with you? You're so interested in how I spend my nights, why don't you spend one of them with me? Just because you were caught in bed with the Viking, you think everybody else in this place is a degenerate."

"So far I haven't seen anything to suggest otherwise. Eddie, I'm not interested in how you spend your nights. I'm interested in how Amanda spends hers."

He glared at me. "Why? You think Amanda went over to Gartner's apartment? That's ridiculous!"

"Why ridiculous?"

"Because she is a class act, that's why. Look, you want to know what Amanda and I did? We took a cab to her place on the Upper West Side. She lives in a brownstone that you would kill for. Amanda got out of the cab, and I stayed in it. The next night I picked her up at eight—"

"I'm not interested in the next night. I don't know why talking about this annoys you. You both had to talk to O'Hagan."

Eddie muttered into his keyboard. "We talked to O'Hagan because it was mandatory. You, as far as I know, are not connected with the police. And gentlemen don't discuss their private lives with coworkers."

I took the hint, rolled back into my cubicle, and took out my book. I suppose that if there was anything to be happy about that morning, it was the fact that I had no work to do. The limbo that had affected C.F. since Mr. Gartner's death continued, and for me that was fine. Doing anything more than languishing was out of the question. Unless it was bugging Eddie about his private life.

Why did I care about that anyway? Whatever Eddie and Amanda had told O'Hagan had been enough to keep her out of jail and that was all that mattered. I had problems of my own to deal with. The love of my life had gone sour, my career path led nowhere. My future was in turmoil.

Was I ever shocked when I discovered the vast extent by which Eddie's problems and turmoils dwarfed mine!

A face floated around and a hand pawed me delicately, but the other hands stayed on my throat.

A voice said softly—

"Oh, Edwin, can we get together for a moment, please."

It was later that afternoon. The now-familiar musical-comedy soprano floated over our cubicles, a rude interruption to my detective story. I had by that time honed my paperback concealing tactics to a fine art. I shoved my book under a stack of computer printouts. Eddie's usual reply came a second later.

"On my way, Charlotte."

On the opposite side of the partition, Helen's eager, scrubbed face appeared. After a quick look into Eddie's bay—just long enough to see he would be a minute or two—she started toward Charlotte's office. She was wearing this anxious, tight smile I was seeing more and more of. If she didn't soon get a chance to butter Charlotte up, her face was going to crack from the strain.

"Charlotte, do you have a minute to talk to me about—"

"Not right now, Ellen. Catch me later."

I peeked into Eddie's cubicle. The metamorphosis was under way—the collar-buttoning, the tie-tightening.

"And the battle for Fast Eddie's body beautiful still rages," I whispered. "Will it be the beautiful but lowly secretary, or will the high-powered lady executive—"

"Edwin?" Charlotte's voice was rising.

"Yes, Charlotte. Coming."

When he stood up, he was Edwin the Company Man, combed and buttoned and knotted, an altogether different person than Fast Eddie Fong.

As soon as the Company Man and Charlotte were shielded behind her closed office door, Helen skulked into my territory.

"Did you hear that? She doesn't even know my name."

I shrugged. "She's probably got a lot on her mind."

"She's only got one thing on her mind, and it's that . . . moron, Eddie. You know what's going on in there?" she added with a peevish nod at Charlotte's door.

"No." Quite honestly, I had never seriously thought that something was going on between Charlotte and Eddie. The idea was within the realm of the physically impossible, especially with Helen bringing it up.

"What do you think is going on in there, Helen?"

"Sex," she hissed. "Why do you think he's getting all the interesting projects?"

I rubbed my forehead for a second, as if I was giving this a lot of thought.

"I don't know," I finally admitted. "Do you think if you and I offered to have sex with her, we'd get some interesting projects too?"

Helen blinked, straightened her shoulders, and said

105

primly, "You're no better than he is." With that, she marched away.

When Eddie finally emerged, he was all business. The rest of the day he had his nose in his work. He was in his cubicle when I left that evening, and when I got in the next morning.

"How about lunch today, Eddie."

"You're on. But cool it this morning." He nodded toward Charlotte's office. "She doesn't like me socializing so much."

"You mean she thinks I'm after you too?"

"She thinks every woman is after me."

It was a little before lunch when Charlotte walked out of her office with a handful of papers and carried them past my bay into Eddie's.

That time she almost got me by surprise. I slammed my paperback into a computer-operating-system manual and began beating on my keyboard. It didn't matter. I could have had a game on my monitor and Charlotte wouldn't have noticed. She had eyes for no one but Eddie.

Charlotte's wardrobe had finally reached a plateau of vivid but more or less sensible work dresses. There hadn't been anything to equal the purple spandex fiasco since the Christmas party. The same was true of her haircut, which now fell somewhere between the barbershop number she'd had when I started and the Christmas party glitter. Don't misunderstand. This was not Miss America. But at this point Charlotte looked—presentable. A not-so-attractive fortyish businessman would not have been out of place with her on his arm. Eddie and Charlotte, though, that was another matter.

They talked business for a few seconds, then their voices dropped. From my side of the wall I couldn't make out their words, but after a minute I heard behind me:

"Remember, Edwin, we need to meet on that later today."

"You've got it, Charlotte."

She continued past my cubicle and into the corridor. It

was by chance that I happened to look up in time to catch what happened next. She had pulled her coat from the closet. As she stretched her arm into the sleeve, she raised her shoulder and blew Eddie a kiss over it. Her lips formed a soundless "Tonight."

What an awful awakening for me! Thinking back on it, I'd almost swear Charlotte hesitated until she knew I was looking. Maybe she did. Maybe this was Charlotte's way of marking her territory, like a dog urinating on a fence to warn off the rest of the neighborhood dogs.

I'd seen examples of Eddie's bad judgment before, and I'd known he was trying to get on Charlotte's good side, but this was beyond flattery. This was grotesque. It can't be, I told myself. Eddie's cute and appealing and bright. He could have Amanda, if he tried hard enough. Charlotte, in comparison to Amanda, was an out-and-out disaster.

Noon finally arrived. I pounded on our mutual wall until it swayed under my onslaught.

"Lunchtime, Eddie!"

Keys clattering against Eddie's keyboard answered me.

"Come on. You promised to tell me all about your personal life." By that time I wasn't kidding. Eddie's personal life was more than a curiosity now. It had become a burning issue.

"In a second, Bonnie."

Standing, I looked over the wall. He was staring hard into his monitor. On his desk beside him was a pad of bookkeeping paper.

"Eddie?"

He made one final note, then stretched his arms over his head and groaned, "Free at last. I should eat lunch here, though. I'll bring you something from the cafeteria. My treat."

"The cafeteria's no treat. I'm sick of that eyeball staring up at me from my plate."

He cast an uneasy eye toward Charlotte's office.

"I know what you mean. We'll have to make it fast, though. Charlotte's . . ."

"Yeah, I know. Big Sister's watching."

Maybe I was a little hard on him, but Eddie's reaction was more than I expected. He got up and slammed his chair into his desk.

"Bullshit! She doesn't control me. Let's get the hell out of here. I know where we can get the best sesame noodles in Manhattan. Or at least the cheapest."

I'd sworn never to return to Chinatown with Eddie, and on the walk to that restaurant I began to regret breaking that vow. Leave it to Eddie. He didn't know where the beaten track was.

We walked up Canal to Mott and turned right. Those two streets teem with a surface life visible to every tourist: the phone booths topped with red pagodas; the open-air food stalls with their fresh fish and exotic vegetables; the poultry shop windows with plucked chickens dangling by their feet. Smells are pungent, the sounds of the stall-keepers' voices sharp. The Chinese language signs are lovely brushstrokes. The prosaic English translations under them announce: "Fish. No Credit. No Check. No Return."

As Eddie and I zigzagged deep into the belly of Chinatown, we left the tourists behind. Soon almost everybody on the street was Chinese. Many of the shop signs displayed only the Chinese characters without English translations. Here's where you start getting a sense of a real foreign country. It's not like Disney World, where the workers in the Chinese pavilion go home to tract houses at night. Here, one bolted door hides a population of nervous aliens running sewing machines fifteen hours a day. Walk under a dilapidated arch into a seedy alcove and you can watch an incredibly shabby chicken play tic-tac-toe.

At Doyer, a short curving street, we took another right. Eddie stopped me where the bend in the street was sharpest.

"This spot right here, Bonnie. During the Tong wars early in the century so many bodies were dumped here that it was called the Bloody Angle."

I looked down at the street and at the shops around us. Not terribly sinister, but not a place I wanted to linger either. Chinese New Year was a month away, but groups of bored teenagers already gathered on tenement steps, setting off firecrackers. Old women's faces showed through upper-floor windows behind torn shades. On a cold, moonless night I'll bet you could almost hear the spooky dark echoes of those bodies dumped on the Bloody Angle screaming their outrage.

"Nice," I said. "Where are we going?" The day was cold and my feet, even in my boots, were feeling it.

Grinning wickedly, Eddie said in an ominous voice, "To an opium den, my pale-skinned beauty."

We stopped at an unmarked door in a nondescript building. There was nothing on the door or building to indicate there was a restaurant inside. The two small windows were so grimy and steam-smeared it was impossible to see through them.

"What is this place?"

Eddie whispered. "It's the headquarters for a white slave ring. As soon as the knock-out drops in your noodles take effect, we're going to smuggle you out of the country and turn you into a sing-song girl."

"Good," I joked. "I could use some action."

We walked into a room not much bigger than our C.F. cubicles. It was filled haphazardly with mismatched Formica tables and chairs. The walls were unadorned except for big sheets of paper with Chinese characters in crayon, and one huge poster of a dragon, the astrological sign of the coming new year. There was no counter, no register, no waiter. If the place had been empty of its crowd of Chinese lunch patrons, I'd never have known it was a restaurant. Except for the smell, that is. The combination of ginger, garlic, and sesame oil turned it into heaven. Noodle heaven.

We found a table by ourselves along the wall.

I nodded toward the poster. "This is going to be a big new year, isn't it? The Year of The Dragon."

Eddie glanced at the poster, then back at me. "It's going to be a big year, but it's going to be the Year of the Monkey."

"What are you talking about? There are dragon posters all over the place."

That drew a grin from him. "My year, Bonnie," he said. "I was born in '56, The Year of The Monkey. And this is going to be a year when this monkey makes it big."

What ideas Eddie had about himself! I could only roll my eyes at that announcement.

He shrugged. "You'll see. I'll be right back." Eddie disappeared through a door at the rear of the restaurant, and a second later he returned carrying a couple bottles of beer and trailed by a middle-aged Chinese woman. She was wearing the traditional loose black silk pants and blouse. Her hands were on her hips, her eyes had fire in them. I couldn't understand a word she was saying to Eddie, but she was sure giving him hell. That comes across in any language.

Eddie ignored her tirade, just like he ignored the rest of his problems. He sat down across from me, and as soon as the woman paused for breath he said:

"Bonnie, this is my Aunt Chen. Aunt Chen, my coworker Bonnie."

Aunt Chen returned my smile with a polite nod. When Eddie had reeled off our order, she gave him a filthy look and spun on her heels. A second later a young waiter placed a chrome pitcher and two water glasses on our table. Eddie poured hot tea from the pitcher into our glasses.

"Your aunt doesn't seem very happy with you."

He shrugged. "She's pissed. I haven't been home much. You women give me nothing but trouble."

"So I've noticed." I took a sip of my tea. It was strong and hot enough to warm me right to my toes. "What's with you and Charlotte, anyway?"

He rolled his eyes. "Give me a break, Bonnie. Yesterday you couldn't leave me and Amanda alone, and now it's Charlotte."

"Yesterday I didn't know there was anything to ask about you and Charlotte."

The waiter returned with a big ironstone bowl. Placing it on our table, he lifted the lid. The fragrant, spicy steam from the noodles rose around me and I was transported.

I picked up my chopsticks. "Eddie, sometimes I wish I'd never met you. But not right now."

"See. Don't I always make everything all right? And take a look at this." He turned one of the bottles of beer so I could see its label. "Remember?"

"Double Happiness Beer," I read. "Sure I remember. I remember our horse too. What ever happened to him?"

Eddie grimaced. "He's still a few furlongs short of the finish line."

"So what about my forty-three dollars?"

"Drink your beer." Eddie served us each a great mound of noodles.

God, he was so annoying. "No wonder everybody is always mad at you. You gave my money to those thugs—"

"Not so loud." He put his finger to his lips. "I don't want the wrong people to hear us. Those guys aren't thugs."

"I know. They're business associates."

"Some of them used to be, sort of. I ran with one of the gangs for a while."

I raised my eyebrows.

"Hey, Bonnie, it was a long time ago. I've changed. Those guys on the subway—they're sort of like private cops—for one of the businessmen around here."

"I can't believe it," I said. "You, with a Columbia MBA, three-piece suits, and a Chase Manhattan training program on your resume. Can I ask you something personal?"

"As long as it's not about my sex life."

"Why are you at C.F., in the same crummy job that I'm in? You know more about computers than I ever will. Why did you leave the brokerage, and before that, Chase?"

"What do you mean, 'crummy job'? It's a great job. The brokerage? Let's just say I found their policies too rigid. And Chase—that place was impossible for a guy like me. A bunch of yuppies. They give me a free checking account, with unlimited overdraft protection, and then they get bent out of shape when I use it." He smiled from the memory.

I never knew when to believe Eddie, but I was beginning to understand a lot about him. He was one of those people who like to impress you by dropping hints about how worldly they are. One thing for sure: He laid waste to the myth of the inscrutable Oriental.

He was twirling the empty Double Happiness bottle across the table. "You got any room in your file cabinet?"

"I've got nothing but room in my file cabinet."

"Maybe I'll bring a couple six-packs of this back to the office."

"And drink beer there?"

"Relax, Bonnie. I'm in control of everything at the office."

"Oh, yeah?" I gave him as evil an eye as I could. "You in control of Charlotte?"

He hesitated. "I'm working on it," he finally said.

I wasn't going to let the subject go that easily.

"Eddie, are you and Charlotte . . ." What were the right words? When I thought about Eddie in a relationship, the right words were "hanging out" and "partying." With Charlotte, the idea of "hanging out," or "partying," was ludicrous. "Seeing each other?" I said after a moment.

He refused to look at me, which all but confirmed my fears.

"Charlotte is a charming and sophisticated woman," he finally said into his bowl of noodles. "We have many things in common."

That did it. Helen's incredible suggestion was true. How in the world had it started? Not at the Christmas party, where I'd taken my first turn down the road to ruin. That night Eddie had been blind to everybody but Amanda.

He went on without my prodding. Maybe he had been wanting to tell somebody about this. "Last Monday Charlotte and I both hung around the office a little late."

Eddie told me she had been feeling bad about Mr. Gartner's death. He had felt bad about the way he'd treated her at the party, or so he said.

"I invited her out for a drink and we got to talking, and one thing led to another and . . ." He smiled, sheepish, hoping for my approval.

"It's your life," I said. "But what about Amanda? I thought you two were interested in each other."

He finished his noodles Chinese-style, tilting the bowl to his mouth. When he had finished, he pushed the bowl aside.

"We are, but we're cooling it temporarily. At least around the office." He managed a wry smile. "Amanda's a lot of fun, but . . ."

"Eddie, girlfriends are supposed to be for fun."

"Yeah, sure. I know that, but . . ." He shrugged. I had the feeling there was something more he wanted to say about Amanda, but when he went on, the subject had been changed.

"You should understand, Bonnie. You're like me."

"Wait a second," I protested.

"I mean, you're one of the peons. My aunt and uncle got me out of China with nothing but the shirt on my back." He looked around the little restaurant. "They've done okay, if your idea of okay is running a chop suey joint. My idea of okay is about a thousand light years away from this. There comes a time when you've got to make your move, and for me, the time has come."

He picked the beer bottle off the table. "Double Happiness. That's what I'm going after. I've got a chance to go places at C.F. I mean, a place that structures tax shelters was made for a guy like me."

"Hey," I interrupted. "That reminds me. What ever happened to that offshore account you found in the computer that you thought was for one of the secret Chinese organizations?"

Eddie shook his head, dismissing my question. "I was wrong about that address. But listen, Bonnie. Here's the thing." He leaned across the table. "I have a master plan. You want to hear this?"

"Sure."

"I get Charlotte right where I want her, under my thumb.

I can do it too. Then I play my cards right, and before you know it, I'll be an officer in C.F. That will be my first happiness." Tilting the bottle into his cup, he finished it. "And after that, I'll work on my second happiness. Maybe Amanda. Maybe somebody with a little more up here." He tapped his knuckles against his forehead.

I sighed. "That's awfully mercenary, Eddie. Charlotte has feelings, you know."

Eddie's smile was shrewd. "Right. She's a delicate little lotus blossom." He smiled then, sort of as if we were co-conspirators. "It will all work out, Bonnie. You'll see. It's just that sometimes a guy's gotta do what a guy's gotta do."

That was the Wednesday before the long New Year's weekend. The following Monday, it became clear that Eddie had done what he had to do pretty well.

PART 2

Success

CHAPTER 9

◆◆◆◆◆◆◆◆◆◆◆◆◆◆◆

Change was in the wind at Creative Financial Ventures. We'd all known it was coming. The question was, in what form? The proposed merger with the bank was off. Discussions had been dropped after Mr. Gartner's death. So now what? Would Gartner's widow take a part in the company? Or would Fike or Smoot, or both of them, purchase her fifty-two percent? The office tingled with anticipation. Rumors buzzed like bees at a picnic. Then came one incredible display of histrionics and we all knew that Morton Fike was firmly in control.

"Out with the old! In with the new!"

With those words Morton Fike set off his reign of terror at C.F. We employees—there were almost a hundred of us—had been told to meet in the gigantic penthouse boardroom at nine A.M. on the Monday after New Year's weekend.

My work habits had slipped. I walked into the boardroom ten minutes late. Still, I was one of the first there. I took an aisle seat near the middle of the room.

Fike, Charlotte Smoot, and several others were already standing by the podium at the front. I didn't know much about Fike, but it was plain that the man was working himself into a lather. Every minute or so he glared into the slowly filling auditorium, then down at his watch. By nine-twenty he had the watch off and was thumping it into his palm. I couldn't help grinning. Meet your staff, Mr. Fike.

At nine-thirty the room was almost filled. Fike wasted no time. Stepping onto the podium, he began what would be a memorable speech by calling for a moment's silence for our deceased founder.

I closed my eyes. I was a bit on edge, but not overly nervous. We were about to hear a pep talk, I was certain. One of those "keep up the good work" and "your jobs are all secure" numbers that follow company upheavals. That those talks generally precede massive layoffs was something I'd worry about later. Fike didn't know me from Adam, so whatever he had to say wasn't going to have much to do with me, at least not for a while.

Around me my fellow employees were restive, whispering, twisting in their seats, popping open coffee cartons and unwrapping muffins. I opened my eyes when Fike's impatient throat-clearing noise sputtered through the microphone.

He was on a stool behind the podium, his head barely visible. What a ridiculous-looking chief executive officer he was, a squatty, toadish man, peeking bug-eyed over the lectern's top. Perhaps he knew he wasn't at his most effective up there. Stepping down abruptly, he snatched the microphone from its stand and walked forward until he stood directly in front of us. When he stopped, his feet were slightly apart. He balanced on their balls like a street fighter facing down his opponent. His grip on the microphone was tight enough to turn his knuckles white.

"I have heard rumors that it is going to be business as usual around here." Fike had a high-pitched, abrasive voice. His words chaffed through the air. Pausing, he glared out at us.

"You may rest assured that those rumors are not true."

Behind me on the aisle there was a ruckus as some late arrivals took their seats. Another throat-clearing from Fike put an end to that. Then his diatribe began in earnest.

"I had originally thought I would spend no more than a minute or two on the subject of rumors, but over the past week, after a great deal of serious reflection, I have decided to make rumors the subject of this, our first, get-together.

"I've heard rumors that the Off-Track Betting facility across the street gets so much business from Creative Financial, during office hours, that they've started offering our employees favorable group odds."

Oh, boy! I thought. Eddie's had it. Someone sitting near me tittered. Fike's eyes darted across my row.

"You think that's funny? I don't! I don't think it's the least bit funny that our employees feel free to abandon their workstations whenever the trumpets blare at the Meadowlands. And do you know another rumor I'm not particularly amused by? How about liquor on the job?"

That was scary. Had somebody—like maybe Helen—squealed about the six-packs Eddie had hidden in my file cabinet?

"Oh-ho!" Fike said, drawing back his head back and widening his eyes. "Just look at your shocked faces. Hard to believe, isn't it, but I've heard we have employees who have the unmitigated gall to keep liquor in their desk drawers. Does that make anybody here laugh?"

It didn't make me laugh, or anyone else in the room either. The hush that had fallen over Fike's audience was deathlike, but I would almost have sworn I could hear almost a hundred hearts quickening.

He was really working up a head of steam, pacing, glowering, his eyes bugging out from their sockets. His face had turned as red as an engorged blood vessel ready to burst.

"What about drugs?" he snarled. "Marijuana in the back stairwell. I didn't have to wait for the rumor there because I've smelled it myself. Then there's the one about cocaine in the ladies' room. How's that for a joke." He punctuated this by slamming the microphone against his leg.

Out of the corner of my eye I took a quick look across the aisle, where Derek was sitting. With Amanda, wouldn't you know. I was surprised to see him raise his hand to his mouth and yawn. Talk about arrogant! Next to him Amanda was white-faced, her hands clenched in her lap. She seemed frozen in place. Maybe the gossip about Amanda supplying Ashley Gartner with drugs was true. And just maybe—though I didn't like to think this—Derek was the source of those drugs.

"Here's another one for you," Fike screeched. "Calling in sick on Friday, then showing up at Thunder Road after work. Bet you thought you were putting one over on your stodgy old managers, didn't you? Anyone feel like giggling now? No? Let's try coming in late. Or taking the back stairs to another floor and sneaking out early? No laughs? I thought this was a fun crowd. I'll give you one of my favorites. This one is sure to get a chuckle."

By now Fike was shouting, gesturing wildly with the microphone. His face was scarlet.

"Inappropriate fraternization on company time!" He positively screamed his next words: "Why aren't you laughing?"

You could have heard a pin fall onto the inch-thick carpet. I think I had even stopped breathing. Suddenly, unexpectedly, my handbag began sliding from my lap. I made a desperate grab for it but only succeeded in banging Derek's Christmas watch against the chair in front of me. The purse's metal clasp clanged on my chair leg. There was a dull thump as the purse hit the floor.

"What? Is there someone here who wants to argue?" Fike's eyes shot to the area where I was sitting and hunted across my row. They stopped on me, moved on, hesitated, swept back. Or was that my imagination. Beads of perspiration broke out across my forehead.

"That's right! Hide! The only thing any of you are good at

is sneaking around. And you're not very good at that, either. My grapevine has told me all about the illicit hand-holding in empty conference rooms. Your sordid little romances in the back stairwell are public information. Don't play innocent with me. I know your names."

I could have sworn the man was looking right at me. He was demented, spitting his words, his face contorted into a fist of fury. Believe me, this dyspeptic gnome, this beet-faced homunculus, had me terrified. I had disobeyed all my career commandments and I was going to be fired.

I stole another look at Derek and caught him looking at me. For a moment our eyes locked. His lips began turning up in a smile. I felt my face growing warm and lowered my gaze quickly.

Fike's ranting went on and on, a laundry list of the staff's debaucheries: Theft of office supplies? Was that funny? Dozens of place-settings missing from the cafeteria? Personal long-distance calls charged to the company? No ha-ha's there? What about somebody's MBA project being composed on company equipment on company time, hidden away in a computer file? At last the list dwindled into our small atrocities—the crossword puzzles secreted under blotters, the paperbacks in desk drawers. I was thoroughly worn down, ready to confess to everything and slink out, tail between my legs, when he wrapped things up with this happy note: "Apropos the season, let me say, 'Out with the Old; In with the New.' From now on, there is a new way of doing things at C.F. My way! When I was in the army they called me 'Can Do' Fike because there was nothing I couldn't do. I can create a new Creative Financial, and I am going to. It's going to be lean and mean. Any of you who don't like the 'can do' way had better start looking for another job now because there's no place for you at C.F."

Fike let out a breath that bordered on a growl, crashed the microphone back onto the podium, and started toward the door. And then the most astonishing thing happened, almost as fantastic as the speech itself. Fast Eddie Fong, the notorious OTB habitué, the insatiable fraternizer, the guy with his bottles of beer stored in my cabinet drawer, the same Eddie Fong who had introduced me to the back stairwell's various pleasures, jumped up, shouted, "Way to go!" and started clapping.

A moment later Amanda was on her feet, tapping those pinkies. I saw Helen rise. Dumont, several rows behind her, was already up. In front of the room Charlotte Smoot began leading a chorus of "Bravo"s. In seconds almost everyone was standing, shouting "Bravo" and "Way to go" and clapping to beat the band. It was obscene. I held back. I already had guilt and fear to deal with. Was I going to let myself be forced into hypocrisy? I couldn't help taking another look at Derek. I expected him, that infamous liar, to be clapping and shouting along with the rest of them. Instead he was still in his seat, shaking his head as if he couldn't believe what was going on around him. Leaping to my feet, I began clapping like a maniac.

At the boardroom door Fike paused, nodded briefly, and left. We filed into the aisles, noisy now. Fike's diatribe and the farce that followed it had had a peculiar energizing effect on us. Like a mob with a charismatic leader we had been whipped into a frenzy. Amanda, for one, was transformed. Her pale skin was flushed, her amber eyes wide.

"Wasn't he magnificent," she gushed.

"Magnificent," Eddie echoed.

"Unbelievable," Derek said from somewhere close behind me. A second later I thought his hand brushed mine. Maybe I hoped. Whichever, my whole body trembled. I glanced up, but he was already moving away. As he disappeared into the crush of our fellow employees around us, I had to stop myself from calling his name.

I was still having my problems with Derek. I mean, the problems were with me. Hardly an hour passed when I didn't remember something wonderful about him. A day we spent together, a night, a conversation, a meal, a ride in the car. He'd even won over my mother in the end.

That was part of the problem. If everything hadn't been so perfect, his imperfection wouldn't have been so tremendous.

It wasn't the fact that Derek had a lot of money to spend that upset me. I'm not insane. I know that more money is better than less money. It wasn't even the money's secret source. Oh, in my most paranoid moments I wondered where the money was coming from and feared the worst— whatever that was: he was a big-time drug smuggler, or the partner-in-crime of that other C.F. employee with too much money to spend, Amanda Paradise.

But when I thought about it seriously, I couldn't imagine Derek doing anything too awful. The Interpol thing may have been true, but sixteen years before Derek had been eighteen years old. At eighteen I had married the hind end of a donkey because he had sensitive bone structure. You have to forgive the crazy things people do when they're eighteen. It's a bad year.

The big problem was the lies. The elaborately thought out, carefully planned lies. The nonrelationship with Amanda. The fake wealthy friend, the fake sublet, the fake loaned Mercedes. The fortune in paintings on his wall. If I carried this to its ultimate, was anything at all real? Was his affection fake? Did he transform himself into his imaginary friend when we made love?

I had agonized over this for a week now. The man of my dreams, feeding me a string of lies. Maybe I should have heard him out, a part of me said. Another, sensible part countered, "Keep away from the bastard."

Now, following Fike's speech, I had an even more sensible part of me saying, "Forget your love life. You've got bigger things to worry about than your libido."

It was only a matter of hours before the flurry of blue interoffice memos began. The first to cross my desk announced one promotion and two resignations in the Offshore Enterprises Division. The second let us know that the head of accounting was leaving. The purge had begun.

It really hit home late the next afternoon when Perry Dumont stopped by my desk. I cringed as he slithered into my cubicle. He looked even more disreputable than usual, if you can picture that. A little more red-eyed, a little more greased down. Completing this picture was a cigarette, an inch of ash hanging precariously from its end. I looked at it, surprised.

"I didn't know you smoked, Perry."

"I stopped for six months. But . . . you know how it is." He waved his hand, the one with the cigarette. The ash fell onto his pants leg. I wasn't about to touch it. I pointed to the red spark. Perry flicked the ash away, leaving a tiny black-rimmed hole. He stared at it for a second, then looked back at me.

"This is good-bye, Bonnie. I want you to know how much I've enjoyed working with you."

You cannot imagine the effect those words had on me. I thought I'd just been fired. My intestinal tract went wild. As I gulped for air, Eddie came into my cubicle.

"Understand you're leaving us," he said to Perry.

"That's right," Perry said. "I'll be working out of my house at first, doing consulting."

Perry, consulting? Maybe if Lee Iacocca consults, it pays. For most of us, though, consulting is a euphemism for unemployment.

"Well, good luck with it."

The two men shook hands. By then I had realized what was going on. "Yes," I said. "Good luck."

Perry leaned down and gave me a peck on the cheek. A lecher to the end, even in the face of adversity, he managed to give my thigh a squeeze as he straightened up. Then he was gone. He passed Helen's cubicle without looking her way.

What a relief! Better him than me. My relief didn't last long, though. Why him rather than me? Maybe Perry wasn't my favorite fellow employee, but he was a competent technical person and a capable teacher. If they were getting rid of him, what was going to happen to me?

The blue memos continued. Wednesday morning there was such a deluge I could hardly keep my phone list updated. That afternoon's interoffice mail brought one even more surprising than Perry's sudden departure. It announced Eddie's meteoric rise to the top of C.F.'s heap.

"As of January 11, Charlotte Smoot will assume the title and responsibilities of Senior Vice President and Director of Technical Services. Mr. Edwin Fong has accepted the position of Manager, Leasing Data Base Facilities, under Ms. Smoot's direction."

Nobody who knew the parties involved, except perhaps Morton Fike, thought that Eddie's promotion was due to anything other than his blossoming romance with Charlotte. But nobody could argue with his end result, either. He may have paid a hefty price, but it looked as if Eddie had done what he had to do pretty well, and pretty fast.

For several days after Fike's speech I lived under a cloak of quiet anxiety. It wasn't necessarily rational—I was far from Creative Financial's worst employee. In the total scheme of things, if you overlooked the fact that I never did much work, I was probably one of the better ones. Still, I had a feeling my name would be showing up on one of Fike's memos before long. I wasn't wrong. It was the memo's content I was wrong about.

"Indermill. Call Morton Fike ASAP," the phone message waiting on my desk Friday morning read. The message had been taken at 7:52. Can you believe that! Maybe it had been 7:52 the evening before. Either way, I hadn't been there to take the call. What kind of a nut's going to be in the office at 7:52, A.M. or P.M.? Less than a week and the place had turned into a sweatshop.

It was 9:09 A.M. when I called Fike's number. At that point I was still okay, fingers steady on the dial. The phone rang two, three, four times. He didn't answer. I was about to cradle the receiver when—

"Fike here!"

His bellow unnerved me so that I dropped the phone on my desk. It clattered, teetered on the edge, then slipped off. Before the receiver hit the floor it gave my trash basket a hefty whack. "Fike! Fike!" screamed from the receiver under the desk. Pure, unadulterated terror took over. My stomach felt as if it had dropped about a foot. My knees weakened. I snatched up the receiver. The last thing I heard before I slammed it down was a shriek: "I'm not amused!"

It was ten minutes before I was composed enough to dial the number again. Thank God Amanda answered. Yes, Morton Fike wanted to see me immediately. I ran his list of no-no's over in my head as I combed my hair into its business "do." About the only things I wasn't guilty of were sneaking out to the OTB and stealing the eyeball dishes. So this was it. Napoleon was going to drop the guillotine.

I walked down the executive corridor to his office, trying to calm myself on the way. So what if I was fired? I'd find another job. This is America. Nobody starves to death. Right? Wrong. I already had visions of myself on the bread line.

Amanda was at her desk, hands poised gingerly over the keys of her typewriter, brow wrinkled in concentration as she stared at a steno pad.

"Hi! I'm here," I said bravely.

She jumped. "Oh." Accidentally her hand dropped onto the typewriter keyboard. The keys sprang up against the paper in the machine. A look of despair crossed Amanda's face.

"Not again!" Tearing the page from the machine, she wadded it angrily and threw it into her wastebasket. With a deep sigh she rubbed her hand over her forehead. Then she leaned down close to the steno pad.

I glanced at the pad. Her notes were a real mess. "Do you take Gregg or Pitman?"

"Neither. I just try to write real fast."

"Does that work? Can you read your notes?"

Squinting, she pulled the pad to within inches of her eyes. "Sometimes."

"Mr. Fike wanted to see me."

"I know." She glanced at the phone console on her desk. "He's on the phone right now. Can you wait?"

"Of course." Would I dare walk out on my own execution?

I settled into the settee and for several minutes enjoyed the travesty of secretarial efficiency in front of me so much that my own problems faded. With each fresh sheet of letterhead, Amanda's fingers trembled harder, her jabs at the keys became more tentative. And with each typo her lower lip edged out farther, the throw into the basket grew more violent. The last straw came when one of her increasingly manic jabs went totally awry. Spinning away from the machine, she examined one of her fingers and wimpered:

"Now look what's happened! I broke my nail! Do you have any Crazy Glue?"

"Not on me."

"He wants this letter perfect," she whined. "No typos. It's only half a page, but I can't do it. I just can't."

"Do you want me to type it for you?"

Her jaw dropped. "Can you type?"

I walked over to her. "Hop up for a second."

I batted out Fike's letter, a luncheon invitation to a prospective client, with no trouble. Amanda was amazed when I handed it to her a minute later.

"Oh, Bonnie. You're always so nice to me. How can I ever thank you?"

"It's nothing. Want me to do the envelope?"

She was ecstatic by the time I pulled the envelope out of the machine. "Look, are you going to Thunder Road tonight? Let me buy you a drink."

Right then her intercom buzzed. Fike was ready for me. I smiled at Amanda. "Thanks a lot, Amanda. But"—I nodded toward Fike's door—"I don't think I'll be feeling sociable this evening."

"Oh, I don't know about that," she singsonged brightly as she reclaimed her chair.

"Indermill?"

"Yes, sir."

Fike nodded to a chair on the other side of his desk. "Take a seat please."

For a few seconds he thumbed through a file, ignoring me. Then, without looking up, he said:

"I've heard a bit about you, through the office grapevine."

More rumors? This was going to be awful. I didn't want to hear it. I didn't *have* to hear it. I drew myself up, ready to stand. I wasn't going to sit still and be abused. I'd just flat out quit.

"Mr. Fike," I began, but my voice was so little it might have come from a frightened six-year-old.

"Yes, quite a bit," he said, not hearing me. He shuffled the papers in front of him and I recognized my resume. My knees started knocking, ending any chance for a dignified exit.

"I hear through Charlotte Smoot, by way of Edwin Fong, that you're one of our most promising technical people." He looked up from the papers. His bug eyes caught mine. After a moment they narrowed.

"Are you all right, Indermill?"

By then I was having trouble breathing. What was he talking about? My "Yes, sir" was scarcely more than a gasp.

"Fong, who has accepted the position of Data Base Manager for our Leasing Department, is particularly impressed by the way you've grasped the technical complexities of our operation. In addition, Fong tells me you embody the attitude the new Creative Financial management team needs." He banged his fist on my resume. "The 'can do' attitude, Indermill!"

Management? Had he said management? The M word? Surely I wasn't having auditory hallucinations. I found my voice. My "Yes, sir" was quick and smart this time, a management "Yes, sir."

"Indermill, I am pleased to offer you the position of Assistant Data Base Manager for Leasing, working under Fong. You must understand that for the present there will be no additional remuneration. However, once I've gotten C.F. down to fighting weight, there's no telling how far you'll go with us."

I felt like laughing out loud, like jumping up and down for excitement. I took a deep breath.

"Thank you, Mr. Fike. I'm happy to accept."

"Thank you, Indermill. You can look forward to a lot of hard work, you know."

"Mr. Fike," I said in all seriousness, "I thrive on hard work."

He nodded sagely. "I know people, Indermill, and I know this is a choice I won't regret."

He showed me out of his office into Amanda's. I was grinning ear to ear. She returned my smile, then proudly handed her boss the letter I'd typed a few minutes earlier.

"At long last. Knew you could do it, Paradise. Just remember what I told you."

"Yes, Mr. Fike," she chirped happily. "Can do!"

It didn't take long for me to figure out that being the assistant to the biggest screw-around in the office had its drawbacks. They were the kind I should have foreseen when I was offered the job, knowing what I did about Eddie. I guess I'd been too excited to think, then. Soon enough I was being asked to perform duties that had nothing to do with my job description. Duties I'll bet would have given Morton Fike apoplexy.

"Eddie, are we going to have a meeting?" I asked the Monday morning after my promotion. "I'm not quite clear what it is I'm supposed to be doing." That was an understatement. I was in a total fog about what the assistant data base manager did.

Eddie had his eyes glued to his monitor. He didn't answer me.

"What are you working on?" I asked.

129

"Nothing."

"Come on, Eddie. I'm your assistant and I'm not sure what you do." About the only thing I was pretty sure of was that Eddie was writing a program to handicap horses.

He looked up briefly. "Don't sweat it. Reorganize something. Where's your initiative, anyway? Why do you think you were promoted?" He tapped his knuckles on the side of his head. "Think, Bonnie. Use your noodle. It's good for you."

"Some supervision and training wouldn't hurt either," I snapped.

He groaned. "You women are making me crazy. If I wasn't too far gone, I'd become a monk." He looked down at his watch. "All right. There's something I need you to do for me right now."

"Okay! Let me get some paper so I can write instructions." Finally something. My first assignment as one of C.F.'s managers. I was rummaging for a sharp pencil when Eddie leaned across our partition.

"Forget the paper." He gestured for me to come closer, then whispered, "I want to run across the street and place a bet. If Charlotte or Fike call, cover for me. Tell them I went down to accounting."

Some things never change. I nodded, but my disappointment must have been obvious. Eddie rolled his eyes. "Don't be such a Girl Scout, Bonnie. You're going to get plenty to do eventually. More than you can handle." Poking his face toward me he bugged his eyes. "You're going to get lean and mean," he hissed in a real good imitation of Fike's crazed Napoleon voice. "A 'can do' manager. But the first thing you've got to learn to do is cover for your degenerate boss. Got that?"

I nodded.

"Thanks, doll. I owe you one."

As he walked away, he looked back over his shoulder. "Seriously, Bonnie. Before you know it, you'll be in over your head."

In retrospect, truer words were never spoken. At the time, who knew?

I smiled back at Eddie. Once he had gone, though, I sat there in a little sulk. I've never been a big believer in the Protestant work ethic, but this was getting ridiculous. If my new position was going to entail nothing more than covering for Eddie, and I didn't dare pull out a paperback for fear Fike would rip it out of my hands, what was I going to spend my days doing? With no "fraternization" allowed in the back stairwell, and nobody to fraternize with anyway, my days at C.F. stretched ahead, long and dull.

I turned on my monitor and logged in, but after a minute I flicked it off again. What did it matter? I didn't have anything to do. What was it Eddie had been working on, anyway? He'd been busy. Maybe I could help. I was his assistant.

I walked into his bay. The monitor was dark, but the small green light at its corner was burning. I gave the contrast knob a twist. The screen flooded with amber light.

Knowing Eddie, I half expected to find his handicapping program on the screen. No. It was work. Real work. This made me even sulkier than I had been. Why hadn't he wanted to share it with me?

There were three columns running down a page. The first was a series of dates, the second, some combination of numbers and letters that meant nothing to me. The third column contained what might have been dollar amounts. I had no idea what I was looking at.

I pushed the page-up button several times, until I found the first page of the account. Where there should have been a name, though, there was a number. It looked to me like one of the Offshore Division's account numbers. But how could that be? Those accounts had nothing to do with Commercial Leasing. I had leaned in close, trying to figure out what these numbers meant and how they related to each other, when a hand suddenly reached past me and flipped off the screen.

131

"What do you think you're doing? I come back for my wallet and catch you messing around with my stuff."

Eddie was standing right behind me. When I turned, I was surprised to see how furious he looked.

"I'm sorry," I said. "I wanted to see what you were working on. You were so busy and I thought I could help."

"I'll let you know when I need help." He motioned for me to get out of his chair.

"It's some sort of personal betting thing, isn't it?" I whispered. "That's why you won't show me. You're handicapping horses."

He slid into his seat. "You've got it, Bonnie. It is my own, personal secret work, and the second you get out of my bay, I'm going to bury it so deep in this computer you'll never find it again."

"You're some terrific boss." With that I stomped back into my bay, dug out one of my paperbacks, and plopped it open on my desk. My blatant show of disdain had no effect on my boss. He finished whatever he had to do at his desk—burying his program from my prying eyes, I suppose—and then left. Passing my desk, he leaned down and whispered, taunting, "Name the secret file and collect a fortune."

For the next few days my job consisted largely of lying to Charlotte when Eddie snuck out to meet Amanda for lunch, lying to the receptionist when Eddie was two hours late, and telling a whopper to Fike when Eddie missed a meeting. The only worthwhile work I did was to type a couple more letters for Amanda. She would call in this panic-stricken voice. "Bonnie, he wants another one perfect." It was no trouble for me. In fact, I started looking forward to Amanda's calls. They broke the monotony.

By the end of the week I was thoroughly disgusted, not only with Eddie but with myself. I had this sick feeling that Eddie had chosen me over Helen not just because he couldn't stand her, but because she would never have put up with his crap. Helen would have insisted on being involved. I berated myself over and over for my weakness. The only thing I had drawn the line at was sneaking over to the OTB to place Eddie's bets.

The only hint I got that Eddie had any real work in mind for me was when he took enough time to arrange clearance for me into the data base. My password was "Moses." When I plugged that word in, rather than getting the usual "access denied" warning, I got a list of commands: Open, read, write, list, create. It wasn't much, but it was a step in the right direction.

Thankfully my drooping spirits got a lift on Friday. Eddie, who now spent about half his time in Charlotte's office, walked out of it in the middle of the afternoon and gave me my first assignment.

"With my help you're going to create a company mailing list. Eventually Fike wants to start doing mailings to clients and potential clients, maybe holding workshops and seminars."

The workshop and seminar part sounded like fun. Writing the mailing list sounded like a bore. I shrugged. "How do I get the names of these potential clients?"

Eddie held up a hand. "Slow down, Bonnie. One thing at a time. It's important work," he added. "Particularly for somebody who is going to be learning how to do it as she does it."

"I'm not complaining. When do we start?"

Eddie glanced at his watch. "Aw, it's already after three. Too late to get into something like that this week. How about Monday morning, if you can manage to get here on time?"

I ignored that crack. "Great!"

"All right. Oh, yeah," he added. "There's something else."

"What?"

He hesitated for a second, and I figured he was going to ask for another favor. I had my "NO" all ready.

"A week from tomorrow Charlotte's having a dinner party. She's going to invite you."

"Fantastic."

Eddie rolled his eyes. "We'll see about that."

I felt a lot more secure about my job after talking to Eddie. It wasn't the prospect of working on the mailing list that did it. It was the simple fact that if Fike decided C.F. should get still leaner and meaner than it was, I was doing something substantial enough to justify my paycheck.

Charlotte's invitation lifted my spirits too. Not that I was so eager to socialize with Charlotte. I still found her daunting, and visiting her and Eddie in their love nest was sure to be odd. But maybe this invitation signaled the start of something—the proverbial fast track I'd always heard existed but had never managed to stumble onto. Who would be at Charlotte's party? I wondered. Some of our clients? Charlotte, as an owner and officer of C.F., surely knew some interesting people. And what would I wear? Not my Christmas party silk again.

I was getting ready to leave for the day, loading my briefcase with some documentation on the database, when Amanda called and offered a potential answer to one of my questions.

"Would you like to go shopping with me tomorrow? I know all the discount places. We could have dinner after, if you don't have plans."

I did some quick mental calculations. Financially I was in good shape, for me. I had about two hundred and fifty dollars in my checking account, to last for another week. There was over two thousand dollars in my savings, leftover reward money. I had vowed to keep that for emergencies, which in my life are not rare. But I also had a couple credit cards that I hadn't violated in ages. "Okay," I said, "but I have to watch my money."

"Don't worry, Bonnie. I'm a great shopper."

CHAPTER 10

◆◆◆◆◆◆◆◆◆◆◆◆◆

She wasn't just kidding. Some of us can type; some of us can shop. A profound failure at the keyboard, Amanda found her niche in the racks of ladies' wear. She knew all the wholesale outlets, knew their best departments, knew whether they took credit cards or checks. No doubt about it; Amanda knew how to get the most for her money.

For me, Saturday turned into a spending orgy of unbelievable proportions. Amanda's enthusiasm for clothing was infectious. I lost all control. Everything in my checkbook went. I ran one of my credit cards up to its limit. When occasional waves of caution hit as I released my credit cards into some eager salesclerk's hands, I beat them back. I was a manager now, with fast-track social obligations. I needed clothes.

I'm not sure I needed the mid-calf-length black velvet skirt and ecru silk blouse I let Amanda talk me into, and I surely could have lived with less expensive boots and without the rose cashmere sweater. As for the red leather miniskirt Amanda went into raptures over, that will go down in my personal history as one of my all-time most foolish expenses.

Shopping with Amanda was not like shopping with my mother. Every time I pulled a sensible suit off the rack, she shook her head no. When I held up a navy-blue shirtwaist dress, or a pair of plain black pumps, she gave a little groan. "Oh, Bonnie. No." Amanda was a Cosmo girl, who lit up at the slinky bias-cut rayons, the brocades, the suedes. That I managed to bag one suit, an office-type dress, and the plain pumps is a miracle. That I didn't buy the $680 baby-blue coat was, to Amanda, nothing short of a crime.

"But it's perfect on you, Bonnie," she said, hands folded under her chin. The saleslady, needless to say, nodded agreement.

"It brings out . . . everything." That was Amanda, giving a passionate shake of her head. "Everything."

It did, too. My blue eyes looked like the sky on a spring day, my middle-of-the-winter complexion glowed a healthy pink. My reddish-blond hair shone with light when I put that coat on. But no way was I spending that much money.

And what did Cosmo girl buy? A form-fitting, almost backless lamb's-wool dress. Purple leather pants. Spike-heeled boots no human being could possibly walk more than a few feet in. And a nightgown. Not a working girl's sensible cotton or flannel. A long black satin spaghetti-strapped number. She spent a staggering amount of money on these things. It amazed me. Sure, she had been at C.F. a long time, but from what I'd seen she did nothing but provide a decorative diversion for the men. How much money could she have been making? How much did being decorative pay? Had Fike given her a raise when he took over, and not me?

We were leaving our final store, the one where I passed up the coat, literally weighted down with our shopping bags, when she made a last-minute purchase. Two luxurious cashmere mufflers, plaids, one green and black, the other red and black.

"Two?" I asked as we walked out the door.

"They're for presents."

It was after five by then. The winter sky was already dark. Amanda looked at her watch. "Are you hungry?"

"Starved. Do you still want to have dinner, or do you have plans?"

"I'm meeting somebody later, but let's get something to eat now. I'll treat. We never celebrated your promotion."

We took a cab to Mulberry Street in Little Italy for my celebration dinner. To me it was excessive. I would have been happy with a good hamburger.

The restaurant was a scream, the kind of place that Mafia capos are machine-gunned down in. Where there wasn't a mural of the sun setting over a canal, the pink stucco walls were encrusted with plaster cupids, sconces holding fake candles, and trompe-l'oeil Corinthian columns. The ceiling was woven with white lattice through which a tangle of plastic grape leaves climbed.

When a coat check woman with several feet of blond hair piled straight up had taken our coats, a tuxedoed maître d' rushed us. As soon as he had deposited us in a booth, a squadron of waiters in pale gold boleros that matched the stripes down their pants descended.

"Amanda," I said, looking at the menu. "We better get out of here. This is expensive."

"My treat, Bonnie. Remember? What kind of wine do you like?"

"The house wine."

We ordered a carafe. Even before I drank anything, I was feeling giddy, and a little bit strange. The giddy was natural enough. I mean, a promotion, all these new clothes. It was enough to unhinge anybody.

As for feeling strange, that was natural enough, too. Working women don't generally spend the kind of money this meal was going to cost on people they hardly know. I couldn't help wondering if Amanda didn't want something of me. Other than help typing Fike's letters, I couldn't imagine what I could give her.

On the other hand, there was something she could give me. An answer to the question that had been nagging me for weeks: On the night of the Christmas party, had Amanda left her apartment after Eddie had dropped her off? Perhaps to go over to Ashley Gartner's apartment? And if she had, what had she done there? Had she carried out her threat to kill him?

The only problem with that, my first and only theory about Ashley Gartner's murder, was that I liked her. We didn't have much in common, but she was, as Derek had said, uncomplicated and fun. Though my reasons for liking her may have been different from his, I couldn't imagine Amanda, no matter how enraged, as the prime mover in a brutal murder.

"How do you think you're going to like working for Mr. Fike?" I asked as we looked over the menu. "He seems pretty tough. Not like Mr. Gartner."

She smiled. "Oh, but he's fair, too, Bonnie."

Amanda waited to go on until the waiter had taken our orders. I asked for pasta primavera at a breath-catching $15.95. It was far from the most expensive thing on the menu. Amanda surprised me. "*Tagliatelle verdi con maiale uso piemontese*," she reeled off, as if she ate it every day. "Are the truffles fresh?" she asked.

"But of course, *signorina*."

"Good. We'd also like the clam appetizer. And your house dressing on our salads."

"You speak Italian. What is that you ordered?" I asked when the waiter had gone.

"Oh, no. I don't speak Italian. But I know how to order here. A friend taught me. I ordered pork shoulder with green noodles."

I laughed. "It sounded better the other way. Anyhow, you were talking about Mr. Fike."

"I was? Oh. Well, one thing's for sure. Everything is going to be fine. Mr. Fike is going to buy Mrs. Gartner's share of the company. He's a genius, you know."

That made me smile. I'd heard Morton Fike's employees describe him as many things, but never a genius.

"I heard he and Mr. Gartner weren't getting along, even before Mr. Gartner got sick."

Amanda shrugged. "That's probably because they were both such strong personalities. Right from the beginning—"

"You were there?"

"Yes. It was Ashley Gartner, Morton Fike, Charlotte Smoot, and me. I was their only employee. At first I was only part-time, because I was a model."

"A model. How exciting!"

Amanda squirmed, evidently uncomfortable with the subject. "Well, I wasn't a real model. I wasn't tall enough. I used to . . ." She looked around, sheepish, then lowered her voice. "I used to pose for art classes."

A light flicked on in my brain. "You mean like Derek Thorensen's art class."

She giggled into her glass. "The first time Derek ever saw me, I wasn't wearing a stitch."

Had I been wrong about them? "And then," I said, casually as I could, "you two started going out?"

"No! I never dated Derek. I would have. He's cute. But he never asked me."

I was at a loss for words. All I could think of was that terrible night at the bus stop.

"I did get Derek his job," Amanda continued. "He was bored with not working. I used to have a lot more to do at C.F. than I do now. More variety. I opened the checking accounts, set up the billing. Everything. But then we started growing so fast and it all got to be"—she extended her hands, palms up—"too much for me. I'm not really very good at office work."

"Sure you are," I said halfheartedly, thinking at the same time that with Amanda setting things up it was a wonder C.F. had ever gotten off the ground.

"No. I'm really not," she said. "Once I even heard Charlotte telling Mr. Gartner and Mr. Fike that they should get rid of me. The men stuck up for me, though."

That, I imagine, was the story of Amanda's life. The women would always want to get rid of her, the men would always want her around.

A trio of waiters covered our table with food—mountains of pasta, a platter of clams, bowls of cheese. There was enough to feed a small Third World country for a week.

139

"Creative Financial would have been so much nicer if Charlotte had never become a partner," Amanda said, digging into the clams.

I sort of agreed with her. I speared a clam, noncommittally arching my brows.

"She almost didn't, you know. Mr. Gartner and Mr. Fike, especially Mr. Gartner, were going to finance C.F. Charlotte was just going to be an employee, like we are."

"Really?"

"Charlotte didn't have the money to become a partner. Her father was a British military officer, and I think she got a small pension, but it wasn't enough."

"I didn't know Charlotte was British."

"Oh, she's not really. Not anymore. I heard that when her father died, her mother married an American and they moved here. She was still a teenager. Honestly, Bonnie. Can you picture Charlotte as a teenager?"

The thought was pretty funny. "So how did she get to be a co-owner?"

Amanda lifted her shoulders. "I don't know. She came up with the money from somewhere. She and Mr. Fike each put in twenty-four percent. Now I'm always worried about her firing me."

I smiled reassuringly. "Well, as long as you make Mr. Fike happy, you won't have to worry about that."

"I'm certainly trying my best."

"*Signorinas.*"

One of the yellow-boleroed waiters was hovering over us. On his tray were two drinks in long-stemmed glasses. "The gentlemen at the table in the corner send champagne cocktails, with their compliments."

Turning, I glanced toward the far corner. Four dark-haired, mustached men raised their glasses and nodded. I looked back at Amanda, dumbstruck.

"This is like in the movies. What should we do?"

She made a prudish little face, totally out of character. "Men! Honestly, this happens all the time." Nodding stiffly across the room, she allowed the waiter to put the drinks on our table. Then she said, "Please thank the gentlemen for us, but tell them we are otherwise engaged."

"Is that how you do it," I asked. "Take their drinks and then tell them you're not interested?"

"Of course. What do you do?"

"The problem doesn't arise that often."

I gave the men a guilty sideways glance. The waiter hadn't delivered our bad news yet. They were looking our way, expectant, ready to spring en masse. One encouraging look from our side of the room and the quartet would decamp and charge across the restaurant to our booth. I pushed my champagne cocktail aside, too embarrassed to drink it. Amanda sipped hers delicately.

"After all, Bonnie, they probably make ten times the money we do."

"That's not the point, Amanda."

"Of course it is." She put the drink back on the table, nudging one of her packages in the process. It fell onto the floor. As she rearranged things, I commented:

"I've never had enough money to buy frivolous clothes. I've always had to spend my clothes budget on things that I'll get a lot of use from."

The smile that answered me was arch and suggestive. "This will all get used a lot. An awful lot. Actually I've sort of wanted to talk to you about something. It's a little embarrassing, but I need some advice."

Here it came—the reason for this lavish dinner.

"I have a special boyfriend who likes me to wear nice things. He gives me money for clothes."

I don't know what I expected, but that bomb wasn't it. If Amanda wanted advice about taking money from men she was talking to the wrong person. I was having a problem with a six-dollar drink. Once over my initial surprise, though, my curiosity was aroused. "Wow! Really?"

She nodded, a dreamy smile spreading across her face. "He's wonderful. I'm meeting him later tonight."

Could she possibly mean Eddie? If she did, this was a side of my many-faceted supervisor I hadn't even imagined. I shook my head in wonder.

"What's the matter?" she asked.

"You just never know, do you. Eddie's a lot of fun, but he's never seemed like"—I nodded at the packages—"that type."

Amanda blinked and her expression went from dreamy to incredulous. "Eddie? You think he's the man I'm talking about?"

"Aren't you?"

"No, no. Oh, that's too funny."

"But I thought you and Eddie were seeing each other."

She burst into giggles. "We are. But it's not very serious. Eddie's a lot of fun, but . . . well, actually, he's pretty sexy too, when we're alone. But I only started going out with Eddie because my special friend and I had a fight. Bonnie, can I ask you something? I really do need to talk to someone."

"Sure."

She began toying with her food, pushing the green noodles from one side of her plate to the other. "The thing is, my friend . . ." She took a sip of wine before she went on. "My friend is married. He says I should try to be mature about our relationship. That I should see other men. I just want to know if you think I'm being taken advantage of."

I shook my head. "Amanda, I don't even have a boyfriend. How can I give you advice? You have to decide how you feel. It sounds to me as if it's hard for you, so maybe . . ." I hesitated for a second. "How do you feel when you see other men?"

"They're not very exciting to me. Not compared to him."

"Hum," was all I could say to that.

"Would you be mature?" she asked.

"Probably not," I said. "But I probably wouldn't handle it the way you do, either."

"What would you do?" Amanda's expression was so hopeful. I knew what she wanted me to say. She wanted me to lend emotional support to this craziness. I couldn't do it.

"I'd tell him to choose between me and his wife. He'd choose his wife. So I'd tell him to get lost, then I'd spend a few days in tears, then I'd go out with every man who asked me out until I got the bastard out of my system."

"Oh, but he's not a bastard. Not really. You know, Bonnie. He's hinted that someday, once his children are older, he may leave his wife. She doesn't understand him."

What a mass of cliches Amanda had fallen for. "How old are his children?"

"Two and four."

I stared at the poor woman. How naive she was! It was like talking to a child, or a Martian. "Where are you from, Amanda?"

"How come?"

"Curious."

"A farm outside of Richton, Mississippi. You should have heard my accent when I first came to New York. I've worked hard to lose it."

Poor Amanda. She had lost her accent and learned to dress, and to order in Italian, but some city slicker was still having his wicked way with her.

"I'd heard you were seeing Mr. Gartner," I said. "I guess that wasn't true."

Her chin dropped. "Mr. Gartner? Bonnie, I swear, I never, never . . . I'll bet Helen told you that, didn't she? She's so nasty. She told the police a vicious lie about seeing me fighting with Mr. Gartner before the Christmas party."

Whoops! I had stepped into dangerous, or at least potentially embarrassing, territory. I was the one who told the police about Amanda's slapping incident, the one who assumed her "bastard" was Mr. Gartner.

"Helen lied to the police?" I said, all innocence.

"A terrible lie. She's such a sneak, spying like that. I wouldn't even have known it was her if she hadn't been wearing her red coat."

143

Well, that was it. The end of my good red coat's short life. I'd never wear it again. "You mean Helen made that story up? You didn't slap him? I'm surprised at her."

"Well, she didn't exactly make it up. But it wasn't Mr. Gartner I was fighting with. It was my friend."

"He works at C.F.?"

Amanda nodded. "I'm not supposed to tell anybody about us. Oh, Bonnie, he's so wonderful you can't imagine. Like a combination of Cary Grant and . . . and Rambo."

"Rambo!"

"You know what I mean. He's sophisticated, and sensitive, but at the same time he's supermasculine. Women can't keep their hands off him. I can understand why his wife is so possessive, but I have a feeling that, in the end, he's going to choose me. Except that, now . . ." Her voice trailed off.

"Now what?"

"Now she's pregnant again. He told me that afternoon before the party. That's why I slapped him. I just lost control. It's his wife I should have slapped. I hate her!"

"Amanda," I said gently, "she's not getting pregnant alone. It's not osmosis. Those old jokes about the pants on the bedpost aren't true."

"Well, I know that. But I'm sure he loves me, Bonnie." She nodded at the packages in the booth beside her. "Just look at all the wonderful things he buys me."

I wasn't too talkative during the rest of our meal. I pretended to be too involved with my pasta to speak, but frankly, I felt kind of downhearted after talking to Amanda. This beautiful woman, who I had thought had everything, who I'd actually been jealous of, was the proverbial "other woman." The fact that I liked her made me feel even worse. Amanda never noticed how reserved I'd become. Why should she? She was so worked up about seeing her "special friend" later that night she could hardly think of anything else. She talked enough for both of us, about all the wonderful things he'd done for her, and all the places they'd gone together.

144

"This restaurant was one of his choices," she told me proudly.

I looked around me at the cupids and plastic grapes, at the sconces with their fake candles, at the busload of noisy, over-dressed tourists being herded through the door. What kind of a man would choose a place like this? Unless he'd chosen it because no one he knew was likely to see him here.

By the time Amanda got our check, she was giddy with the idea of showing her "special friend" her purchases. I had nobody to show anything to. Still, I was heading home to a cat who slept on my bed every night, and who, through thick and thin, was all mine. There are worse things in the world than not having a boyfriend.

"Here," I said, pulling out my wallet. "Let me get the tip."

"No. It's all right, Bonnie. Besides"—she lowered her voice—"my friend will give me some money tonight, if I ask him."

With a shudder I managed to conceal, I plunked a twenty-percent tip on the table. "I insist. Are we ready to go?"

Amanda got all "hedgy" when I said that. She looked down at her watch with an "Oh, gee, how time flies" expression.

"It's almost eight," she said. "You're probably exhausted, after shopping."

I nodded. "You go up the West Side, don't you? We can share a cab as far as your place."

"Oh, I'm not going that way tonight," she responded, not looking at me. "I guess I'll stay here for a while, before I go to meet my friend. Let's ask one of the waiters to get a cab for you."

Before I could protest, Amanda waved her hand in the air, gave the waiter her instructions, then settled into the booth. Her whole act was so transparent it wasn't hard to figure out what she was doing. I would have bet that her friend was picking her up at that restaurant, and she wanted to make sure I was long gone when he showed up.

I went through all the motions, gathering my purchases, thanking Amanda profusely, collecting my coat. All the while this idea was percolating in the back of my mind: If it wasn't too hard, I just might stick around until I got a look at Amanda's mystery man.

It was quite dark outside now, but the streets in Little Italy pulsed with life. Fur-coated tourists milled up and down its neon-lit street, pausing to read menus and stare into restaurant windows.

My cab was waiting for me in front of the restaurant, one of the restaurant's unctuous captains holding its door open. I dismissed it with an imperious gesture, then stolled casually across the street.

I'd become obsessed with Amanda's special boyfriend. Who at C.F. could possibly be considered a Rambo–Cary Grant combination? It wouldn't hurt to spend a few minutes trying to find out.

Dodging crowds making their way along the sidewalk, I walked into the first shop I came to that wasn't a restaurant. It was a big corner butcher shop and deli and was very gross, at least for someone who'd just eaten as much as I had. Whole animal bodies, skinned but still intact, hung from ceiling hooks. The display cases held a medical student's nightmare of mucousy animal parts.

Thankfully the place was so busy nobody had the time to glance my way. I nudged myself through a line of waiting customers until I was next to a window. I could see the street and the restaurant on the other side of it with no trouble.

So, what now? I wondered, once I'd been there for a minute or two. Above me, its head only inches from mine, hung the still-bloody carcass of a lamb, larded with fat. If I dropped my gaze too far, it came to a tray of ice filled with raw livers. I couldn't take too much of this. I would give this escapade exactly five minutes of my time.

It took no more than two. The door to the restaurant opened and Amanda stepped outside, buttoning the top of her coat. Not five seconds later a big car pulled up at the curb and the passenger door swung open. Amanda slid into the seat, and the car joined the heavy traffic on Mulberry Street. Hiding my face in my collar, I walked out of the shop.

Amanda's friend's car hadn't gotten far. The traffic around it had it hemmed in. I squinted to see better. It was easy enough to pick out Amanda. Her long hair shone under the almost carnival lights of the street. The man behind the wheel I couldn't make out. He was shorter than Amanda. Much shorter. His head barely showed above the seat. As traffic began moving and the car started pulling away, I happened to notice the license plate.

"Oh-my-God!" I said out loud. A woman on the street looked at me curiously. I didn't want to make a fool of myself, so I buried my face deeper in my collar. But this time it was to stifle my howls of laughter. The license plate on Amanda's friend's car was a personalized one. It read, "CAN DO." Her supermasculine friend, her Rambo, her Cary Grant, was none other than Morton Fike.

I giggled to myself all the way home. The cabdriver probably thought I was deranged. I just prayed that if Amanda did break up with her Rambo, she didn't tell him she was doing it on my advice. Wouldn't that do a job on my career path!

It wasn't until later, after I'd put away all my purchases and flopped down on the couch to watch a late movie, that the not-so-funny side of what I'd seen hit me. With a start I jumped up and retrieved Mr. Gartner's reorganization chart from my desk. Spreading it on my coffee table, I once again looked at Fike's name in that little box on the bottom.

If anyone had gained from Mr. Gartner's death, it was Morton Fike. Had Gartner's reorganization taken place, Fike, though retaining his twenty-four percent, would have ended up under not only Mr. Gartner, but under Charlotte Smoot as well. Now, like I said, he was firmly in control.

From what I had heard, Mr. Gartner had trusted Amanda, even after his kerosene-in-the-coffee episode. Had

147

his trust been misplaced? Had he unknowingly let Morton Fike's devoted girlfriend into his house after the party? And had that devoted girlfriend, whose world began and ended with Fike, killed Gartner so that Fike could take over C.F.?

The biggest hitch to this, from what I could see, was Amanda herself. She didn't seem like a likely murderer. But she could have been a perfect accomplice. Adoring, subservient, willing to go to all lengths to preserve her relationship with her "special friend." Maybe all she did was create an opportunity for Fike.

I mulled this over for a while that night, but when I began drifting to sleep my thoughts shifted to Derek. I missed him. He hadn't lied about Amanda. Maybe I should listen to what he had to say about the money and the lies. That was, if he still wanted to say anything. I gave Moses a good-night hug. He purred and snuggled closer. Sweet, but a poor substitute for the real thing.

CHAPTER 11

◆◆◆◆◆◆◆◆◆◆◆◆◆◆

Charlotte Smoot's Brooklyn Heights apartment was in a big, modern high rise. It towered above its neighbors on the tree-lined street, dwarfing the neo-Gothic church next to it and putting the brownstones across from it forever in a shadow. If you wanted to get snooty about it, the building was so far on the edge of Brooklyn Heights that it was probably officially in downtown Brooklyn. Still, it was a long way from the ghetto.

A uniformed doorman behind a counter in the lobby rang Charlotte's apartment to announce me, and then he directed me to a cramped elevator at the back of the lobby. I planned to make a grand entrance, so on the ride to the twelfth floor I slipped out of my down coat. There's no way of looking grand in a three-year-old down coat that leaves a trail of feathers wherever it goes.

My outfit was the result of a monumental debate with myself and several discussions with Amanda. I was wearing my new velvet skirt and silk blouse, the Italian leather boots, and carrying Amanda's beaded evening bag, borrowed for the occasion. Everything on me had been chosen by Amanda and charged to Visa. I'd even charged the haircut Amanda's beautician had given me that morning. From head to toe, I was guilty of imitation and ripe for repossession.

At Charlotte's floor the elevator doors opened onto a narrow hallway with doors on both sides. It looked as if the builders had squeezed every apartment they could out of the space they had. Fluffing my hair one last time, I walked down the hall and rang Charlotte's bell. The lady herself opened the door a second later.

What a sight! I wasn't the only one who had done herself up "à la Amanda." I only hope that I did a better job of it.

To begin with, Charlotte was made up to beat the band, with deep-purple eyeshadow and crimson lipstick. But that wasn't the worst of it. Her outfit was an ill-fitting near-duplicate of Amanda's red Chinese-style Christmas-party dress. Its mandarin collar cut into her chin. Across her hips the silk had tugged itself into a series of ripples. When she stepped forward to greet me, the slit up the dress's side displayed charms best left hidden.

"Why, Bonnie!" She shrieked and raised her eyebrows. If I hadn't known better, I would have thought my arrival at her door was a complete surprise. "How elegant you look tonight! Come in! Come in!"

This was the first time Charlotte had ever called me by name. I had sometimes wondered if she even knew it. Behind her stood a black woman in an honest-to-God maid's uniform, little white apron and all. As the maid took my coat, Charlotte and I exchanged one of those fake kisses-on-the-cheek that are de rigueur in some circles of women.

While the maid disappeared into a room at the end of the hall with my coat, I followed Charlotte through a narrow foyer into the living room.

What a surprise the apartment was. From Charlotte, who knew what to expect, except perhaps the worst? This wasn't it. The furniture was Queen Anne, with upholstery in shades of rose and blue. Expensive-looking Oriental rugs covered the floors. The one in the living room was gorgeous—a pastel that must have cost a small fortune. The apartment was everything its owner wasn't—delicately appointed, tasteful, and somehow perfectly feminine.

I paused as we walked past the small collection of Chinese sculpture displayed behind the leaded-glass doors of an ornate black lacquer curio cabinet. The Oriental goddess I'd seen the day I met Charlotte was proudly displayed on the top shelf, surrounded by several smaller figures.

"Oh, you've noticed my deities. You remember my goddess, Padmapani. Isn't she perfect? The marble Buddha next to her is Tang dynasty. That's from six hundred to nine hundred, A.D."

"That's older than Ming?"

"Much older." Charlotte opened the case. "And look what I've added. A little boy. An early Ming acolyte, to attend her. Every goddess needs an admirer," she mused. Charlotte carefully lifted a wood figure of a boy from the cabinet. He was bent forward, his hands in prayer. His hair was covered with black lacquer, dressed in double loops atop his head. There were traces of gold and red on his long-sleeved robe.

"He's beautiful," I said.

"Yes, isn't he. I often think of Keats's words when I look at my collection. 'A thing of beauty is a joy forever: It's loveliness increases; it will never pass into nothingness.'" She smiled fondly at the figure, then put it carefully back in its place. "But enough of my showing off. What would you like to drink? Edwin is playing host tonight."

Eddie was sitting on a pink satin love seat by a door that led to a balcony. He was plainly more interested in charming the attractive Chinese woman next to him than in playing host. He waved carelessly when he saw me.

"Could I have a white wine spritzer?"

"Certainly," Charlotte responded. "Edwin? Could you fix Bonnie's drink?"

Right then Morton Fike walked into the room from the separate dining room. In his hand was a mug of beer.

"Bonnie!" He gave me a thump on the shoulder that just about knocked me over. "Hey, Charlotte," he said around my shoulder. "I like that quote. Keats, did you say? I may use that one of these days. What are you drinking, Bonnie? I'll get it."

"No, no, Morty. Edwin's our host. Oh, Edwin! A spritzer for Bonnie, please."

"Got it, Charlotte."

By now I knew Eddie well enough to get pretty good readings of his emotional state. Anyhow, he was far from complicated. From the set of his jaw as he crossed the living room, he was hating every minute of his hosting duties. He took his time ambling to the makeshift bar that had been set up between the living and dining rooms.

"One white wine spritzer, coming up."

Charlotte watched as he poured my drink.

"Give her some more ice cubes, Edwin."

"Yass'am." After his clenched-teeth parody of a put-upon servant, he thrust the glass at me with a sugary smile. "Enjoy."

Charlotte held out her glass. "While you're at it, dear heart, would you mind?"

The veins in Eddie's temple went into a spasm. I scooted back a couple steps toward the dining room and pretended to look at some Chinese prints on the wall. Then, thankfully, the maid called from the kitchen, "Miss Smoot. Where do you keep the napkins?"

Charlotte shook her head. "Honestly, the help you get these days." She hurried away.

Eddie walked over to me. "How's your drink?"

"Not worth the trouble it caused," I muttered.

"Sorry about that, but this 'houseboy' bullshit gives me a pain." He looked past me toward the curio cabinet. "Did you catch her bit with the Eddie doll? Fuckin' Barbie and Ken. For a nickle I'd toss them both into the river."

There was nothing I could say to that except perhaps, "So who forced you to start going with her?" I didn't say it though. Eddie's temper was so short he might have exploded.

"What do you think of Fike's wife?" he asked a second later.

Fike had joined the Chinese woman on the love seat. It looked as if he was delivering a monologue. Nothing unusual for him. The woman was nodding, all rapt attention.

"That's Fike's wife?"

"Yup," Eddie said softly. "An MD, yet. A pediatrician. And she comes from a filthy rich family. That's probably where Fike got the money to buy Gartner's share of the company. That guy is some operator."

More than you'll ever know, I thought. As we watched, Fike stood up and took his wife's hand. She rose and trailed him across the room. The closer she came, the prettier she looked. And the more pregnant.

She was small, with short blunt-cut black hair that curved across her cheeks. Her eyes were wide and expressive, her lips full like a thirties silent-screen siren's. Looking at her, I felt even sorrier for Amanda than I had.

"Linda, darling, this is Bonnie Indermill, Eddie's new assistant. Bonnie, this is my wife and much better half."

With that, Fike wrapped his arm around her waist, made this awful growling noise, and took a big pretend bite out of his wife's arm. Linda giggled behind her hand. "Morty! Stop it!"

Better half was right! Here was my CEO, Mr. "Can Do" Fike, acting like a jerk. Wedged where I was, between Eddie and the wall, I couldn't ignore him. I smiled and extended my hand to Linda. As she reached her hand toward mine, her husband tickled her ribs.

"Oh, Morty!" she squealed.

Oh, baloney! So this was it for Charlotte's dinner party? Morton Fike making a fool of himself with the wife he regularly cheated on, Eddie drafted into playing host and sour as a pickle about it, and Charlotte, the perfect parody of a overwrought hostess, gushing and fussing all over the place. For this I'd blown fifty-five dollars on a haircut that would be grown out before I paid for it?

Just then the maid passed behind us. She must have nudged Fike a bit because he swayed into me. The arm that wasn't goosing Linda in the ribs was the one holding his beer. Half the glass slopped onto my skirt. I watched in dismay as the beer soaked into the black velvet. No one else noticed.

"Hors d'oeuvres?" the maid asked, her West Indian accent slaughtering the words.

I took a minuscule cracker with Brie and caviar, swallowed it in one bite, and consoled myself with this thought: Apart from Linda, who had her nutso husband to contend with, and the maid, who was an unknown, I was probably the least likely person in the room to make an ass of myself. No matter how bad things got as the evening wore on, I would leave with both reputation and career path intact. Things could be worse.

And then, almost as if I'd willed it on myself, they were. The doorbell rang one more time. Charlotte fluttered from the room, and seconds later I heard Derek greeting her with his unmistakable accent.

Well, that about did it. The taste of caviar surged up into my throat until I almost gagged. If he walked into that living room with a date, I was going to excuse myself, go to the bathroom, throw up, leave, and mail in my resignation. I was starting to hate the crummy job anyway. There were limits to what I was willing to endure for it.

I was some mess by the time Derek came into the living room. Thank God he was alone, because he looked great. I am telling you, he may have been the world's biggest liar and a thorough scoundrel, but my resolve just about collapsed as soon as I saw him. In his tweed sport coat and gray flannel pants he knocked me for a loop. The courteous, impersonal "Hello" I thought I could get away with vanished when he smiled and took my hand.

"I'm glad to see you." He glanced around the room. "And I'm particularly glad to see you alone. You are alone, aren't you?" I was paralyzed, unable to retrieve my hand, unable to do anything more than nod.

"Derek! Happy you could make it. You got your packing done?" That was Morton Fike. He took care of the problem of my lingering fingers by snatching Derek's hand away and pumping it violently.

"Yes. All packed. I'm not going to be able to stay very late. I've got a seven A.M. flight."

"What a shame." Fike nodded toward me. "I see you've met Bonnie, Eddie Fong's new assistant. I'd think you'd like to stick around just for her company."

"I'm not sure she would want my company."

"Of course she would. Wouldn't you, Bonnie?" Another thump on my back followed. Maybe this was what Amanda meant by Rambo. The Cary Grant side of Fike's personality had yet to appear. "A good-looking, unattached man?" he added, grabbing Derek's arm. "There aren't too many like this around."

Didn't I know it. I forced my face into a dumb smile. A second later Fike dragged Derek away.

Linda and I made small talk for a while. Once removed from her husband, she was bright and interesting. I asked how she had met Morton.

"Through Charlotte. Charlotte and I grew up together."

"Oh, in England?"

154

"England?" Linda looked puzzled. "No. Hong Kong. Her father was with the British Army Quartermaster Corps. When he died, her mother married an American."

Hong Kong? For a second I was confused, as if I was at the wrong dinner party. The first time I'd met Charlotte she'd said she'd never been to the Orient. If Hong Kong wasn't the Orient, what was? What a dumb thing to lie about!

"They came to the States long before I did," Linda was saying, "but when I got here to go to medical school, I looked her up." Linda smiled and made a gesture toward her husband. "By that time Charlotte was already working with Morton, and she introduced us. And here we are." She looked at me seriously. "I'm so lucky. Morty's one in a million."

What did Fike have that attracted these beautiful women? Okay, Amanda was no genius, but she was nice. Linda was not only beautiful and nice, but smart. And rich, too, according to Eddie. This was amazing.

I looked across the room. Morton Fike had backed Derek against a wall. His, Morton's, mouth moved rapidly. He made quick, sloppy gestures with his glass and the beer in it rolled like surf on a windy day. Every now and again Derek nodded thoughtfully.

Linda bent closer to me. "Aren't you just thrilled about Charlotte and Eddie? Don't they make a wonderful couple?"

I looked at her, searching her face for traces of sarcasm. She was beaming happily.

I nodded.

"Meeting men hasn't been easy for Charlotte. With her passion for the Orient, Eddie seems—perfect."

I couldn't imagine what to say to that, but a second later Charlotte wedged herself between Linda and me, saving me the trouble of answering.

"You're probably wondering why I invited Derek."

That was Charlotte, anticipating my unasked question.

Wondering? I was almost beside myself with curiosity. I shrugged.

"He's very handsome," Linda said. "That should be enough."

"Morty's trying to entice him to come with C.F. full-time. He's quite brilliant. Made an absolute fortune on the Exchange. And single," Charlotte added with an arch and meaningful look my way. "I seated you together."

Oh, hell! This was as bad as one of Noreen's family dinners. Worse. I had to be nice to Charlotte. She was my boss's boss, as well as one of his girlfriends. I had to be smart, too, but not too smart; fun, but always ladylike; helpful, but never interfering. And above all, nonthreatening. Had to watch those chats with Eddie.

Dinner was atrocious. I can't even remember what was served. Every swallow went down my throat like a boulder. Derek, sitting next to me, congenial and attentive, unleashed in me a mass of feelings I could barely conceal. When he refilled my wine glass, my body temperature soared until I felt as if I had a fever. Over the soup course when no one else at the table was paying attention, he leaned to me and quietly said, "You look wonderful tonight." Steam from the hot soup rose in a suffocating fog, and I became so faint I feared I'd collapse facedown into my bowl.

"Thank you," I stammered. I glanced around the table. Across and to my right Fike, Linda, and Eddie were involved in a three-way conversation. Charlotte, on the end to my left, was half out of her chair, hissing orders at the maid. "So do you," I whispered back. "Where are you going?"

"Copenhagen, for two weeks. Maybe we can have a talk when I get back?"

I nodded happily, my spirits lifting like I'd had an injection of helium and was about to fly around the room.

"Hey, Bonnie," Eddie called from the end of the table. "What are you so red about all of a sudden?"

He was some awful host. "Nothing, Eddie."

Conversation continued around me. When I wasn't in a

dither over Derek, I watched Linda interact with her husband. With me and anyone else, she was articulate, full of interesting opinions. With her husband, Linda was a child, a cooing, eye-batting babydoll. And he ate it up. From what was going on across the table from me, I wouldn't have put any money on Fike's choosing Amanda in the end. It looked as if Linda was there to stay.

When the talk turned to business, I was outclassed by everyone but Linda. I managed to hold my own, though, except during one terrible moment. Conversation had died down and Fike suddenly fixed me with his beetle-browed stare.

"So, Bonnie." He slapped the table. All the glasses jumped. "Eddie showing you the ropes? Teaching you all about our data base? You going to be able to take over if he's ever away?"

This took me by surprise. Silence fell around the table. Not a pregnant silence or a tense one. Just a silence, with everybody waiting for my answer.

Down at his end of the table Eddie was alerted. "She's doing fine. Going to be a real pro."

Fike kept staring at me. Under his gaze I squirmed. I would really like to have slugged Eddie right then, but finally I said, "Oh, yes. Eddie's shown me so much already."

"There," Fike said, turning to Derek. "That's the kind of team you'd be playing on." He waved, expansive. "Eddie, Charlotte, and now Bonnie."

Derek grinned. "I must admit, the idea of 'playing' on that team is in some ways appealing."

I spent the rest of the meal reeling with anticipation, occasionally saying a word or two, but mostly . . . anticipating.

Derek was amazing. He talked to these people about business and knew what he was talking about. He knew the ins and outs of leasing and tax shelters and had an impressive knowledge of the stock market. Fike and Charlotte listened attentively when he spoke. Even Eddie dropped his cynical role to join the conversation. Finally, as we were leaving the table, Fike stretched up to reach his arm around Derek's shoulder.

"Derek, I hope you'll consider my offer. You're the kind of 'can do' finance person C.F. needs. Think it over while you're on vacation."

My back was turned by then, so I couldn't see Derek's expression. Finance person? What was Fike talking about.

"Thank you," he answered, "but as I said, my decision was made several years ago and I haven't regretted it yet."

"Well, if you ever do, you know where my office is."

Derek said his good-byes and left almost immediately. I was half-hoping he'd ask if I wanted a ride, but considering the state of our relationship, I wasn't surprised when he didn't.

Coffee and dessert were served in the living room, and at long last the evening was over. I was, by then, wild to get out of there, exhausted by several hours of unrelieved stress.

In Charlotte's luxurious bathroom I splashed cold water on my face. I'd get a cab on Montague Street, be home in forty-five minutes, take a hot shower, and sleep like a log.

As I stepped out of the bathroom, I heard Fike and Linda saying good-bye to Charlotte by the front door. Turning down the hall, I went toward the den in search of my coat.

I paused as I passed the bedroom. What a love nest Charlotte had created in there, all pastels and laces, with a king-size bed smack in its center. There, on that huge bed, Charlotte and Eddie did—it. The big IT. I suppose there have been stranger lovers, but right off hand, I couldn't think of any. Shaking my head, I wandered back toward the den.

The room was in darkness. I ran my hand along the wall, searching for the light switch. When I didn't find one, I made my way toward the closet on the far wall. Suddenly on the other side of the room there was a noise, a drawer closing.

"Oh." I jumped back toward the door. As I did, my shoulder rammed into the wall switch. I flicked it up, flooding the room with light.

"Eddie. You scared me."

"Bonnie. You scared me too."

He was crouched in front of Charlotte's antique rolltop desk, his hand on a drawer pull.

"What are you doing down there in the dark?"

"Shush. Looking for leverage." Standing, he lowered his voice. "Don't say anything to Charlotte about this."

Right then the front door slammed. Not a second later Charlotte called, "Edwin, where are you? You missed Morton and Linda."

"Gee, what a disappointment," he called back, his voice syrupy sweet. "I'm getting my coat."

It wasn't two seconds before Charlotte rushed into the den, her face full of panic. "Are you going out now?"

Eddie glanced down at his watch. "Gimme a break, Charlotte. Even obedient Chinese houseboy gets to party on Saturday night." Yanking his leather jacket off its hanger, he pulled it on.

I threw my coat over my arm and, in something of a panic myself, squeezed behind Charlotte and out of the den. I sure didn't want to be in the cross fire when those two got going.

"Good night," I called over my shoulder. "Thank you both for a lovely evening."

Charlotte didn't answer. I hadn't expected her to. After her brief stint as the "hostess with the mostest" she was reverting to type.

Was I ever glad to step through her front door. As it closed behind me, I heard her say to Eddie, "You better not have any ideas about seeing that tramp tonight."

The elevator had just arrived when Charlotte's door opened and Eddie walked into the hall, nonchalantly winding a red plaid scarf around his neck, the one Amanda had bought a week earlier. "You are a brave man," I said, eyeing it.

Eddie grinned. "What's life without a little danger. It makes my blood race. How are you getting home? You want a lift?"

"No thanks. I'll get a cab."

"Why throw your money away? I'm driving up your way and I've got new wheels I want to show off. Toyota Celica Supra, white with black trim. Hot!"

When the elevator reached the first floor, Eddie lead me out of it, away from the doorman's reception desk, and through a door at the rear of the lobby. I followed him down a flight of concrete steps.

"Charlotte took me to pick it up from the dealer today," he said.

We walked through a vast underground parking area past rows of cars, until he pointed proudly.

"You like?"

How could I not like. It was beautiful, brand-new, gleaming white under the fluorescent garage lights.

"Does one hundred and twenty in third. More my style than driving around in that hearse of Charlotte's." He nodded toward a big green four-door next to the Toyota.

Eddie's car had that wonderfully distinct new-car smell. I glanced at the odometer. Less than a hundred miles showed.

"Your raise must have been better than mine," I said.

"Raise? What raise? Charlotte advanced me the money."

Good grief! And I'd been racked with guilt about charging nine hundred dollars' worth of new clothes.

When we drove past the parking attendant, Eddie handed him a card. The kid jotted something on a tablet, then returned the card to Eddie. "Have a nice evening, Mr. Fong."

Eddie smiled broadly as he drove up the driveway that ran alongside Charlotte's building. "Man, this is the life."

"Is it?" I said, wondering how he felt about coming home to Charlotte every night.

"You bet! Remember what I said about The Year of the Monkey? It's happening. I have one or two kinks to work out, but after that, it's all gravy."

Manhattan's night skyline glittered beyond the Brooklyn Bridge, reflecting into the water beneath us. Heavy metal blasted from the car stereo. Eddie's head and shoulders bopped up and down to the music.

"What do you think? Rides fine, doesn't it?"

"Fantastic."

"Not like Derek's Mercedes, but give me time. Man, that guy kills me. I don't blame you for breaking up with him."

"What do you mean?"

"He's crazy. London School of Economics. Made a fortune out of a small inheritance by playing stock futures. He could name his price with Fike." Eddie glanced at me, truly perplexed. "Why's a hot shot like that working part-time in graphics?"

I didn't want to let Eddie know that both the London School of Economics and the fortune's source were a surprise to me. "Maybe he already has enough money," I said finally.

To Eddie that statement was mind-boggling. "Enough money!" he hooted. "How much money is that? There's no such thing as 'enough money.'"

"Sure there is. How many cars can you drive? How many fancy restaurants can you eat in? How many clothes can you wear?"

Eddie shook his head in wonder. "Bonnie, I can't imagine enough money. You know what the first Chinese immigrants called the U.S.? *Gum shan*. Mountain of gold. I won't have enough money until that's how much I have. A mountain of it."

I shrugged. "Look, Eddie. Since we're alone, there's something I'd like to talk to you about. You heard that lie I told Fike tonight about how much you're teaching me. He wasn't kidding, either. He thinks I'm learning from you."

Eddie glanced over at me, shook his head, and looked back at the road. "Bonnie, you're too hung up on this work bullshit. I'll teach you the entire system as soon as I get a chance."

"And when will that be? I can't even find you half the time anymore. What if you got sick?"

"Don't sweat it. I'm not going anywhere. Hey, I'll take you all the way home, but there's somewhere I've got to stop first."

We were in Manhattan by then. "Why don't you just let me out and I'll get a cab?"

"Take it easy! I've just got to pick something up. Two minutes, I promise."

He turned up Canal and we cruised past all the neon-bright restaurants of Chinatown. That's just what Eddie was doing. Cruising, like kids where I went to high school used to cruise.

I expected him to stop in the center of Chinatown or maybe go to his aunt's restaurant. To my surprise Eddie drove past Bowery and turned down a narrow street that runs almost directly under the approach to the Manhattan Bridge. Though still in Chinatown, the streets here were darker and more sparsely populated. It was a dank, fetid place hard to imagine the sun ever touching, even at noon. Now, in the middle of the night, it was spooky.

Finally he turned on to Forsyth Street, a block that wasn't much wider than an alley. Along its length were only a few lighted windows. A sign at the entrance read "Dead End."

"Look, Eddie. I don't want to wait here. Take me back to Canal and I'll get a cab."

"Bonnie, you're safer here than in your own living room. This block is patrolled. There's a private club down at the end. I've just got to run in for a second."

We moved past gloomy tenement buildings with crumbling steps and graffiti-covered walls. Here and there lights were on, but an awful lot of windows were covered with the sheet metal that tells you an apartment is deserted.

In a run-down four-story building at the end of the street, a dim light burned over a metal doorway with a small barred window in its center. Whatever occupied the bottom-floor shop space was protected by heavy wire-mesh windowguards and hidden by dark curtains. Beyond this building, blocking the street, was a scruffy, trash-strewn park. Eddie pulled up in front of the park.

"Just be a second."

He disappeared into the building, leaving the ignition running. Sliding into the driver's seat, I shifted into reverse and maneuvered the car around a black Trans Am with tinted windows and a dragon on its hood until I faced out away from the park toward the intersection. I pulled right in front of the building before climbing back to the passenger side.

It wasn't all that bad, I assured myself after looking around. In the center of the block, several doors up, a small Chinese grocery was open. Men and women went in and out. A couple men walked past me and into the park. They paid me no attention. If I looked out the car's side window, I could see the faint outline of a television through somebody's gauze living room curtains. There were a lot worse places in New York City. If worse came to worse, I could always get out and walk.

Two minutes became three, four, five. I watched the time flip by on the dashboard clock, growing edgy in spite of myself. Above me, traffic on the bridge rumbled.

A flare of light from the door of the brick building Eddie had gone into attracted my attention. Two men stepped from a dark hallway into the thin night light. One of them held the door open for a moment, and behind him I saw a steep flight of stairs. The taller lit a cigarette and took a drag, all the while watching Eddie's car. After a minute the two men leaned their heads together. Then the tall man threw his cigarette onto the ground, stepped down off the narrow porch, and walked toward me. I quickly checked the lock on my door.

The stranger tapped on my side window with his knuckles and leaned in close. I recognized him now. He was one of the men who had chased Eddie onto the subway. The babyfaced one. He made a couple small circles with his hand. I rolled the window down a few inches.

"Fong's new car?" Babyface asked through the narrow opening.

"Yes. I'm waiting for him."

"You should find yourself some other friends."

"Get away from my car, punk, and leave my friend

alone." Eddie had come out of the building in a fury. It looked like there was going to be a fight. I stiffened with fear, waiting for Babyface to pull out his knife. To my relief he stepped aside.

Eddie walked up to the car and I unlocked the driver's door. He tossed a gym bag he had carried from the building into the backseat.

"Dumb punk." He slid into the car seat. "Right off the boat. One of these days I'm going to be his boss. Then we'll see about him messing with anybody in my car."

We sped up the street to the intersection, burning rubber. A few minutes later we were on the West Side Highway. Almost home.

My relief was premature. We were approaching Fourteenth Street when Eddie cut across traffic to pull into the turn lane.

"Bonnie, when I go around this corner, you look and see if you can spot a black Trans Am back there."

I twisted in my seat. Seconds later the black car with darkened windows followed us onto Fourteenth Street.

"It looks like it, Eddie. You don't think they're following us, do you?"

"Seems that way. How's that for trust among friends, huh?"

There was a canyon of space between Eddie's ideas about trust and mine. For that matter, there was a canyon separating our ideas about friendship, too.

"You said you paid back their money. Why would they follow you now?"

"Why? Maybe they want to know where I'm going. I'm going to lose them."

"No way, Eddie! Not with me in the car. Drop me—"

"Can't stop right now, Bonnie." He took the corner at Eighth Avenue on two wheels, throwing me against the door. The next five minutes was a nightmare, Eddie dodging in and out of traffic, taking sharp corners, looking in his rearview mirror every few seconds. Finally he slowed. We were approaching Columbus Circle.

"Lost them," he said.

By then I had lost all patience with Eddie. Boss or no boss, he was a fool. "Pull over by the subway. I'm getting out."

"What's the matter with you? Fifteen minutes you'll be home."

"My joyriding days have been over for a long time. Now pull over!"

"Yes, ma'am! You bossy women are going to kill me," he said. "The subways are dangerous this time of night. All kinds of weirdos down there."

"There are all kinds of weirdos up here, too."

He let me out near the newsstand by the entrance to the A train and pulled around the circle onto Broadway. As I started down the subway steps, I happened to look back at the street. A block behind Eddie's new Toyota, the black Trans Am was rounding the circle, dark windows concealing its occupants. I ducked down another step to shield myself. It wasn't me they were interested in, though. The black car continued around the circle and followed Eddie up Broadway.

What a headache the evening had given me! Not only seeing Derek. That had worked itself out as well as it could for now. As for later, when he got back from Copenhagen, we would see. At least it was clear that I was no more out of his system than he was out of mine.

It was the rest of the evening that got my temples throbbing. My immediate boss was a compulsive gambler and risk-taker with these crazy ideas about making it the easy way. His immediate boss and lover, Charlotte, was so peculiar she gave me the willies. Then there was Fike, the boss of us all, a squatty despot with an appetite for beautiful women.

Maybe, I thought during the subway ride home, I should think about updating my resume. How would I manage that, though, with barely seven weeks' experience at C.F., only one as a manager? And I didn't know how to do anything. This career path I'd been so hopeful about was turning into some muddy road.

CHAPTER 12

◆◆◆◆◆◆◆◆◆◆◆◆◆◆◆

My next week at C.F. passed slowly, with my mailing list project slogging along. The problem was, as usual, Eddie. After much nagging from me, he'd spent about twenty minutes getting me started. Then I was on my own. Fine if I'd known what I was doing, but whenever I ran into a snag, I had to ask Eddie's advice, and his appearances at the office had become so sporadic there were whole mornings when I didn't know where he was.

For all that, the week was pleasant enough. With Derek's impending return on my mind my concern with my career path had faded. No one at C.F. except Morton Fike cared what I was doing anyway, and after not very much soul-searching I'd decided that if he ever confronted me, I'd put the blame where it belonged: on Eddie. It wasn't until the following week that my job situation became so desperate that I couldn't ignore it.

"Edwin!"

It was Monday morning, the first of February and a week after Charlotte's party. For Eddie, things were starting out with a roar.

He hadn't gotten to his desk until close to eleven A.M. It was obvious Charlotte didn't know where he was. Every few minutes she opened her door and peered over the row of cubicles, her expression growing darker. By the time Eddie slung his coat over his chair she looked ferocious. Whatever Eddie had done, he was going to pay dearly.

Without acknowledging Charlotte, who was hands-on-hips in her doorway, Eddie casually unbuttoned his shirt sleeves and turned the cuffs up. I had rolled into his bay to say good morning. Charlotte's next call sent me back to my own territory in a hurry.

"Edwin!"

"Morning, Charlotte." He slid into his chair and dialed his phone. A second later there was his familiar refrain:

"Louie, can you get me a line on what's happening in the third at the Meadowlands? I've got a few bucks burning a hole in my pocket."

Charlotte came out of her office like a hurricane coming across the Gulf of Mexico, gathering speed until she stopped dead in Eddie's cubicle.

"When you're settled down, I'd like to have a word with you." Her voice was quietly drenched with anger.

"Yass'am."

I could actually hear Charlotte take a deep breath and slowly let it out.

"ASAP, Edwin!"

With that she turned and stormed into her office.

All this time my face was buried in my monitor, as if I couldn't tear myself away from the mailing list. As soon as Charlotte's door slammed, I peeked around our mutual wall. Eddie had tilted his chair back. In one hand he held a container of coffee, in the other the *Daily News* sports section.

"Eddie, what's going on?"

"Heathen Chinee houseboy didn't come home last night." He grinned, a sly disturbing grin. "By the way, you owe me twenty bucks."

For a moment I didn't know what he meant. Then I realized it was the twenty dollars he'd wanted to bet on making it with Amanda. As if she wasn't abused enough.

"Take it out of the forty-three dollars you owe me," I

snapped. "And I hope both of them rip you apart one of these days."

He shrugged. "Female trouble. The story of my life. If one of you isn't pissed off, another one is." Laying his coffee and paper aside, he stood and stretched as if he had all the time in the world. As he walked past my cubicle, he leaned over to me. "Do I look like I'm worried?"

Eddie hadn't been in Charlotte's office thirty seconds before Helen paid me one of her rare visits. She looked unsure of herself for a change, and when she apologized for interrupting my work, I braced myself for something unpleasant.

"I know you and Eddie are friends, and that he's your boss, but don't you think that has gone far enough?" She nodded toward Charlotte's door. "It's a disgrace to the company."

What a pill! I could not imagine what lengths of depravity an employee would have to sink to to be a disgrace to C.F. "Helen," I said, "they're both adults. And I assume they're both consenting. They have the right to disgrace themselves any way they want. And haven't we been through this before?"

"But now she's keeping him. It's all over the office."

I sucked in my breath. "If that is true, and I'm not sure it is, what do you expect me to do about it?"

"As his assistant, you have a responsibility to report it to Mr. Fike. I can't believe he would—"

I held up my hand, stopping her. "First, I have no intention of passing unfounded gossip on to Morton Fike, and second, Morton Fike knows Eddie and Charlotte are involved because last week he and his wife went to a party at their apartment."

Helen's reaction was what I should have expected, a wide-eyed, "Were you invited?"

"Certainly. It was fantastic, Helen. Dozens of us business types, all networking like crazy."

Giving one of her fed-up sniffs, she turned away. I thought the episode was over, but no such luck. When she reached my wall, Helen looked back at me. "I might have known you'd protect Eddie. Everybody knows you've been covering up for him." With that she stalked off.

Eddie and Charlotte must have fought in whispers. Once Eddie closed Charlotte's door behind him, there was nothing. Not a sound. The room could have been deserted.

Time passed and I lost interest in what was going on in Charlotte's office. Though I hated admitting it, Helen's accusation had struck a sensitive spot. I *had* been covering for Eddie. Storing my mailing list, which was nothing but pretend work, I logged into a word processing program, pulled my resume from my drawer, and read it over. What a mass of lies and exaggerations! Just looking at it depressed me. How on earth was I going to update it? I shoved it back in the drawer untouched.

A few seconds later Charlotte's door opened and Eddie walked back to his bay. When he didn't stop to say anything to me, I poked my head around our wall.

Eddie's back was to me, his elbows were on his desk, and his face was buried in his hands. This was scary. Had she fired him? If she had, it was all over for me too.

"Are you all right?"

He sat up and stretched. "Yeah. Sure. I'm okay, I guess."

This was the closest I'd ever heard Eddie come to admitting he wasn't okay. Rolling into his cubicle, I took a closer look. My lively, hell-raising boss looked beaten and kind of gray.

"You don't look okay. What happened? Did she fire you?"

Eddie made an effort to yank himself to life. Straightening his shoulders, he gave me a forced smile.

"Fire me? You've got to be kidding. The only way she'll ever let me go is in a pine box."

"Eddie," I said, "what have you gotten yourself into?"

He hesitated for a second, then gave me a dose of his usual. "I'm kidding you. Everything's cool, Bonnie. You're such a worrier. Like I said, do I look worried?"

I was on my way back to my own area when he added, "So, Bonnie. How'd you like to go to a wedding?"

It took a moment for the Eddie's words to sink in. When they did, I had to steady myself before I could turn around and face him.

He was chewing his knuckles, staring at me.

"Eddie. You can't mean that. Not . . ." I was having trouble even saying it.

He nodded. "Why not?"

"You and Charlotte?"

"Sure. Me and Charlotte. What's wrong, Bonnie? You got something against mixed marriages? Let me tell you something. When Charlotte's ancestors were still beating on each other with sticks, mine were already blowing each other up with gunpowder." He was cocky now, the Eddie I knew. Only this time I knew it was a front.

"You know what's wrong. You can't marry her."

"You don't know what I can do. You don't know anything. Charlotte's a very . . . giving woman." After that outburst he turned his back to me and began shuffling papers on his desk. The conversation was closed.

Giving? You better believe she was giving. He'd gotten the promotion for escorting her and, if my instincts were right, the Toyota for sleeping with her. What could she give him to make him marry her? Her share in the business? Whatever it was, it couldn't possibly be enough.

For the rest of the morning we didn't speak. I was too upset about what Eddie was doing to himself to pretend I wasn't, to put on a "Congratulations, best wishes" act.

Eddie was at his desk when I got back from lunch. Maybe he'd never left. His behavior was so odd these days I never knew what to expect. I'd spent my lunch hour taking a long, cold walk, trying to talk myself into being civil about Eddie's engagement. If I thought what he was doing was gross, so what? It was Eddie's life and his business who he married.

"Congratulations," I choked. "When's the big day?"

He smiled. I could tell he was glad we were speaking again. "Pretty soon. Charlotte wants it to be soon."

I'll bet she did. Before the groom chickened out.

"A big wedding? Are you going on a honeymoon?" I tried to sound enthusiastic, but I'm sure my smile looked as strained as it felt.

Eddie shrugged. "I don't know. Maybe. That's all up to Charlotte." Reaching over, he put his hand on my shoulder. "It will be cool, Bonnie. You'll see."

"I hope so, Eddie, because you're the one who's going to have to live with it."

There were other questions I wanted to ask, like: "What did your aunt and uncle say?" "Have they met the blushing bride?" "What about Amanda?" "Are you going to continue working here?" And naturally, "Who's going to run this department if you and Charlotte go on a honeymoon?" That last one was the real killer for me. No doubt about it, I had to get my resume updated, fast.

Late that afternoon I got the first hint of trouble in paradise. Or I should say, trouble with Paradise.

"Hey, Bonnie," Eddie said, rolling into my bay. "I need a favor."

"You always need a favor."

His voice dropped until I could hardly hear him. "Come on. Just this once. Charlotte and I are going to the diamond district to look at rings. Amanda's on her damned phone again, as usual. Go tell her I'm going to be late tonight. Probably around ten or so. I'm going by Hector's first."

"Are you kidding?" I couldn't believe this. Eddie actually intended to keep seeing Amanda.

"Not after last night, I'm not. Why?" He held up his left hand. "You don't see any ring here yet, do you?"

"No. It's the one through your nose I'm thinking of."

It's next to impossible to make an effective angry exit rolling in an office chair, but Eddie almost pulled it off. He could fume all he wanted to, though. And Amanda could wait till doomsday for his message. I was through doing Eddie's dirty work.

An icy wind swept through the city that night. The temperature, which had been warm for midwinter, fell sharply. By the time I reached my apartment I was shivering through my down coat.

A surprise was waiting in my mailbox. A letter from Derek. It was dated a full week earlier. I waited until I got into my apartment to open it, fearing that I was going to find a Dear John—or Dear Jane—letter.

My dear Bonnie—

The time without you has been difficult and I was looking forward to our being together once again. Now, however, I find that my father's illness is much worse than I had expected, and I will not be returning to New York for several more weeks.

My reasons for lying to you about my money now strike me as foolish. You are not the type of woman who would be involved with a man simply because he was well off. Still, I have made it a point not to tell people about my money until I felt I knew them well. Unfortunately, with you I waited too long.

Derek said that he had inherited some money from his industrialist grandfather and had made still more investing in stock futures. The letter continued—

I accept that your career path is important, but should you want a break from it, I will purchase airline tickets for you. It would be wonderful to show you my country. I'll call you Sunday night and we can talk about this.

He closed with "Love." When I read that, my career path, which had been steadily losing ground, plummeted into nothingness. I fell into a dreamy, lovelorn sleep. My only concern about my career path was how much notice I should give before I left for Denmark.

"Bonnie! Bonnie!" My name, whispered again and again, alternating with taps and scrapings.

I woke slowly, coming out of a dream. And what a dream! It took me a few seconds to realize I was alone in my own bed. Opening my eyes I looked through the darkness to the dial on my clock. Eleven-fifteen. At the foot of the bed Moses was wide awake, his ears pitched forward. I listened for a second, but there was nothing. No sound at all. It had been part of the dream.

"Come on, kitty-kitty." I patted the bed next to me. Moses got up, stretched, and wandered to the top of the bed. In the middle of making himself a nest in the extra pillow, he stopped, rigid. A second later I heard the noise again. This time it was more real. There was something, or somebody, on the fire-escape landing by my bedroom window.

Moses was on full alert, his tail puffed as big as a raccoon's.

Jumping up, heart pounding, I grabbed the phone next to my bed and started dialing 911.

"Bonnie!" Tap-tap-tap. "Come on, Bonnie. Wake up."

I could hardly believe what I was hearing. It sounded as if Eddie Fong was on my fire escape. Replacing the receiver, I tiptoed to the window and cracked the shade. Eddie's face, pressed flat against the glass, scared me so badly I jumped back with a shriek. Moses freaked out. The last I saw of him was his puffed-up tail disappearing under the bed.

I opened the shade and lifted my window. Eddie threw a gym bag through the opening and tumbled in after it.

"Shit, I thought you'd never wake up. I almost froze to death out there. Pull down that shade. And don't touch the fuckin' lights."

He crouched on the floor by the radiator, rubbing his hands against his thighs. As soon as I'd closed and latched the window and drawn the shade, I yanked my blanket off the bed and threw it it over him.

173

"Sorry," I said, "but I'm not used to my company coming in through the window."

"Keep your voice down, Bonnie. You don't know these guys."

He stayed crouched for a few minutes, rocking back and forth on his feet, rubbing his hands on his thighs. I knelt down and tucked the blanket around him.

"Eddie, what's going on? Should I call the police?"

"No, no. No cops." He doubled over at the waist and groaned. "Man, I'm dying. You wouldn't believe what I've been through tonight."

I remembered Babyface and Scarface on the subway and that knife. Had Eddie been stabbed? "Eddie, you've got to get to the hospital. Can you walk?"

He looked up and shook his head. "Hospital? Shit. I need something for my stomach. My ulcer is killing me. Maalox, or Tums. You got anything?"

I shook my head. "How about a glass of milk?"

Grimacing, he hoisted himself onto the bed and dropped back on the pillow. "Milk! That's like trying to put out a forest fire with an eyedropper."

I sat next to him. He looked awful, drawn and gray. "Should I call Charlotte? She's probably worried sick."

"Charlotte!" His eyes shot open.

"You remember. Your fiancée."

"I think the engagement's off." Smiling weakly, he sat up and looked around my room. "Listen, Bonnie. I may have made a big mistake. I mean, real big. Like the biggest mistake ever. I need to hide something."

"Here? What? If it's drugs, forget it."

"Drugs? What kind of a guy do you think I am?"

That was one question best left unanswered. "What is it?" I asked again.

Eddie nodded at the dark-green gym bag that had fallen near the foot of the bed.

"What's in it?"

"My pajamas! Come on, Bonnie. If I'd wanted to play twenty questions, I'd of gone to my aunt's house."

"If you can't tell me what's in the bag," I said, "I don't want it here."

Eddie groaned. "It's nothing for you to get excited about. Some private business papers. No big deal." He wrapped his arms in front of his stomach and doubled over again. "Aaah. I'm dying."

"Did you park outside? I could take you to the emergency room at Presbyterian Hospital."

Eddie shook his head. "Do you think I'd leave my car outside and come in the way I did? Get serious."

That reminded me—how had he even known which apartment was mine? I asked him.

"Remember, you said 'top-floor corner, with a view of the river.' It wasn't hard to figure out."

He was clenching and unclenching his fists. "I need time to work out an angle. Maybe you're right. Maybe I should call Charlotte. Or maybe Amanda." He smiled. "You women are usually pretty understanding. Right? Always ready to forgive a guy?"

I wasn't sure I belonged in the same category as Charlotte or Amanda, but this was no time for a debate. "Sometimes. You mean, they're both fed up with you?"

"Bonnie," he said bitterly, "you don't know the half of it. I've got shit coming down around me you wouldn't believe."

"I have a pretty good idea what's responsible for this. Gambling. Right?"

"You don't know anything. And that's the way it should be. I don't want you messed up in this." He clenched his stomach. "Oh, man. You know what I need?"

"A favor?"

"Yeah. Is there a store open around here where you could get some Maalox?"

I nodded.

"Would you mind picking up a couple bottles?"

Mind? I'd been minding the favors Eddie wanted since I'd met him. With him threatening to die on my bed, what was one more.

"Okay, sure. But then, Eddie . . ."

175

"Yeah?"

"You've got to tell me what's going on and let me decide whether we should call the police."

"For sure. We'll talk. After you bring back the Maalox."

He slipped back onto the pillow, closing his eyes. I fished through my drawer for some jeans to slip over my nightgown.

As I was leaving the room, Eddie said, "Remember: no cops. And no Charlotte."

"I promise. Not until we've talked."

"Thanks, doll. I owe you one."

"You owe me dozens."

Upper Washington Heights is quiet at night, especially wintery weeknights when the wind off the Hudson is so cold it burns your lungs. Across the street a man walked a big Doberman. Far down the curving hill, light came from an all-night garage. I turned the other way, bundled my coat around me, and walked to the bodega.

"*Como está?*"

"*Muy malo.*" I paid for two large bottles of liquid Maalox—more money Eddie would owe me forever—and was about to push the glass door open when something in the street stopped me cold. The black Trans Am with the dark windows and the dragon on its hood rolled by, quiet as death. God! One second later and I would have been out there.

I waited a minute, then stuck my head out the door again, expecting to see the taillights disappearing down the hill. The Trans Am was double-parked at the next corner across from my building.

It took only another second for the real horror of the situation to sink in. How did those thugs even know who I was, much less where I lived unless Eddie had told them. What a fool he was!

I watched the street through the bodega's window. The headlights on the black car dimmed, but puffs of smoke drifted from the exhaust pipe into the black night. Hopefully this meant they didn't plan to stay. If anyone got out of that car and went to my building, I was calling the police. Hell with Eddie and his stupid ideas. No one did, though. Whoever it was just sat there with the engine running, waiting.

I turned to the proprietor. "Do you have a phone?"

He nodded to the rear of the store.

After hurrying down the aisle, I dropped in a quarter and dialed my number. Busy! Honest to God! Eddie was every kind of a moron. Probably talking to a bookie! I slammed the receiver down.

Back at the door I watched the Trans Am. The driver was getting fidgety. He pulled up directly in front of my building, paused there for a second, and then reversed to the corner. What was he doing? Trying to figure out which apartment was mine? That thought made me even more furious at Eddie.

I went back to the phone and tried my number again. This time it rang. I heard it lift off the receiver, but there was no "Hello."

"Eddie! It's Bonnie. Are you there?"

"Where else would I be? What's keeping you?"

"Listen, asshole! I can't get home because you told those thugs where I live and they're outside my apartment right now."

"I didn't tell them, Bonnie. I swear. I never mentioned your name to them."

"Then why are they parked on my corner?"

"These guys have friends in places you'd never suspect. Just be cool and don't let them see you. They don't know I'm here. Wait them out. They'll leave."

Five minutes later the car pulled away. It was hardly out of sight before I left the bodega and hurried home. I'd had enough. Eddie was going to get a piece of my mind and my resignation with his Maalox. Then he could get out of my apartment and handle his problems without me.

He was gone. I knew it as soon as I stepped into my apartment. There's some way, when you've lived in a place for a while, that you know when you're alone. It can be a good sensation or a bad one. In this case I had an immediate sick feeling.

"Eddie?" I walked into my bedroom, softly calling his name. The room was empty. The window shade was slightly askew, and when I examined the window, I saw that though it had been closed tight, it was now unlocked. Eddie had left like he had arrived, by the fire escape. Tucked under my clock radio I found a note:

Played a hunch and called a sympathetic lady. Feeling better. See you tomorrow. Be on time. You have a long way to go on that mailing list.

Be on time? Me? Of all the nerve! I wadded the note and threw it onto the floor. What a jerk Eddie was. Reckless, inconsiderate. Hands down the worst boss ever.

It was midnight. Moses slinked from under the bed. "A pit bull you're not," I told him. He blinked, ready for action now. I was wide awake too, and on top of everything else, my recent adventure had left my stomach churning. Maybe Eddie's ulcer was contagious. His traumas certainly were. I took a couple slugs on one of the Maalox bottles, then crawled into bed.

It was a long time before I fell back to sleep. And as I lay there tossing around, wondering if those hoodlums were gone for good, I made a decision. In the morning I would write Derek and tell him I had given two weeks' notice and he could send the tickets. Then I would tell Eddie exactly what he could do with his preposterous job. During the coming week I would put my abundant spare time and C.F.'s computer to work composing a new resume, and when I got back, I would apply for every job in the *Times* that I was remotely qualified for.

The way things turned out, I never got the chance.

PART 3

◆◆◆◆◆◆◆◆◆◆◆◆◆

From Bad to Worse

CHAPTER 13

◆◆◆◆◆◆◆◆◆◆◆◆◆◆◆

I was on time Tuesday morning. Eddie didn't show at all. So much for the mailing list. I had no intention of touching the damned thing again. So much for my resignation too, at least for that day. Normal office procedure is that you resign to your boss first.

Charlotte didn't make it to work either. That, I figured, settled the identity of Eddie's softhearted lady. It looked as if whatever he had done to upset Charlotte and end their engagement, he had managed to undo after going out my window the night before. Now they were sleeping off their reconciliation in Charlotte's king-size bed.

It wasn't until the next day that I started to worry.

Charlotte was in when I got there. Her coat, as usual, took half the closet, and I had to fight with the dead animal to fit mine in. Eddie, however, there was no sign of. So where was Charlotte's hapless fiancé? She must have known; she didn't do any glowering over the partitions.

I thought long and hard before bringing up the subject of Eddie's whereabouts with Charlotte. Finally, when he hadn't shown by noon, my curiosity got the best of me. Though Eddie's performance in both areas left a lot to be desired, he was my friend and my boss. After the problems he'd had Monday night, I wanted to be sure he was okay.

I knocked tentatively on Charlotte's ever-closed door.

Charlotte answered my tentative knock on her ever-closed door with a marine drill sergeant's "Yes?"

I opened the door cautiously.

Gone was the oversize nymphet of the past weeks. The sturdy blue suit was back. The navy bow was squarely under the assertive chin, right where it belonged, rather than in the hair or at the waist. The unpolished nails were short and square cut. Gone was the mascara, the violet eyeshadow. Charlotte's sole concession to color was the mud-colored lipstick making a faint slash across a face otherwise as blank as a bucket of putty.

She stared up from the work on her desk, fierce. Woe to the sucker who crossed her threshold that Wednesday. It would have taken a cattle prod to get me into her office. I poked my head through the door, trying to be as unobtrusive as I could without seeming like a ninny.

"I was wondering when Eddie was going to be in."

"I haven't the foggiest idea. Do I look like the receptionist?"

So much for our cheek-kissing relationship.

"Oh, the receptionist. Yes, I'll check with her. Thank you."

I closed the door fast.

This put a new slant on the situation. If Charlotte didn't know where Eddie was, who did? Was it possible Amanda was the softhearted lady he'd paid his late-night call on?

I found Amanda agonizing over a typo. Nothing out of the ordinary there, at least.

"Amanda, have you seen Eddie?"

She glanced nervously at Morton Fike's door.

"No! And please! I can't talk about that right now," she whispered.

I bent over and whispered back, "Did you see him Monday night?"

She blanched. I didn't imagine it. Her porcelain skin turned whiter still until it looked almost transparent. "Only for a little while. Please, Bonnie. We'll talk later."

She'd no sooner said that when Morton Fike burst from his office with a fistful of crumpled typed pages.

"How is it, Paradise, that one day you can give me perfect letters, and the next I can't tell what language you're typing in?"

Amanda flinched. I got out of there fast, too.

By afternoon Eddie's whereabouts had become more than a matter of curiosity. I was so concerned that I called his aunt at her restaurant. She hardly spoke English, and what I got out of her amounted to, "Eddie not here. Try Eddie at office."

Office! I didn't tell her that was where I was calling from. There was no point in worrying her needlessly.

Eddie had always accused me of being a mother hen, a worrier. How many times had he said, "Don't sweat it, Bonnie. You worry too much." But now, once again, he had put me in an impossible position. Was he holed up in one of his favorite haunts? Did he have some "softhearted lady" I didn't know about? With Eddie nothing was impossible. Had he skipped off on one of the tong gambling tours to Atlantic City for a few days?

I kept trying to convince myself that Eddie had gone to Atlantic City, that as I worried myself into an ulcer he was standing at the craps table losing his last dollar or, more likely, somebody else's. I couldn't get away from that terrible nagging feeling that kept passing through my mind, though. Had those guys in the Trans Am gotten him? I could just hear Eddie accusing me of being a mother hen, but by the end of the day I was scared. I had to do something.

He had planned to visit Hector before going to Amanda's apartment Monday night. Picking up the Manhattan directory on Eddie's bookshelf, I looked up a Rodriguez on Gramercy Park.

It was strange standing in front of Mr. Gartner's apartment house. The last time I'd been there I'd been too involved with other things to bother looking at it. Now, under the streetlights, I could see that it was old and graceful, a building from a more genteel time.

Around the side I found the ground-level door to the Rodriguez apartment. SUPER was painted over the buzzer in big white letters. A plump, middle-aged woman answered my ring.

"No vacancies," she said.

"I'm looking for Hector Rodriguez."

"Hector? Hector's upstairs, painting. First floor. Number one." She pointed straight up.

I walked back around the building. Thick, well-tended shrubbery bordered the front steps on both sides. When I got to the landing, I looked over the wrought-iron railing. I didn't know which side Mr. Gartner's body had been found on, and the bushes gave up no clues. I could understand, though, how it was the body wasn't spotted until morning. Against the white of the snow a body, pulled to the back of this dense shrubbery, would be just another dark clump.

There were five buzzers, only one for each floor. That's why there was no doorman. A building with five tenants didn't warrant one. Too bad.

I had no trouble spotting the apartment Hector was working in. Its curtainless front windows faced the street. Lights were on. If I stood on my toes and peered through the ornate black window bars, I could see the apartment was empty of furniture. It had obviously been the Gartner's apartment. I pushed the button labeled 1. A second later Hector buzzed me in.

I felt terribly awkward. Except for our brief messages through Eddie, we hadn't communicated since this mess started. For that matter we'd scarcely spoken before it started, either. I only had Eddie's word that Hector didn't hold a grudge. And Eddie, though I was determined to remember him for his good points, wasn't famous for reliability.

Hector, in his painter's clothes with a brush in his hand, looked far more comfortable than he had playing "yes-man" to Amanda.

"Hi, Hector."

"Hi, Bonnie. What's new?"

"I can't find Eddie."

Hector laughed. "That's nothing new."

I followed him through a foyer into the apartment's big, airy living room. It was a wonderful place, with a high, domed ceiling, arched windows on two walls, and a brick fireplace.

"Was this the Gartners'?" I asked, already sure of the answer.

"Yeah. Mrs. Gartner didn't want anything to do with New York anymore. Gave up her lease." He turned down a transistor radio that was tuned to a rock station. "It's already been rented. Made the landlord happy."

He shrugged, a wise-to-the-world shrug beyond his years. It was a long time since I was Hector's age, and I'd never been a tough city kid. I hardly knew how to talk to him, and I could see that he felt the same about me. After a moment he started absently dabbing paint on a radiator.

"Hector, I'm wondering if you've seen Eddie around? He hasn't been at work in a couple days."

"No." Looking up briefly, he said, "Eddie was supposed to come by Monday about eight to give me a few bucks he owes me, but he never showed. He's probably off gambling somewhere. He's into that really big."

"If you hear from him, tell him I'm worried."

"Sure. That's if I hear from him. He's something else. Not real reliable."

"Well, thanks." I glanced down at the parquet floor. Most of it was light and looked freshly cleaned. Around the edges,

185

though, the wood was darker. There had been a carpet on this floor recently. That, and the fact that this was an old building from the days of foot-thick concrete floors, made me wonder if Hector's story about Mr. Gartner's female visitor was true.

"That night Mr. Gartner got killed, you heard him talking to a woman through this floor? They must have been shouting."

"No. Not through the floor." Leaning down, he tapped his knuckles on the radiator. "Through this. O'Hagan tell you about that?"

"No. Eddie did. What happened that night, anyway?"

"Jesus! I told Eddie about the woman in confidence. I'm never going to trust that guy again." Wiping off the brush, he laid it across the paint can. Then he sat down on the windowsill and told his story in a bored monotone. No wonder. He'd probably told it to O'Hagan a thousand times.

Hector had, indeed, intercepted Mr. Gartner as Mr. Gartner was opening the building door and asked him for a loan.

"He was a good guy," Hector explained. "Always willing to let me have a couple bucks."

"Hector," I said, sounding like the school marm Eddie always accused me of being, "it was a couple hundred, wasn't it?"

He shrugged. "A couple, a couple hundred. Gartner had plenty. Anyway, Gartner said to me, 'Let's get in out of the snow,' and he handed me his briefcase while he finished unlocking the door. I followed him in and put the briefcase on the floor. He gave me the bread, I promised I'd pay him as soon as he got back from Florida, and I split."

"And you went downstairs and heard the woman?"

He shook his head. "It was later. An hour, maybe less. First I walked over to Second Avenue. There's this pool hall. Some of the guys hang out. I had to pay somebody back fifty bucks. Then I came back to our apartment. Our living room's right under this one." He tapped the floor with his sneaker. "Right down there. Everybody but me's asleep. I turn on the TV low and stretch out on the sofa. That's when I hear that Mr. Gartner's got a girl up there."

"You could hear clearly?"

"No. Not what they were saying. Just voices. But let's face it, I know a chick's voice from a guy's. I'll take you downstairs and show you."

He turned up the transistor radio to about the level of normal conversation. After that, I followed him down to his family's apartment.

The Rodriguez place was was low-ceilinged and cramped, with none of the grandeur of its upstairs neighbor. The living room was full of children, television noise, and cooking smells.

"Keep it down for a second," Hector said to the kids as he lowered the television volume. A little girl stuck out her tongue, then darted out of his reach.

He was right about the sound from upstairs. The closer I got to the radiator, the more clearly I heard the radio. An old Carole King song was playing. I couldn't have made out the lyrics if I hadn't known them, but I could tell it was a woman's voice.

"You see?"

"I sure do," I said. "And what happened then? You said Gartner went out."

Hector shook his head. "That I couldn't swear to, except you got that letter from him. All I remember is the two of them walking across the floor, Gartner's door slamming, and then I either fell asleep and didn't hear anything, or there wasn't anything else to hear."

Thanking Hector, I left. It had been an informative visit. Not where Eddie was concerned. I hadn't learned anything there I didn't already know. The time element in the Gartner killing, however, was news to me. About an hour had passed between the time Derek and I dropped Mr. Gartner off and when Hector heard the female visitor. A lot can happen in an hour.

When Eddie didn't show up Thursday morning, I cornered Amanda in the ladies' room. She was in front of the mirror, makeup case open on the ledge over the sink, searching her chin for a nonexistent pimple.

"When did you see Eddie last?" I asked.

"I don't want to talk about Eddie. I'm through with him. If you only knew the trouble he caused me." Snapping the makeup case shut, she shook her head so that her hair fanned around her face. "Do you think I should get a perm?"

"A perm, Amanda? I'm worried about Eddie. Seriously worried."

"I better get back to my desk," she said, as if she hadn't heard me. "Mr. Fike doesn't like me to leave it." She tried pushing her way around me. I stepped into her path. My heart started to thump. The only friend I had left at the office and I was about to get into a tussle with her. She gripped the edge of one of the sinks.

"I don't know where Eddie is, and I don't care. I haven't seen him since Monday night."

"What time Monday night?"

"Eight forty-five, exactly."

She was all but writhing with embarrassment. What was the matter with her? I gripped her shoulder.

"Eight forty-five? It was more like twelve forty-five, wasn't it, Amanda? I've got to know."

Wiggling from under my hand, she stooped to look under the stalls. When she was satisfied they were empty, she said, "I know it was eight forty-five because I wasn't expecting Eddie until about ten. He got to my apartment and refused to leave." She took a quivering breath. "And my special friend stopped by to drop off a present for me and caught Eddie there. It was awful."

I'll bet it was awful. It was possible Morton Fike knew about Amanda and Eddie, but poor Eddie had no idea about Fike. What do you do when you find out, in a face-to-face confrontation, that your competition is the president of the company you work for?

Amanda managed to shove past me. "Bonnie, I've got to get back. Mr. Fike is going to be looking for me. I'll talk to you later."

I returned to my desk worried. It was getting harder and harder to take—to "be cool" about this. The hoods in the Trans Am were no longer in the back of my mind. They were right up there at the front, knives drawn, ready to do something terrible to Eddie.

As soon as I got back to my desk, I called Eddie's aunt again. This time I explained that I was from the office and that Eddie hadn't been at work in days. When it became clear to me that he hadn't been sleeping at her house, I called the police department and got the number to report missing persons.

At Missing Persons there was a snag. The woman I had been referred to logged in my call, but told me that Eddie hadn't been gone long enough to be considered missing. "Relax," the woman said. "Your friend's sure to turn up. Ninety-three percent of missing adults do."

My lunch hours were getting longer and longer and I didn't care. I wandered all the way to the Bowery that noon, hoping the cold air would clear my head.

Bowery Street has been called the Street of Forgotten Men. It isn't all hoboes, though. Where it cuts through Chinatown there are several blocks of more or less respectable-looking shops. Walk a few blocks south and you come to City Hall and the staid government office buildings that surround it.

The lunchtime crowd was heavy. It seemed that everybody in New York wanted to eat in Chinatown that day. I strolled in a half-daze among the rushing throng, worrying about Eddie, letting the crowd carry me along at its own speed.

As much as I had on my mind, it's a wonder I noticed anything at all, and a fluke that I looked up into the dirty window of the crack-in-the-sidewalk office that sold bus tours to Atlantic City. Stepping out of the crush of pedestrians, I studied the address. 704, in peeling gold letters over the door. I couldn't remember the exact address Eddie had found in the wrong computer file when we started at C.F., but 704 sounded about right. I did remember the name. W.B. Ent. Ward Broadcasting, I had assumed at the time. If this was W.B. Ent., I now understood why Eddie had been surprised to find them on our client list.

A faded poster of waves on a beach crowded with oil-slicked bodies hung askew in the door. The window was a bit livelier, with colorful pictures of Atlantic City casinos at night: Harrah's, Sands, Tropicana. "Come to play," a poster with ragged edges begged. There was nothing on the window indicating the proprietor's name.

Squinting, I looked through the window. The office was empty except for a young Chinese woman behind the counter. Without considering what I was going to say once I got inside, I opened the door and walked in.

"Can I help you?" the young woman asked.

"Maybe." Picking a brochure from a stand, I thumbed through it. On its back page the stamped name on the bottom all but jumped out at me: "W.B. Ent.," it read in smudgy black letters.

Now what? I looked up at the clerk. "I'm thinking of booking a tour for a group of senior citizens. A huge group," I added, sweetening the pie.

The woman nodded enthusiastically. "We handle very big groups."

"I'd sort of like to speak to the manager. You're part of Ward Broadcasting, aren't you?" I pointed to the "W.B. Ent." stamp. "Is the manager here?"

"That's not Ward Broadcasting," she said with a smile. "W.B. Ent. is Woo Brothers Enterprises. There are two brothers: Herman and Kee. But Kee Woo is mostly in Hong Kong. I can have Mr. Herman Woo call you, if you'd like."

I left after giving the woman a fake name and phone number.

If I'd been distracted earlier on my walk, I was now totally out of it. Eddie had told me he was mistaken about the Bowery address, but there it was, and it was just what C.F.'s file had called it: "W.B. Ent." I didn't remember the exact amount W.B. Ent. had transferred to an offshore tax haven account, but it had been substantial. If that tiny office cleared twenty thousand dollars a year, I'd be surprised. Why had Eddie, after first pointing it out as part of a secret Chinese association, later lied to me about it? Well, that was a nutty thing to ask myself. Why had Eddie done most of the things he'd done?

Was I ever surprised when Sergeant Vincent O'Hagan knocked on my door later that night!

"Understand you reported an Edwin Fong missing."

I nodded.

"I thought I'd stop by and check into it," he said. "Can we come in?"

"But . . . you again?"

O'Hagan and and a middle-aged Chinese man walked into my living room. "Funny thing, Miss Indermill. I was going to say the same thing to you," O'Hagan said. "You again?"

I shrugged. "Just lucky."

O'Hagan sank into one of my chairs as if he was exhausted. "This is Captain John Lee from Organized Crime down at Police Plaza."

A police captain, to look for Eddie Fong? A captain is a big deal in the police department. I shook hands with Captain Lee. He was short and square, like a sumo wrestler. He was wearing the ugliest light-green-checked topcoat ever.

O'Hagan asked the questions and I answered them. This was getting to be a routine with us. As with the Gartner killing, I kept nothing back. Eddie's visit to the building under the Manhattan Bridge didn't surprise either man. Neither did the W.B. Ent. tour office and its possible connection to C.F. When I talked about the Trans Am with the dark windows and the dragon, O'Hagan glanced at Captain Lee.

191

"I know the car," Lee said. "I'll have somebody check it out."

"And this gym bag Eddie brought through your window and wanted you to hide? When you got back from the bodega, he had taken it with him?"

I nodded. "I looked everywhere."

"Everywhere." That was O'Hagan, of course. "You have no idea what was in it."

"Eddie said it was his pajamas."

O'Hagan rolled his eyes. "Pajamas. You're trying to tell me, Miss Indermill, that you believed Eddie Fong wanted you to hide his pajamas for him?"

I wasn't going to let O'Hagan rile me up this time. "No," I answered calmly. "I asked him if it was drugs, and he said no. He said it was papers."

O'Hagan looked at Lee. "Papers."

While the policemen weren't as forthcoming with me as I was with them, I learned from Captain Lee that Eddie was well-known in Chinatown's underworld of illegal gambling operations. "A compulsive gambler who borrows from the loan sharks," Lee said. Eddie had been in over his head before, but he'd always managed to come up with the money.

"Have you ever heard of a 'smurf'?" Captain Lee asked me.

All I could think of was some kind of stuffed toy. Lee smiled when I said that.

"A 'smurf' is what we call an underling in a money-laundering operation. The guy who carries the cash and converts it into something that's not going to get the authorities excited. Cashier's checks are the most popular."

Lee explained that under the Bank Secrecy Act, financial institutions are required to fill out detailed reports when there are cash transactions of more than ten thousand dollars. The smurfs kept their transactions under that amount.

When I heard that, I told Lee about the transactions I'd seen in the W.B. Ent. file. "I can't remember the amounts, but they were all just under ten thousand dollars."

Lee then asked me how C.F. handled money transfers to its tax-haven accounts.

"I'm not too familiar with that part of the business, but we do wire money. We're licensed to," I added.

I learned from Captain Lee that it wasn't unusual for dirty money—money somebody wanted to make look respectable—to move through a dozen currency transactions before it returned to the originator. "By that time," Lee explained, "the money is impossible to trace. It's clean."

"Did Fong ever hint to you that he was carrying money for one of the gambling operations, like maybe that place on Forsyth?" O'Hagan asked.

I shook my head. "No. All he hinted about was that he was going big places with them. But he was always talking big. Is that what that place is? A gambling operation?"

"A little of this, a little of that," said the always garrulous O'Hagan. "By the way. Did you ever get the feeling Eddie Fong was suicidal?"

That surprised me. "Eddie, suicidal? Not from what I saw."

Once more, the two men exchanged glances.

"Why?" I asked.

"We received information that he may have been. His car was found yesterday about a block from the pedestrian walkway to the George Washington Bridge. Not far from here," Captain Lee added. "A scarf that might have belonged to Fong was knotted around one of the cables on the walkway. One of the men working on the bridge found it. Cashmere. Red and black plaid."

I nodded with a sinking feeling. "Amanda Paradise gave Eddie a scarf like that."

That was something the two policemen wanted to hear more about. Not the scarf. Eddie's relationships with Amanda and Charlotte. I told them as much as I could. When they were through with their questions, I brought up something that had been bothering me:

"Do you think this is related to Mr. Gartner's murder?"

O'Hagan scratched his eyebrow. "Why do you ask that?"

"Because it's so much. Two"—I didn't want to say deaths; hopefully Eddie was still alive—"two incidents."

"Could be coincidence," O'Hagan said. "You did hear about Gartner's autopsy, didn't you?"

"No. What about it?"

"Coroner's office found a tumor in the temporary region of his brain."

"'Temporal,'" Lee corrected.

"That's what I said. The medical boys tell me that people with brain tumors sometimes have these fits. Think they smell things that aren't there."

"Olfactory hallucinations." Lee, again.

"Right." O'Hagan stood and picked up his coat. "Too bad the killer didn't wait. Gartner would have died anyhow."

"Maybe the killer couldn't wait," I said as I walked the two men to my door.

Captain Lee was already in the hall when O'Hagan turned to me. "Keep out of it, Miss Indermill," he said ominously. "You hear from Fong, call me or Captain Lee immediately. These guys play rough."

Friday morning the deepening gloom I'd felt hanging over Creative Financial Ventures Leasing Department since Eddie's disappearance turned black and ominous as the shadow of a bomber. For once, the trouble had nothing to do with Eddie. Congress had introduced legislation to plug the AMT loophole.

Fike's maniacal mailings and belt-tightenings, Charlotte's endless slaving over her printouts. None of it meant anything in the face of this legislation. Derek had been right. Leasing would keep going for a while, but if this legislation passed, and that was rumored to be likely, their efforts would amount to nothing more than the desperate heaves of frightened people, trying to drown out the death rattle of a department going under.

Six weeks earlier the situation would have horrified me.

Now I planned to be long gone by the time Leasing's name was once again peeled off the mahogany door.

The office felt deserted. Most of the people I liked or even felt comfortable with were gone. Derek on vacation, Mr. Gartner violently killed, Eddie simply gone. Those last two were unbelievable. Within five weeks I'd lost a CEO and a boss. Was it coincidence? O'Hagan said it could be, but that was mind-boggling. What were the statistical probabilities of two people, coworkers in a small, white-collar company, encountering violence within little more than a month of each other?

Something Helen said late that afternoon hit me like an ice-cold shower. We were putting on our coats, getting ready to brave the cold outside. Helen sighed and shook her head.

"I've never known any good to come from being involved with men who are beneath you. Unstable personalities."

I thought she meant herself and Perry Dumont and whatever had gone on the night of the Christmas party. What a dumb thing to bring up now. And the phrase, "unstable personality." Only Helen would refer to somebody drunk out of his mind as an "unstable personality."

"Everybody makes mistakes, Helen, especially at office parties. You're not the first," I said, not really giving a damn about Helen's wretched love life.

Her reaction, when she realized what I meant, would have been laughable if I'd been in a better state of mind. Her chin thrust out. Her eyes narrowed to pinheads.

"I meant Charlotte and Eddie," she snapped.

"What are you talking about?"

"Well," she said, buttoning her coat, "Charlotte told me she had been trying to break up with Eddie, but he refused to let her go. Charlotte felt sorry for him. He was such a mess. She was hoping she could help him. Eddie was the one who insisted on the engagement."

"Charlotte said that?"

"Yes. I went in to talk to discuss my work and it came up."

Sure it did. I could just see Helen figuring that, with Eddie gone, she could wheedle her way into Charlotte's favor and get a decent job out of it. And I could see Charlotte, trying to disguise the fact that she had been left standing at the altar by telling people she hadn't wanted the engagement in the first place.

Helen and I were all the way to the reception area when she added in a low voice, "Eddie was suicidal, you know."

That stunned me. Had the police talked to Helen? "Where did you hear that?"

"Charlotte," she said over her shoulder. "And she should know. You coming?" Helen poked at the elevator button.

I shook my head. "Go ahead without me."

I went back to my bay and sat for a while, trying to get my thoughts focused. It looked as if Charlotte was the source of this suicide rumor the police had repeated to me. The Eddie I knew did have many problems. He was compulsive, impulsive, irresponsible. But suicidal?

As the old saying goes, you never know a man until you live with him, and Charlotte had lived with Eddie, however briefly. Was it possible he was up all hours, threatening to dive off her terrace or hang himself from a curtain rod? It didn't sound like the Eddie I knew. It sounded impossible. One more impossibility to add to all the other impossibilities.

I wished that Derek was there, for more than the obvious reasons. He always made such sense, except when he lied to me. I would love to have talked to him, use him as a sounding board for all these things I was thinking.

Pushing back my chair, I rolled into Eddie's windowed cubicle. How often had I done that in the last eight weeks? At least three or four times a day. Now I could have the window for myself, if I wanted it. I didn't.

I opened one of Eddie's drawers. It was packed with yellow lined tablets and graph papers, everything written on and stuffed in his drawer. The rabbit's-foot key chain lay on top of the stack. For somebody so neat about his appearance, he'd been a real slob about office housekeeping. Taking out the key chain, I tossed the keys in the air as Eddie had done so often. What keys were these, anyway? I didn't see anything like a car key on the chain. For no particular reason I dropped the keys into my purse. Pushing that drawer closed, I opened the one above it. A bottle clattered to the back of the drawer. Double Happiness Beer. I turned the bottle over in my hand. All Eddie had wanted was everything.

Outside, the little daylight left was fading to gray. The office around me was quiet. I'd stopped thinking of it as a workplace. Over eight weeks I'd been there. The irony of that almost made me smile. My probation was over! Twisting open the bottle, I took a long swallow, then leaned back in my chair, put my feet on the windowsill, and watched the lights of New York flickering on outside. When I closed my eyes, I saw Eddie just like this, feet up, admiring the view.

Forget it, as soon as you can, common sense told me. Forget Eddie, and Mr. Gartner, quit this ridiculous nonjob, and get on with your life. Or in the words of Eddie, "Don't sweat it."

By the time I came out of the subway station into the cold air a few blocks from my apartment, it was almost eight P.M. A light, wet snow was falling. I was hungry, distressed, my thoughts were jumbled, and I couldn't even think about cooking for myself.

A block away from my apartment is a street of small businesses—the bodega, of course, a Korean greengrocer, a dry cleaner, a pizza parlor where the neighborhood hoodlums hang out, and around the corner, a Chinese carryout.

I'd halfheartedly decided on pizza and was about to turn into the pizza carryout when, at the edge of my vision, I saw something that jolted me awake. Babyface, the Chinese hoodlum, crossed the street up ahead and turned the corner toward the Chinese carryout. What would that thug be doing back in my neighborhood with Eddie gone? We had our own thugs.

Rushing to the corner, I looked up the block. No

Babyface. It had been my imagination. This business with Eddie was destroying my nerves.

I had passed the pizza place and it was too cold and damp to backtrack. Ahead, the steamy windows of the Chinese carryout beaconed.

I was relieved to find myself the only customer in the place. Giving my order to the Chinese man who did the cooking, I sat down on one of the battered kitchen chairs in the front of the shop.

The big ceiling fan spun slowly over me. The massive griddle sizzled. The soft-drink machine in the corner hummed. Everything normal. I smiled at the cook when I realized he was watching me from the corner of his eye. He looked away quickly.

My order was finished in record time. The cook, this man who I'd spoken to at least once a week for several years, shoved it across the counter and backed off. His fingers fumbled when he made change.

"Good night," I said. The man nodded, speechless.

Once home, I fed Moses and spread my meal on the table. A carton of stir-fried beef and broccoli, a carton of rice, a couple of fortune cookies. Some wild Friday night, Bonnie.

I didn't have much of an appetite. I picked at the beef and broccoli, ignored the rice. Was it possible, even remotely possible, that Babyface was still hanging around my neighborhood? But why would he be watching me? What did he want? Unless he and his friends were still looking for Eddie. Which meant that Eddie was all right.

You're obsessed, Bonnie, I told myself. Your job is making you crazy. Think about something else. Think about Derek and what you're going to say when he calls Sunday night.

Moses squeezed himself onto my lap. Half-standing, he draped his front paws over the tabletop and started batting at the fortune cookies. I grabbed one and cracked it open.

"Do not trust your future to a dark-haired man," it read.

Wasn't that one right on target! Smiling, I gave Moses the pieces and cracked open the second cookie.

"It could be unhealthy to interfere in things that do not concern you."

I dropped the slip of paper as if it was on fire. This was not my imagination. Somebody had slipped me threatening fortune cookies.

I killed the first bottle of Maalox before I got to sleep that night.

CHAPTER 14
◆◆◆◆◆◆◆◆◆◆◆◆◆◆◆

I met my fate through housewifery.

I woke up early Saturday morning, reread Derek's letter, then daydreamed into my pillow for a good hour. It took a stern talking to and several cups of black coffee to energize myself enough to tackle the million projects I'd been neglecting. With a trip to Denmark on the horizon and a job hunt looming beyond that, best to get all the drudgery out of the way. There was washing and ironing to do. There was that overpriced red leather skirt to take back. Maybe the refund could go toward a new coat. And there was my resume. There was always my resume.

I never made it past my dirty clothes.

I keep them in a big duffel bag left over from my wild youth. Royal-blue canvas with the words BERKELEY CO-OP in faded white letters on its side.

It was tucked into a deep, narrow closet in the hallway between my bedroom and bath, shoved between the ironing board and my vacuum cleaner. The closet, needless to say, is not a place that gets much of my attention.

On hands and knees I first pulled out a couple pairs of tap shoes that were collecting dust on the closet floor. I'd tossed them in there when I'd gotten the job at C.F., vowing no more dancing. Wasn't it strange? The only vow I'd kept was the one I definitely should have ignored.

I dusted off one of the shoes until my out-of-kilter reflection glowed back at me through the black patent. Even at its worst, after rejections, after mediocre reviews, after paychecks that never materialized and shows that closed after one performance, dancing had never given me the problems that my mainstream jobs had.

Maybe I gave it up too soon, I mused. New shows are always opening. Maybe my time was about to come. Maybe I'd pick up that copy of *Variety*, just for the heck of it. Maybe forget about getting the resume offset and get some new headshots taken instead.

Maybe you're finally flipping out, Bonnie. How many successful tap dancers can you name? There's Gregory Hines, and without the occasional acting job, he wouldn't be a success either. No. It wasn't a wide-open field, like computers, and for a thirty-six-year-old woman with nothing to fall back on, it was no field at all.

Shoving the shoes back into the closet, I wrestled the duffel bag into the foyer. The miserable thing weighed a ton. Half my day would be spent in the basement laundry room.

I tugged open the drawstrings and began sorting: whites with the whites, darks with the darks. Three washers at least. I was at the bottom of the bag when my fingers scraped over a rough, unfamiliar surface. Now what was that? Some piece of dirty clothing neglected so long it had petrified? Grabbing it, I heaved it from the bag. As soon as it hit the light of day, I gasped. In my fist I was holding on to the corner of Eddie Fong's gym bag.

Oh, hell! I dropped it onto the floor, then sat among my heaps of laundry, staring at the miserable thing. Damn Eddie Fong wherever he was! However I tried to shut him out of my life, he kept seeping back in, spreading like a leaky spot in a ceiling.

I sat for ages, not even wanting to touch the bag. When I did, it was with the toe of my shoe. I nudged it until it sat upright on its bottom.

"Papers," Eddie had said with his street-hustler's voice. What kind of papers does a guy who's running from gangsters hide in a friend's laundry. "Papers." I remembered the effect that word had had on Sergeant O'Hagan and Captain Lee, how the two policemen's "What she doesn't know won't hurt her" looks had given me the feeling everybody knew something I didn't. Wouldn't they be surprised when they found out I had the papers.

Scooting over to the case, I grabbed it by the handle and pulled it onto my lap. The latch was nothing more than a small button, like one on a handbag, but there was a hole next to it for a key. If it was locked, did I dare force the thing open? Taking a deep breath, I pushed the button. The latch popped open easily. Leaning forward, I spread the bag at its hinges.

I was greeted by the sight of a terry-cloth towel. Wouldn't I be surprised if all I found was some smelly sneakers and a damp, sweaty T-shirt. I pulled out the towel and examined both sides of it. It was exactly what it looked like. A towel. The bag's next layer contained a thin, Chinese-language newspaper, neatly folded. Oh, brother! What had Eddie been thinking when he'd hidden this bunch of junk?

Again I reached into the bag. I didn't even get the paper completely out of it before that question was answered by the stacks of green. I tossed the newspaper aside.

Money! Stacks of green bills, gathered neatly in thick rubber bands. I gaped into the bag. God! I'd never seen so much money. Entranced, forgetting all about fingerprints and evidence, I pull one banded stack from the bag and slipped the band off. Bundles of smaller stacks fell all around my legs, a shower of money. How much? There was only one way to find out. Gathering the fallen bills, I started counting.

Twenty, forty, sixty, eighty . . . It took awhile. The small stacks each held a thousand dollars in mostly used twenties, except for one of them, which held $990. So the first bundle of money contained $9,990.

Nine thousand nine hundred and ninety dollars. That's a nice-size clump of money. Has a good heft to it. I looked back in the bag. There were three similar clumps wedged into it.

In a euphoric frenzy I turned the bag on its side and scooped money from it until stacks of banded green bills covered the floor between my legs. I thumbed through a few more stacks. In each of them except for the bottom bundle in each stack, the rumpled bills added up to a thousand dollars. Each of the bottom bundles fell a few dollars short. Not too much short, though. I was the ecstatic holder of almost forty thousand dollars.

For a moment or two all reason fled. Closing my eyes, I leaned back into the edge of the closet door and swayed back and forth. My imagination ran berserk. There were so many possibilities. With this much money I could walk out of my job and not worry about finding another one. I could pay off my charge cards, I could get a new coat, I could do almost anything I wanted.

Moses crawled onto my lap, scattering the money, oblivious to what he was walking on. He nuzzled my neck, asking for food. When he got no reaction, he climbed off. Soon there was a scraping sound. I opened my eyes. For Moses the gym bag was a combination scratching post/love object, something to nuzzle and claw. The money, for him, was no more interesting than a wadded-up piece of scrap paper.

I gazed at the bills again. How many people had I seen hurt by money in the last couple weeks? Mr. Gartner may have been killed for it. Amanda settled for it, cheating herself out of real affection. Derek lied to me about it, hurting both of us. Charlotte tried to buy Eddie with it, but only managed to make a fool of herself. And Eddie. Poor Eddie. His words came back to me: "There's no such thing as enough money, Bonnie." So where was Eddie now? Wherever he was, if he was alive, he was no doubt broke as usual.

There was a tightness growing in my chest. I couldn't kid myself. These stacks of "paper" on the floor around me were the reason the kids in the Trans Am had been looking for Eddie. It was stolen money. Not stolen from those kids, but from the people those kids worked for. The money had come out of that house on Forsyth Street under the Manhattan Bridge.

I pieced together what I recalled of the moment two weeks earlier when Eddie had walked out of that house. He'd been swinging a gym bag in his hand, but I'd been so occupied with getting out of there that I hadn't paid much attention. Scarface and Babyface had both watched Eddie put the bag in his car. The fact that Eddie had carried something from the house hadn't alarmed them, but they hadn't trusted him completely. He'd known that. "How's that for trust among friends?" he had said when the Trans Am followed us.

A dozen questions jumbled around in my mind. Several of them I knew the answers to. What went on in the Forsyth Street house? Gambling or loan sharking or extortion. Maybe all three. And what was it Eddie threw into the trunk of his car? The money from that illegal enterprise, hidden in a navy-blue gym bag. That explained why a police captain was so interested in Eddie's disappearance. But that's where my answers stopped. Was carrying that money something Eddie did regularly? Was he a "smurf"? Was this the same money, or was this another shipment of money? Who did he carry it to? Why did the Trans Am follow us that night? How did the hoodlums in the Trans Am know to look for Eddie not only in my neighborhood, but outside my apartment building, if Eddie had never told them who I was?

That last question brought me back to a frightening reality. That *had* been Babyface in my neighborhood the night before. It was no paranoid delusion. A Chinese warlord had sent one of his thugs to watch me. Babyface was probably still over there, still terrorizing the cook in the Chinese carryout. I continued staring at the money. It was looking less attractive by the second.

I couldn't keep it. I knew that. I reached around on the floor, gathering the stacks into a miniature money mountain. Every last one. I wouldn't even keep one out for myself. When they were all together, I pulled the case over and once again pried it open. I had put the first couple stacks of money back into it when I realized that this gym bag appeared deeper on the outside than it was inside. With the flat of my hand I pushed the bottom of the case. It gave under the pressure. There was something else down there.

The false bottom, made of a sheet of plastic-covered cardboard, came out easily. Secreted between it and the bottom of the case were, indeed, papers. Two papers, to be specific. Two folded, legal-size sheets of paper, stapled at their top.

They were written in Chinese. On the first page there was absolutely nothing, not one mark, that meant a thing to me. On the second, only one thing did: Charlotte Smoot's signature and a date next to it, July 14, 1981.

What was Charlotte Smoot involved in that Eddie would want to hide the evidence of in his gym bag? Were these papers the "leverage" he had been searching for when I caught him in Charlotte's desk?

And what, I finally asked myself, did any of this have to do with me? That was one question easily answered. Nothing.

I dressed quickly, in my warmest slacks, my new rose cashmere sweater, and lined boots. There was only one thing to be done here and it was obvious. All this—gym bag, money, and papers—had to go straight to Captain Lee.

I repacked the bag carelessly, but before I left my apartment I took the precaution of sliding it into a department-store shopping bag. If Babyface saw me on the street, he might not realize I had the money.

It was bitter icy cold outside. After weeks of unusually mild weather, winter had hit New York with full force. The snow from the night before had left the streets spotted with treacherous patches. When I came out of the subway at St.

Andrews Plaza, the thermometer on a nearby building read 9 degrees. With the windchill factor it had to be well below zero. I peeled the edge of my glove down and took a quick look at my watch. It was almost noon. With any luck this business would be done with by one P.M., then I could get back home and take care of my own life.

Putting on my glasses to protect my eyes from the wind and tightening my muffler around my face, I turned up Park Row.

Police Headquarters is several blocks south of Chinatown in a square red-brick building. The entrance is at the left of a wide, covered walkway. At the back of that walk a flight of steps leads to an open plaza where two orderly rows of trees stand like soldiers at attention.

I was almost at the entrance when Captain Lee came out the front of the building. It had to be Lee. There couldn't possibly be two overcoats that shade of green in Manhattan. Lee turned away from the street and quickly went up the steps to the plaza.

I called his name, "Captain Lee," but when he didn't turn, I realized that the sound of my voice had been lost in the wind. Stepping gingerly to avoid the ice, I hurried after him.

The captain moved quickly for a short man, taking long, loping steps. He seemed oblivious to the ice patches on the sidewalk. By the time I reached the top of the stairs, he was halfway across the plaza, heading diagonally toward the Court House.

When I'd been on jury duty, I'd spent several lunch hours in that plaza. Today it was too cold for sitting on benches. I figured Captain Lee was heading for one of the cafe's on the other side. I'd have to hurry to reach him before he disappeared from sight.

I was near the Court House when I saw Babyface again, coming from the direction of Chinatown. A black watch-cap was pulled over his ears and a red scarf tucked into the neck of his jacket. He was carrying a newspaper under his arm.

You're crazy, Bonnie, I told myself. It can't possibly be

Babyface. I squinted, straining to see. It *was* Babyface! In a panic I stepped into a doorway of one of the buildings that abuts the plaza and tried the door. Locked! I flattened myself against the building, hoping he would pass without noticing me.

I waited, scared. Any second now he was going to walk by. Any second he could take a look in that doorway and see his quarry cowering in it. If he did, I'd just thrust the bag at him. That was all. I wouldn't even try to get to Captain Lee. My heart was pounding. A few other pedestrians passed my door—a girl in a yellow coat, two black men carrying lunch pails. No Babyface. Finally I stuck my head out. Babyface had disappeared.

Stepping out of the doorway, I started back into the park. It was almost deserted and I had no trouble spotting Captain Lee's green-checked coat. He was in line at a Nathan's hot dog wagon in the middle of the square.

I hadn't gone more than a few steps when I saw Babyface. This time I was sure. He had taken a shortcut and was now just a couple feet beyond the hot dog vendor and Captain Lee, the folded newspaper under his arm. I took a few steps back until I was partially concealed by a tree.

When he came to a wooden bench on the police headquarters side of Nathan's, Babyface sat down on one end of it and opened the paper. Not half a minute later Captain Lee, hot dog in his hand, sat on the other end of the bench. A chill that had nothing to do with the weather gripped me.

Of all the empty benches in that park on a frigid Saturday, these two men chose the same one. There was something frightening and at the same time fascinating about watching them. Something was going to happen here.

Babyface read his paper. Captain Lee chewed his hot dog and stared at the gray sky. A minute passed. Then Babyface stretched his arms, folded his paper, and rose from the bench. With studied casualness he walked to the nearest trash basket, dropped the folded paper into it, and walked off in the direction he had come from.

I didn't have to wait long for the other half of this drama. Captain Lee was done with his hot dog. Wadding the napkin and paper bag into a ball, he got up and, from where he stood, made an overhanded high toss toward the trash basket. The hot dog wrapper missed by several feet. Lee retrieved the wrapper from the ground. Then, with deliberate care, he leaned over the basket to deposit it. When he straightened up, I had a clear view of him tucking the folded newspaper under his coat.

The horrible implications of what I'd witnessed hit me immediately. Reports of police corruption make the papers periodically. It's an insidious thing that knows no boundaries of rank or race. And I had just witnessed it at its pinnacle. A police captain taking a bribe from a gangster's thug.

When both men had disappeared, I walked up to the vendor's wagon and bought myself a hot dog.

"That man that was just here," I said as I spread mustard over the roll. "The guy in the green coat. He looks familiar. Does he come here very often?"

The vendor handed me my hot dog. "The Chinese guy? Yeah, couple times a week, I think. But you know how it is. They all look alike to me."

"Thanks."

I started walking down the street away from both Police Plaza and Chinatown, taking a bite of my hot dog on the way.

"Hey, lady," the vendor called. I turned around. He was pointing on the ground next to his stand. "You forgot your shopping bag."

Jesus! I'd almost walked off without the almost forty thousand dollars. Hurrying back, I picked it up.

"Thanks."

The vendor smiled. "Sure. You wouldn't want to forget your goodies, would you?"

It seemed at the time that I walked across most of lower Manhattan. That wasn't really the case. It was much too cold to walk very far, but by the time I settled down in the back booth of a coffee shop near my office, both my feet and my head ached.

Over coffee and a piece of apple pie I tried putting my problems into some order. Problem number one, I was carrying around a lot of money that some very rough people wanted. Problem number two, there was no one I could trust, including the police. Problem number three, my boss's disappearance had something to do with this money. Problem number . . . oh, God, there were too many of them. I finished the last bite of pie, then fished through my purse for money to pay my check. Would you believe it? I'd spent my last dollar at the hot dog stand.

For a second I had this awful embarrassed feeling. I'd have to talk the waitress into letting me go to a cash machine before I could pay my check. And then the absurdity of that hit me. I didn't need to go to a cash machine. I had almost forty thousand dollars.

Except for my brief euphoria earlier that day, which could probably be attributed to shock, I hadn't seriously considered keeping, much less spending, any of the money. Now, however, after what I'd just seen in the park, my attitude had swung to "What the hell!" The money no more belonged to the police than it did to me. And it certainly didn't belong to the gangsters. So whose money was it, anyway?

Taking a surreptitious look around the coffee shop, I dug a sneaky hand into the shopping bag, popped the latch on the gym bag, and pulled out one of the stacks of twenties. Peeling off the top bill, I stuck the rest of the stack into my handbag.

By the time I handed that twenty and the check to the cashier, my mind once again swam with possibilities. Forty thousand dollars. The things I could do with forty thousand dollars.

I took a cab to the store where Amanda and I had seen the baby-blue coat two weeks before. The fare was two dollars and forty cents. I gave the driver a five and told him to keep the change. Talk about out of control.

"You've made a wonderful choice," the blue-haired sales-lady gushed. "With your blue eyes, well . . ." She put one hand over her heart and sighed. There were no words to express how terrific I looked in this coat. Her other hand remained palm up next to the cash register.

I counted out twenties, thirty-seven of them, into it. Seven hundred and thirty-four dollars it came to, including tax. I'd never spent that much on an item of clothing in my life. I'd never even spent that much on an item of furniture in my life, either. In fact, there had been times in my life when I could have gotten along quite nicely for several months on seven hundred and thirty-four dollars.

"Enjoy it," she called after me. "And please come back."

"I will." I meant it. There was one sweater in a deep gold that was fantastic. And only $99.99! I walked into the after-noon smirking like an idiot. Seriously. Strangers passing on the street smiled back at me. Why shouldn't I smile? I felt great. I was going to pay my bills, I was going to resign Monday. I wouldn't even bother going in. I'd quit by phone. If I couldn't find anybody to resign to, I'd resign to the re-ceptionist. The hell with C.F. and its filthy tax shelters. The kind of money I had, I didn't need to worry about tax shel-ters.

I walked along in a daze, thrilled with myself, with life, hardly looking where I was going. I was going to take a taxi home even if it cost twenty dollars. What was twenty dollars to me?

At the corner I raised my arm in the air to hail a cab. I suppose I was blocking the crosswalk, because the next sec-ond I was jostled from behind. I glanced over my shoulder, straight into a young man's face. A young Chinese man. I couldn't help myself. I screeched. He drew back, startled. The light changed and he stepped around me, giving me a wide berth. Before disappearing into the sidewalk traffic, he turned back and gave me a puzzled look.

My heart was beating like mad. I leaned against the

bumper of a car trying to calm myself. This was horrible. What was I going to do? Jump out of my skin every time I saw an Oriental man? New York has a huge Oriental population.

There's only one direction from euphoria and that's down, and it took no more than a split second for me to get there. I couldn't keep this money. I was out of my mind to think I could, even for a moment. I might be able to handle my guilt, but if the gangsters didn't kill me, my own fear would.

I had to get rid of it. How, though? I wasn't about to toss thirty-nine-odd thousand into a Dumpster. I could give it to charity. But what charity? Should I walk into the Red Cross and give it to the first person I saw? I couldn't think straight. I should just hide the money somewhere until I decided how to get rid of it for good. But where, I wondered? Not my apartment. What I needed was a place where no one ever looked.

CHAPTER 15
◆◆◆◆◆◆◆◆◆◆◆◆◆◆◆

A phone was ringing when I stepped off the elevator into C.F.'s reception area. At the receptionist's desk I glanced at the switchboard. The red light on Morton Fike's extension blinked on and off. Why would anybody be calling him there on a Saturday? Unless he was expected. I'd better do my dirty work and get out.

Hurrying to my desk, I cleaned my bottom file drawer of Eddie's empty beer bottles. Then I shoved my shopping bag with its ill-gotten contents into the far back of the drawer. When that was done, I filled the front of the drawer with a couple stacks of ledger paper.

What high hopes I'd had for my cabinet when I started! I'd envisioned it filled with computer printouts and memos and correspondence with clients. Here it was nine weeks later and one drawer was jammed with Eddie's beer and the other with stolen money.

After locking the cabinet I took the precaution of taping the key onto one of the center pages of my software user manual. No chance of anyone ever disturbing it there.

Now for the empties. They would go back where they had come from.

Eddie's desk was just like I'd left it the evening before. My empty beer bottle was still on the windowsill. It seemed like so long ago, but it had been less than twenty-four hours.

I lined the rest of the empties up on the windowsill. Six of them, glowing amber in the afternoon light. What did it matter if Charlotte or Fike saw them now? It was too late for Charlotte to break their engagement or Fike to fire him.

Morton Fike. There was one crafty character. If C.F. was laundering money for a Chinatown gangster, which the crooked Captain Lee had suggested, did Fike have anything to do with it? He had a China-born wife, Linda, and a girlfriend, Amanda, who had been at C.F. when its accounts were set up. From what I had seen of Linda, though, she was not only respectable, but she was too smart to get involved in anything underhanded. As for Amanda, what kind of criminal would want her in his organization?

My thoughts kept returning to Charlotte. Charlotte and Eddie. What had the attraction been? What she saw in him was, in part, an elegance and grace she could never hope to achieve herself. That and her enchantment with the "Oriental sensibility" had fueled her passion. Eddie's side of it was harder. He had so much going for himself. Had he sold out for one lousy promotion in a company that had one foot in the grave and the other on a banana peel? I couldn't make myself believe that. Sliding into his chair, I turned on his terminal and logged into a word processing program. Then I started listing everything that seemed remotely connected with Eddie's disappearance.

First, that second week he'd been fascinated by the misplaced account for W.B. Ent. he'd found in the Ward Broadcasting file. That account had listed four deposits of just a little less than ten thousand dollars each paid to an offshore shelter the week before.

Second, when I'd later asked Eddie about that account, he'd said he had been mistaken about the address.

Third, when I'd checked out the address myself, I discovered that he hadn't been mistaken at all. W.B. Ent. stood for Woo Brothers Enterprises, owned by Herman and Kee Woo.

Fourth, Eddie was probably a "smurf," laundering money for an organization in Chinatown. But they didn't trust him and had their men follow him. But why did they bother with him at all if they didn't trust him?

Fifth, Eddie had been running scared. Why was he running? He wanted to work for that organization, so why cut out with their money?

Sixth, the one thing Eddie didn't want to do, despite assuring me otherwise, was marry Charlotte Smoot. So why was he doing it? Eddie could have found another job.

Seventh and eighth, Charlotte lied about being born in Hong Kong. Why lie about something like that? Charlotte also lied about Eddie being suicidal when there was convenient evidence that he had jumped off the George Washington Bridge.

Ninth—and when I realized what this one meant I got very excited—the first day I met Charlotte she was fondling a present from a grateful client, H.W. Was "H.W." Herman Woo of W.B. Ent.?

Tenth, what were the Chinese language papers in Eddie's gym bag with Charlotte's signature on them?

And eleventh, Eddie had become angry when I'd looked at

his work and had started keeping a secret file in his computer. "Name the secret file and collect a fortune," he had taunted.

I'd collected the fortune without naming the secret file. What would I collect if I found the file?

Storing my list, I typed in my password, "Moses." When the prompt appeared on the screen, I typed "Do pmt list."

Thankfully, this file was one of the few I was able to move around in. I found the W's with no problems, went straight to Ward Broadcasting, and followed their entries to the end. There was no W.B. Ent. listed now. I rolled back through the Ward entries. There was nothing to indicate that they did any business with C.F. other than leasing, no hint that anything went on in any of the tax havens. I exited the program.

The familiar c> prompt showed on the screen. "Do Eddie" I typed on a whim. "Invalid parameter" the screen read. I started to type "Do Amanda," but it was inconceivable Eddie would have named a file he was working on after Amanda. Charlotte, Exalted Keeper of the Data Base, would have killed him. "Do Charlotte" I typed. Again the screen showed an invalid parameter.

The late afternoon sun was shining hard through the window now. The beer bottles lined up on the windowsill cast an amber glow over Eddie's desk and up over the monitor.

Okay, I said to myself. This is the last shot. "Do Double Ha—" The computer refused to accept anything more. That's right; there was that twelve-character limit to file names. I thought for a second, then typed in "Do Happiness." For a second I thought I had it. Numbers and characters flashed across the screen. But then, at its bottom, there was another prompt command.

Eddie, give me a break. "Do Happiness" I typed a second time. That was it. Eddie had buried the file two layers down. The monitor now glowed with numbers. I was in Eddie's secret project.

There was no client name, no address. At the top left-hand corner of the file was a series of fourteen numbers. Beneath that were two columns. The first listed dates, beginning in September 1981. The second column was a list of dollar figures. The first entries, the ones in 1981 and 1982, were mostly in the low teens. I pushed the page-down button. The entries continued, growing larger. The last ones, at the bottom of the third page, were dated January 1988. There was an entry almost every week, and the amounts were now running from around $37,000 to $39,000.

I couldn't have filled in the details, but I was almost sure about what was going on. The satchel I'd just hidden had been intended for this offshore account. Eddie was a go-between—a "smurf"—between the gambling organization and C.F. He converted the money into some sort of negotiable paper, and then that paper was sent to the account on the screen. Where it went from there I had no idea, but I had a pretty good idea who at C.F. had set this up. Everything pointed to Charlotte.

How this related to Ashley Gartner's murder was still a mystery, but I was convinced it did. Had Gartner discovered his company was a conduit for dirty money? Had the criminal gotten to him before he or she was exposed? But that didn't work if Charlotte was the one doing the laundering. Hours before his death Mr. Gartner had had nothing but praise for her.

I decided to copy my note pages. Not that I had the vaguest idea what I'd do with the information, but you never know.

The central printer shared a room with the copy machine down the hall from the executive offices. As I walked into the room, the phone in Fike's office was ringing.

Hurrying, I printed out my information. Back at Eddie's desk I logged out of the program. Folding the four pages I'd printed, I tucked them into my user manual, rechecked the lock on my cabinet, and headed for the elevator.

Fike's extension on the receptionist's desk rang over and over as I paced impatiently, waiting for the elevator. Where was it, anyway? Finally I couldn't stand the ringing. I lifted the phone off the hook, planning to lay it unanswered on the desk, but it was no sooner in my hand when an anxiety-stricken voice cried on the other end:

"Morty, thank goodness! I'm scared to death."

It was Amanda, and what on earth was she talking about? "Amanda?"

There was a short pause, then "Who's this?" in a cautious tone.

"It's Bonnie."

"Bonnie? What are you doing in Mr. Fike's office?"

"I'm in the reception area, Amanda. I had to do some work in the data base."

"Oh. Have you seen Mr. Fike there?"

"No. I'm the only one here and I'm leaving now. Why?"

"I don't know what to do, Bonnie. I was supposed to meet Mr. Fike there. He wanted to give me some shorthand."

I almost hooted. Shorthand! In a roundabout way that was as good a synonym as any for a quickie.

"He must be late," I said. "What are you scared of?"

"The Chinese are after me."

The winter days were so short there hardly seemed to be any daytime at all. I stepped out of the subway station at 110th and Broadway into the dark. Barely five o'clock and the streetlights were already on.

I walked down Broadway one block to 109th, Amanda's street. There I turned left toward Amsterdam.

As funky streets go, it's not too bad. At least not to me. Maybe it's because parts of my neighborhood, Washington Heights, are so similar. At any time of the day or night the salsa music blaring through a window or from a passing car might threaten to deafen you. In the summer old men gather on tenement steps, drinking their beer from bottles in brown paper bags. Regardless of the time of year, or the time of day, garbage lines the gutters. And there is always the stripped car, looking like the skeleton of a Thanksgiving turkey a week after Thanksgiving.

Eddie had lied again! From more than a block away I knew that the classic Upper West Side brownstone I had burned with envy over, that last word in trendy elegance my imagination had constructed, was going to be a dump.

Getting from the corner of Broadway to Amanda's building's crumbling, unlighted front entrance was an exercise in courage. It was in the middle the block between Amsterdam and Columbus. Forty, even thirty blocks south, an apartment in the same block would have been a prize, an apartment, in Eddie's words, "to kill for." Up here, it was a place you could be killed trying to reach.

I walked along the wrong side of the street because the lighting was better. At the corner of 109th and Amsterdam I crossed to the south.

It was getting cold. Really cold. The moisture on the sidewalk was freezing solid, and the space between the corner and Amanda's building shone under the streetlights like a glacier.

My eyes were tearing so much I could hardly see ahead of me. As I waited for the light so I could cross Amsterdam, I pulled my scarf over my ears. A frigid blast of wind blew it back off my head.

I was in the middle of Amsterdam Avenue, crossing with the light, when a car pulled up at the crosswalk. I walked past it, not paying attention. All I wanted to do was push against the wind until I got to Amanda's building. I had reached the sidewalk when the engine roared. I glanced behind as I stepped on the curb, just in time to see the Trans Am's scooped-up rear end skid around the corner.

When you're that cold it's hard to think clearly, much less act. But the second that car double-parked at the curb and its doors flew open, I knew I was in trouble. I started running.

They were on me in no time. Two men in parkas, black caps, and red scarfs pulled over their faces. One of them grabbed my right arm and held it tight. The other one took

216

hold of the shopping bag with my new coat in it and yanked, hard. As he did, his scarf slipped off and I recognized Babyface.

Why I held on I don't know. I've lived in New York for a while. I know the rules. Give the creeps what they want and they'll go away. But I couldn't. This was my new coat. This was the only thing I'd decided to keep out of the money. It looked so good on me.

"Let go, you dumb broad!" Babyface said. I tried to scream. The guy holding my arm put his other hand over my mouth. There was a ripping noise as the handle on my shopping bag tore, and my arm was suddenly hanging free.

A half-second later the doors on the car slammed and it raced off, sliding up the icy street.

Every part of my body was shaking. I took two steps, lost my footing, and crashed to the sidewalk. My eyes filled with tears. Damn! Hell! Where had the police been? I looked around the street. Nobody had even noticed. I could have died right in the middle of that sidewalk and nobody would have cared. And my new coat was gone.

It was a Puerto Rican woman carrying a snowsuited baby who got me going again. She stood me up and brushed me off. "*Madre de Dios!* This city, you have to look over your shoulder every minute."

Madre de Dios was right. Mother of God. Those gangsters had taken my new coat.

If getting to Amanda's building from the subway stop was an exercise in courage, getting to her apartment from the building entrance was an exercise, period. She lived at the top of five steep, treacherous flights of stairs.

What a dump! The old wooden banisters along the stairwell swayed to the touch. The stairs themselves creaked and groaned and slanted off at peculiar angles. One dangling exposed light bulb, about twenty-five watts per floor, hung over each landing, giving just enough light to illuminate the graffiti-covered walls and the fact that the floors hadn't been mopped in fifty years. All that, combined with my shattered nerves and my aching bottom, made for quite a journey.

Amanda's metal door looked as if it had been used for target practice by the heavy artillery corps. There was no buzzer. I beat on the door with both fists: "Amanda!"

"It's all Eddie's fault," Amanda whined as she clanged around her minuscule kitchen fixing me a cup of coffee. "We should never forgive him. Either of us."

"Amanda, wherever Eddie is, I don't think our forgiveness is very important to him."

I was sitting in her one chair, a floor-level beanbag. Around me, everywhere, was Amanda's wardrobe. A heap of dresses across the bed, a jumble of shoes on the floor, slips and stockings spilling from the dresser, gold chains and strings of pearls draped over doorknobs.

Even cleaned up the apartment would have been a pretty dreary place to live, at least by my standards. And my standards aren't all that high. My own apartment is a long way from *Architectural Digest*. Amanda's was a plain mess.

If I leaned back in the beanbag, I could see where leaks had caused big dark rings on her ceiling. The plaster walls were cracked and diseased looking, as if something awful was growing on them. Her floorboards ran at a slant, so that no matter where I stood I felt as if I might slide downhill. At the end of the studio, metal grates crisscrossed the two narrow windows that looked out on an unbroken expanse of brick wall.

Oh, she had made some effort to make the place homey. On the windowsill a bedraggled pot of ivy struggled against all odds to catch the sun. A collection of stuffed animals shared the bed with Amanda's clothes.

"I don't spend much time here," she had offered when I staggered through her door.

She handed me my coffee in an eyeball cup and saucer. She was a bundle of nerves, alternately pacing and flopping down on her sagging mattress. Every few minutes she dialed the phone, no doubt trying to reach Morton Fike at the office. That she was doing all this in skintight black leather pants, an almost backless fuchsia sweater, and spike-heeled boots said plenty about the shorthand she planned to take from Morton Fike.

"Amanda, you said you were scared because the Chinese are after you. Which Chinese? How do you know?"

"A Chinese man with . . . with a big scar." She drew a line diagonally across her eye and lip, then shuddered. "He's hideous."

Scarface! I didn't blame her for being scared.

"I saw him looking at me on the subway yesterday after work. Creepy. He followed me off the train all the way here. When I went out to the grocery store last night, I saw him there. And when I started to leave today to go to the office, he was across the street near the phone booth. I got to the front of the building next door, and he started walking too. That's why I ran back here."

"Did you call the police?"

She sighed. Standing up again, she walked to her full-length mirror and struck a pose. "No. I'm tired of talking to the police. That's why I was trying to get Mo . . . Mr. Fike. He always knows what to do."

I'll bet he did. Rambo to the rescue.

I slumped farther into the chair. While Amanda strutted her stuff in front of the mirror, tossing her hair and thrusting a hip forward, I thought about what was going on. Much of it was still a mystery to me, but Scarface and Babyface were easy enough to figure out. They knew, somehow, that Eddie Fong was friendly with both Amanda and me. They either knew, or suspected, that on the night he took off with the money he might have come to either Amanda or me. So they were watching us. I had drawn Babyface; Amanda had Scarface.

That morning when I'd left my apartment, Babyface hadn't been there because he was meeting his police contact, Captain Lee, to pay a bribe. That was why I'd been able to get out of my apartment with the bag of money. But later he and his cohorts had spotted me on Amanda's block with a shopping bag and decided . . . what? Maybe that I was taking the money to her place to split it up? They'd grabbed my package and run with it.

Oh, boy! I must have blanched. Amanda looked at me through the mirror.

"What's wrong?"

"Amanda, those guys may be back. They're going to be pretty unhappy when they open that bag and find a coat."

She shrugged. "Serves them right. What do they expect to find in a Barney's bag? Money?"

Was she ever dumb! No matter how I twisted the situation around, there was no way I could associate Amanda with what was going on. A master criminal wouldn't trust her even as a dupe.

"Amanda, if I asked you a couple personal questions would you tell me the truth?"

She was back at the mirror. She turned sideways and studied her reflection.

"Sure. Except about . . . you know what."

"Don't worry. I'm not going to ask you about your special friend. What I want to know is, after the Christmas party, you left with Eddie. Right?"

She nodded.

"What did you do then?"

"We got a cab."

"And then?"

"Well, he dropped me here, then he took off in the cab."

"And you came up here and didn't go out again?"

"That's the same question Sergeant O'Hagan kept asking me. And I know why. It's because Hector told the police that Mr. Gartner had a woman in his apartment. But it wasn't me, Bonnie. It wasn't."

"You stayed home all night? Alone?"

"I stayed home all night, but I wasn't alone all night," she admitted. "The thing is, I'd had that fight with my friend. I was hoping he would call me."

"Did he?"

"Of course." She grinned happily. "Ten minutes after I walked in, he called from across the street."

So Amanda and Morton Fike had been together later that night. They were alibis for each other. But that didn't mean they weren't lying.

"What did you do the rest of that night?"

"Bonnie! Come on. You know what." She blushed furiously. I followed her glance to the bed.

The bed. It was mind-boggling what went on there. The thing was, with Morton Fike married this had to be where he and Amanda did what Fike had so aptly called hanky-panky. Did Fike, that pip-squeak Rambo, actually drag himself up five flights to do it under that mouldering ceiling with those cheap metal grates casting their crosshatched shadow over his antics?

Maybe I was getting weird about this. Two weeks ago I'd been staring at Charlotte's flowers and eyelet flourishes and wondering the same thing about her and Eddie. Maybe that's what happens when you don't have a love life of your own: You start speculating about everybody else's.

I sipped my coffee. "Does your friend stay here very often?"

"Sometimes." She tugged off the leather pants, then pulled the sweater over her head. She was wearing a little black teddy. Turning sideways to the mirror, she pressed her palms to her stomach. "He says it makes him feel like a bohemian. An artist, you know. Or a poet. Do you want to know what he said the other night?" She had this goofy look on her face now.

I nodded. "Sure."

"He said that my beauty is a joy forever, and that my loveliness only increases." She heaved a sigh. "Have you ever heard anything more beautiful?"

Morton Fike quoting Charlotte Smoot quoting John Keats. "Gorgeous, Amanda." I set the eyeball cup and saucer down on the floor.

"That's how he is. Poetic. Do you think I'm getting a stomach?"

If she was, I didn't see it. I shook my head. "How about Eddie?"

Amanda had pulled on a white wool dress. She straightened the shoulder pads, then twisted her back to look over her shoulder at the zipper.

"Eddie? He's not poetic at all. You know, Bonnie, he had the wrong idea about our relationship."

"What do you mean?"

"Well, I liked him and we had a lot of fun together, but he got this idea that I was serious about him."

"Did you tell Eddie about your special friend?"

"No!"

"Eddie visited you up here often?" I was getting past the bounds of idle curiosity, but she was willing enough to talk.

"When he was staying with Charlotte, he snuck up here a couple times to get away from her. How come?"

"I was wondering. The night he disappeared it was almost midnight when he left my apartment. Are you sure he didn't come here?"

She collapsed onto the edge of the bed and hugged a stuffed pink bunny in her arms.

"Positive. If he had, I wouldn't have let him in. You wouldn't believe the scene my friend and I had after he caught Eddie here earlier. Please don't mention any of this around the office."

"I won't tell anybody." That was an easy enough promise. Amanda was the only person left at the office I spoke to anymore. "Eddie got here first, right?"

She nodded, eyes wide with the memory. "Yes. He wasn't supposed to. He was coming over at ten, and we were going to go dancing. My special friend planned to stop by at nine to drop something off. You can't imagine how surprised I was when Eddie showed up at eight-thirty. I told him to go away until ten, but he wouldn't. He was . . . wild and nervous, talking crazy things."

222

"Like what?"

"He wanted me to run away with him. He said he had a lot of money. I didn't want to run away, Bonnie. I mean . . ." She swept her hands through the air, taking in the entire studio with her gesture. "This is my home."

"You told Eddie no?"

"Of course. I told him he should go back to Charlotte, but he said that was impossible. He still didn't want to leave. I was almost ready to tell him about my friend. Before I could, I heard my friend's key in my door." Amanda shook her head. "It was awful."

"What happened?"

"They just stared at each other for a minute. Then Eddie gave me this hateful look and said, 'Oh, I get it now.' Finally he left."

"What about your friend? Was he mad?"

She rolled her eyes. "He was furious that I was seeing somebody from the office. We had such a fight. When we made up, though, you know what he promised?"

"What?"

Her honey-colored eyes got so soft and trusting it was pitiful. "He's going to leave his wife, any day now."

"Amanda," I said as I hauled myself up from the beanbag chair, "Morton Fike is not going to leave his wife. Morton Fike is a pig. He's using you and he's using her, but she's got him because she's got money. Promise me you'll lock your door and not go out again until you hear from me. If you haven't heard from me in two hours, call the police in Brooklyn Heights and tell them something to get them to Charlotte Smoot's apartment. Tell them anything. Do you hear me? Amanda?"

She nodded slowly.

I left her sitting on her bed hugging her pink bunny, surrounded by her designer clothes, with her honey-brown eyes misting.

223

CHAPTER 16

◆◆◆◆◆◆◆◆◆◆◆◆◆◆

The night attendant in Charlotte Smoot's garage stared at my hand as I unclasped my purse. He was a hulking kid with lank, greasy hair, a rash of pimples over his chin, and a T-shirt with "Harley-Davidson" and a wild-eyed biker blasting across its front. He was also, lucky for me, or so I thought at the time, quite stupid.

His eyes widened as I dropped my roll of twenties casually on the desk between us. Opening my wallet, I flashed him my C.F. identification card. The kid's eyes grew into saucers when he looked at the big eye superimposed over my photo, and the words "Our Eyes on Your Security."

"Jeez! I never met a woman private eye. I mean, I never even met a private eye before. This is something. Wait till I tell my brother."

"Your brother?"

"Yeah. He's a cop."

A cop! Just what I needed. "We're prepared to pay for this information." I picked up what was left of the roll of twenties I'd stuck in my bag at the coffee shop, fondled it for a second, then peeled one off the top. I felt tough and dangerous, Sam Spade in rose cashmere.

The kid stretched out his hand. He had the dirtiest fingernails I'd ever seen, half-moons encrusted with black grime.

"Sure. I know Miss Smoot. She's the light green Cutlass four-door. I signed her out about an hour ago. I can tell you

224

the main thing about her. She don't give no Christmas tips. She wants her car when she wants it, and when it comes time for tips, she's gone."

I shook my head sympathetically. That wasn't precisely the kind of information I wanted, but at least he was willing to talk.

"I'm interested in one night in particular," I told him. "December seventeenth. It was the night of the first snow."

"Oh, yeah. I remember that night. Nobody was ready for that sucker. Cars skidding all over the place."

"What I'd like to find out is, did Miss Smoot take her car in or out late that night?"

The kid nodded thoughtfully. His eyes moved tentatively back to the bills in my hand. "That will take a few minutes. We log them all in and out, and we hang on to the logs for a couple months. But jeez—December seventeenth—I mean like, you know, that was a few weeks back."

I peeled off another twenty-dollar bill. The kid stood up. "I just gotta check through the file."

While the kid rummaged through an old gray cabinet, I kept my back to the door. Wouldn't it be something if Charlotte Smoot drove up and caught me bribing her parking attendant.

"Here we go," he said, sitting down at the desk with a handful of log sheets. "December seventeenth. Late, you said?"

"After eleven. In or out."

"Out, eleven twenty-five P.M. Back in, two-oh-five A.M." He got a kind of trancelike look, then nodded. "Yeah. I remember. Crazy."

"You remember?"

"Yeah. She goes out like a bat out of hell, skidding all the way up the driveway. Comes back the same way. I noticed because she's usually a real cautious driver."

"You think she might have been drunk?" Charlotte sure had seemed drunk when she left the Christmas party. Ac-

225

cording to Derek, though, she sobered up once he got her into the cold air.

The kid shrugged. "I don't know. If you'd asked me that a month ago, I would have told you flat out no. Smoot never struck me as a drinker."

"But now you're not sure?"

"The thing is, she's changed. She used to be a real conservative type, but now . . ." Again his glance took in the money. I put another twenty in his hand.

"About a month back she started living with this Chinese guy. According to the doorman, they were getting engaged. I met the guy. Eddie Fong. Kept a Toyota here. First thing that strikes me is, this Fong's a good-looking guy. You know, sharp dresser, good haircut. A lot of personality. Real hot car. The kind of guy you'd expect to be going out with beautiful women. And here he is, with Smoot. You ever seen her?"

I nodded.

The kid made a face. "A dog! I mean, the doorman says getting married's like going to jail, and getting married to Miss Smoot's gotta be like serving hard time. Attica!"

"Your doorman sounds like a scream."

The kid nodded eagerly. "He is. He's got a million stories. Anyhow," he continued, "according to the day attendant, the cops showed up here the other day looking for Eddie Fong's Toyota. It looks like he's split on Smoot."

"Wow!" I said. "Did the cops ask about Charlotte's coming and going on December seventeenth?"

"If they did, the day man didn't mention it to me."

"What about last month? Did they check on it then?"

The kid thought for a second, then shook his head. "Beats me. If they did, they didn't ask me."

It looked as if Charlotte had never been a suspect in Ashley Gartner's murder. She'd had the opportunity, though. She'd left the party long before Derek and I dropped Mr. Gartner off, and she'd taken her car out later that night.

Opportunity, however, isn't the same thing as motive,

much less proof. I was convinced Charlotte was involved in laundering money through C.F., but why would she kill Mr. Gartner?

Eddie's keys jangling around in the bottom of my purse were just too tempting. Chances were they were the keys to his aunt's apartment, but I was doing so well, why not keep going? I took a long, purposeful look out of the garage office. In the driveway outside, the leafless bushes were being whipped around by the wind.

"I'd like to get up to the lobby. Is there an inside staircase so I don't have to go out right now?"

"Sure. You going to talk to the doorman?"

I nodded.

"Good," the kid said. "He can tell you everything that's ever gone on in this building. Like I said, a thousand stories."

Moments later I opened the door into the rear of Charlotte's lobby and edged around the row of plants, aware that the doorman could see me if he happened to look up and back. Luck was still with me. The elevator was just arriving at the lobby floor. Two couples and a child stepped out of it. They made a lot of commotion, and when they reached the building's street door, the doorman left his post to open it for them. I stepped into the waiting elevator like I belonged there and pressed the button.

On 12, the elevator doors closed behind me and the car glided up. At Charlotte's door I pushed the buzzer just in case the kid in the garage was wrong. There was no answer, not that I had a ready excuse for being there if there was. When I pressed my ear to the door, the apartment on the other side was quiet.

I went for the most likely key first, a big round-topped one that looked like a door key. I tried it one way and then the other. Either way, it didn't fit. Behind me the elevator slipped past on its way down. My fingers began growing damp, slipping on the key. I tried the next-larger one. It slid into the lock without much effort.

Somewhere a door opened and closed. I was really nervous now. My fingers were so wet I could hardly turn the key. I twisted hard. Nothing happened. I tried pulling on the key to readjust it in the hole. It wouldn't budge. The damned thing was jammed into the lock.

My hands were sliding so badly I couldn't get a decent grasp. They started shaking too. I pulled and yanked, my panic growing by the second. I was so wrapped up in getting the key out of Charlotte's lock that I never noticed the elevator car coming to a stop down the hall until it was too late.

The doors had already opened when I turned. Charlotte Smoot was standing in front of them, her lips clenched. My lucky streak had ended.

I started backing away from her door. Maybe I could run for the roof. Charlotte's eyes slid to the keys and the rabbit's foot dangling from her lock. By the time she looked back at me, she was already reaching into her bag.

"The keys to Eddie's aunt's apartment are not likely to fit into my door," she said softly.

I was ready to scream for help when I saw the silver-colored pistol she had pulled from her purse pointing straight at me. "One sound," she hissed, "and you're dead. And don't think for a second that I won't shoot. All I have to say is I caught you breaking in and you threatened me."

With her free hand Charlotte reached for the keys swinging from her lock. Grabbing the one I'd jammed in, she gave it a vicious yank and pulled it loose. She glared at the rabbit's foot dangling from them.

"Filthy thing!"

She pulled another set of keys from her bag, opened her door, and stood aside.

"Get in there."

I had gotten as far as Charlotte's foyer when I heard one of her neighbors' doors open down the hall.

"Good evening," a woman said.

"Hello," called Charlotte over her shoulder. I took a chance and tried pushing past her back into the hall. The shove Charlotte gave me in the middle of my back sent me reeling ahead. The Oriental hall runner in her hall slipped under my feet and I stumbled forward, unable to stop myself. For a split second there was a searing pain on the side of my head. I remember falling, and my shoulder ramming something hard. Glass shattered around me. After that everything went black.

I have no idea how long I was out. As I slipped in and out of consciousness, bits of conversation drifted past me. A phone ringing, and Charlotte saying, "No, no. Dropped a large vase. Everything's fine." It must have been a long time, for as I slowly woke, I realized that Charlotte and I weren't alone in the room.

". . . wants her alive for now," a man said. His voice was strange, an echo, booming and fading.

Something rough was pressing against my face, scraping my skin. I opened my eyes and colors swam before me—pink and pale blue. I was facedown on Charlotte's Oriental living room rug. I shifted my head to the side. Pieces of broken glass were everywhere. Somewhere near me was a sound like a woman crying.

Another man's voice, this one heavily accented, said, "She's awake."

The same voice barked something in Chinese. I was pulled to my feet and shoved into one of Charlotte's velvet-covered Queen Anne chairs. A pair of hands remained on my shoulders. Looking back, I tried to focus. When I did, I saw to my horror that the hands belonged to Scarface. In one, he held a black gun. It was only inches from my neck.

My head throbbed terribly, but the crying wasn't from me. Charlotte gradually came into focus across the room. She was sitting sideways on the settee, staring down at her Ming goddess. The statue lay in several pieces across the cushion next to her.

"It was priceless," she sobbed when I looked at her. "Absolutely priceless."

Turning my head slowly, I looked around the room. The black lacquer curio cabinet was on its side, the glass shattered. That's what I had hit on my way down. The little wooden acolyte—the Ken doll—was near it on the hardwood floor. It seemed to be in one piece.

Propped against the wall, impassively surveying all the destruction, was my shadow, Babyface.

"We've got to get her back to the house." He was speaking to Scarface behind me. "I can handle her. You can stay and help Miss Smoot."

"You crazy?" answered Scarface. "This one get away, he'll kill us all. We go to the club together." He shoved the back of my head. "Up!"

My legs gave and my stomach lurched when I tried to stand.

"I have to go to the bathroom," I said.

The three of them exchanged looks. Finally Charlotte wiped her eyes with a tissue. "I'll go with her."

Charlotte stood outside the bathroom's open door, her round face registering disgust as I abused her luxurious facilities. When the worst of it was over, I washed my face and rinsed my mouth. She handed me a fluffy yellow towel with a flower appliqué that matched her wallpaper.

"Try not to stain it."

I felt well enough by then to wish my nose would start bleeding all over it. I also felt well enough to realize that I didn't want to go wherever it was they wanted to take me. If I could stall long enough, Amanda would call the police. As I rubbed my face with the towel I glanced at my watch. My lovely present from Derek. It was close to nine-thirty P.M. I'd left Amanda's at a little after six. Surely she should have made the call by now.

"I know you killed Mr. Gartner. Did you kill Eddie, too?"

Charlotte's chin shuddered as if she was going to cry again. "Of course not," she whispered. "I loved Edwin. He called me the night he disappeared. I told him I was willing to forgive him, but he never got here."

230

I handed the towel to her. "Why did you kill Mr. Gartner, anyway? He liked you."

She gave me a brief frown. "You're guessing, but where you're going, it's not going to matter. Ashley wanted to merge us with a bank that has rigid requirements about reporting cash transactions. That would have ruined a partnership of mine."

"The one with W.B. Ent.?"

Charlotte's shoulders stiffened. "My God! Edwin really couldn't keep his mouth shut, could he? I suppose it's just as well he's gone."

One of the men called in Chinese from the living room.

"Let's go," Charlotte said. "We're wasting time."

Charlotte's coat was thrown over a chair by the spilled curio cabinet. As she stepped over the glass-splattered rug to retrieve it, her glance fell on the little acolyte. For a brief moment her eyes clouded. It looked as if she intended to reach down and pick up the figure, but then her gaze swung around to meet mine.

"I should never have trusted him, but I can't say I wasn't warned."

Her size nine boot came down hard on the wood figure. The acolyte's head shot from under her foot and careened into the corner. When she lifted her boot, the body was in slivers under it.

She snatched her fur coat off the chair.

They couldn't tie my hands for fear someone on the elevator would see, so we went down the elevator to the basement garage in a tight little knot, one of the men on each side of me, Charlotte behind. I was too woozy to put up a fight, and sure the two guns I'd seen were both pointed straight at me. I knew one thing for sure. The only reason I wasn't already dead was that these people suspected I knew where the money and papers were. If I told them, I'd be killed immediately. If I didn't, what would they do? Even if they believed me, they'd still kill me. I knew too much now. And if they didn't believe me—what would they do to me to find out?

I'm not a complete coward. I can give blood or go to the dentist without first loading up on tranquilizers. But even in my groggy state I knew that I wouldn't be able to deal with anything these people did to me. I had to risk it and try to get away, even if I got shot in the process.

I would cry for help to the first person I saw. Or make a break and run. If they shot me—well, you don't always die from being shot.

The elevator doors slid open on the garage level. It was Saturday night. Surely there would be someone there, getting into or out of a car. I looked around desperately. The big garage was deserted.

Our feet clanked across the concrete floor, echoing through the cavernous space as they hustled me past the rows of cars until we reached Charlotte's green Cutlass.

"Your car's out front?" she asked Scarface.

He nodded.

"I'll drive," Charlotte said. "One of you get in the back with her, the other one picks up your car once we're out of here."

I took a surreptitious look at Charlotte's car. No matter where they put me, I was going to be next to a door. The garage attendant knew me. If there was some way I could signal him, maybe he would he realize I was in trouble. Would he remember my name? If he did, would he have the sense to call his brother, the policeman? Every policeman in the city couldn't be on this gangster's payroll.

They were one step ahead of me. Scarface suddenly grabbed both my wrists behind my back and said something in Chinese to Babyface. The next moment my hands were bound tight behind me with Babyface's belt. Charlotte had opened the back door.

"Down there," she ordered, pointing to the floor behind the front seat. I knelt and fell forward onto the rubber mat. In the distance a car's tires squealed. "Get in fast, both of you," Charlotte ordered. "Throw this over her. Try to keep it clean!"

Charlotte the executive was back in charge.

The next moment I was in the dark, covered by a warm weight. Charlotte's fur coat, so heavy and hot and perfumed that I started to choke. In a panic for air I tried to rise to my knees. Rough hands pushed me back to the floor.

"Cool it, chick," Babyface said from the seat above. "You'll be out soon enough."

The idea struck Scarface as funny. He laughed from the front seat.

The engine started. "Put something in her mouth," Charlotte said as the car began rolling. "We don't want her making any noise when we pass the attendant. Use your glove."

A small pocket of air and light reached me. Babyface had lifted the corner of the coat. The next second a wool glove was scratching over my lips. I clenched my teeth together. He tried to grab my nose, but I managed to get the fleshy part of his palm between my teeth. I bit down hard.

"God damn!"

The car jerked to a stop and rocked back and forth.

"If you can't keep her quiet, hit her over the head," Charlotte said.

There was a snap, and then the point of a knife pressed directly under my eye. The razor-sharp steel gleamed so close to my pupil that it blurred. An involuntary, terrified gasp escaped me. The glove was jammed into my open mouth. Then the coat covered me again and I felt two feet in the middle of my back, pressing me to the floor.

We left the garage without incident. A second later the car stopped on the street and the passenger door opened and closed. That meant Scarface had gone for the other car. Now there were only the two: Charlotte driving, Babyface in the backseat with me.

"Hey, you know," he said, "maybe you should stop and call Mr. Woo to let him know we're coming."

233

I couldn't tell what Charlotte was thinking about this, but one thing hit me: For the second time Babyface was trying to get me alone. What did he want? That long, sharp knife was terrifying. Was he a sadist? Did he want privacy to carve me up?

"Nobody's getting out now," Charlotte answered.

The car hit a pothole and bounced, slamming my head against the floormat. I groaned, not so much from pain as from my growing terror. Again cool air rushed across my face. Babyface had pulled part of the coat back. I couldn't believe what happened next. He patted my shoulder with his free hand as if to calm me, then he dragged Charlotte's fur coat around so that my head rested on it. The last of my control and resolution gave way to my growing terror. I spent the rest of our trip weeping.

CHAPTER 17
◆◆◆◆◆◆◆◆◆◆◆◆◆◆

We weren't in the car long. The tires rolled over the open grating of a bridge. Shortly after that, there was the stop-and-go of heavy traffic. Traffic thinned for a few minutes, then the car lurched as if we were crossing some raised barrier. We stopped a second later.

"Give me my coat, then go in and make sure the way is clear." That was Charlotte. Babyface lifted the coat off me, then the door nearest me opened. I knew, immediately, that we were at that house in the shadow of the Manhattan Bridge. Above us traffic noise roared.

"We should blindfold her," Babyface said.

"I doubt if that's necessary, but go ahead." Charlotte answered. "Here's my scarf."

The scarf was wrapped tight around my head, covering my eyes. The car door slammed shut.

"You can get up," Charlotte snapped.

I crawled onto the seat.

"Don't try anything," Charlotte said. "I have a pistol pointed straight at you, and two of Mr. Woo's boys are standing right outside."

Considering that I was bound, gagged, blindfolded, and terrified, there wasn't much I could try.

Charlotte sighed. "All this time I thought it was that other tramp. You never seemed like Eddie's type."

"I'm not," I tried shouting. The gag soaked up my words. I shook my head no. That made it hurt even more than it already did. I rested my head on the back of the seat until there was a knock on the car window. Charlotte lifted the lock and opened the door.

"He says we should put her downstairs for now," a heavily accented voice said. "You should go in the front and meet him upstairs in the office. He'll be awhile."

The car's back door had opened by now. Somebody—I assume it was Babyface—pulled me off the seat by my shoulders and stood me upright. Here was a chance. If I could throw him off balance, I could start running. I couldn't see where I was going, but at least my legs weren't tied. I slammed into him, hard.

"Shit, she's fainted," Babyface said, catching me from behind.

Another man said something in Chinese and grabbed me around the waist.

"I'll wake her up," Charlotte said. Two quick slaps stung my cheeks. I jerked my head upright. Tears of anger and fear flooded my eyes and soaked into the blindfold.

Babyface and another man pushed me toward the side of the house. I had been able to pick up some light through the scarf around my eyes, but suddenly that ended. We had moved into a darker place. It must have been narrow because we were walking single file, one man in front of me, another behind. I stumbled forward several paces.

A few feet in front of me I made out the sound of a padlock clicking, low on the ground. Hinges squeaked. Babyface pushed me forward. I'd gone less than a yard when the ground gave way from under me. Stumbling, I made a terror-filled noise through the glove in my mouth.

"Watch it," Babyface snapped. "Step down here."

The other man had opened a cellar bulkhead. I counted eight narrow steps as I half-tumbled down them. When Babyface and I reached the bottom, one of the other men followed. The hinges creaked again as the door slammed shut.

We were in a cold basement room. Babyface still had my arm in both his hands. I heard the other man, who was several feet ahead of us, pull on a chain to light an overhead bulb. Once more, light reached me through the blindfold. Then Babyface pulled me across the floor to a wooden beam that seemed to run between the basement and the first floor of the house. A rope was produced from somewhere and my hands, which were still bound behind me by the belt, were lashed to the beam. The second man tested the gag in my mouth and tightened the band around my head. A moment later, after another pull on the chain, I was in darkness.

I listened carefully to the men's footsteps. They walked several paces, then climbed what sounded like a flight of wooden steps. There was a brief, dim second of light and voices, then I was alone. Toppling forward as far as my bounds would allow, I fainted, this time for real.

I woke feeling warmth on my face. It was a light, so bright my eyes watered through the blindfold. I was still bound and tied to the pole, but the hated gag had been removed.

"You're awake now, my dear?"

The voice was soft and comforting, the voice of an older man. He had a beautifully modulated English accent. I tried to speak, to ask him for help, but my tongue was so dry I couldn't get it to work properly. I nodded.

"Here. Drink this," the kind voice said. A paper cup was held to my lips. I drank greedily.

"Now, I'm going to ask you a few questions, and if you give me the right answers, you can go. What is your connection with Eddie Fong?"

No. This wasn't a friend. A friend would have cut me loose. I struggled for an answer. Finally—"Eddie's my boss."

"And has Eddie ever been to your home?"

I shook my head. "No." Clearing my throat, I added, "I've only known him a few weeks."

"Ah. And when was the last time you saw him?"

"The first of the week. At work. I don't know." I had to pause. There was something going on in back of me. Someone was breathing inches from my ear. "I can't think straight."

"That's all right, my dear. Take your time. How did you happen to get hold of Eddie's keys?"

"They were in his desk. I wanted to move to his window cubicle."

"She's lying." Charlotte Smoot's voice, from somewhere behind me.

"Please, Charlotte!" the man said. "My dear. We seem to have an article of clothing that belongs to you. The receipt in the bag indicates you paid over seven hundred dollars in cash for it earlier today. Where did you get that much cash?"

"It was a Christmas present from my parents."

The man made a clucking sound with his tongue. The bright light clicked off. "Charlotte, we must go back upstairs and have a long talk about all this."

I was right. Someone had been behind me all this while. Grabbing my head, he shoved the gag back into my mouth and replaced the scarf. I raised myself to my feet, trying to scream.

"Please try to be patient, my dear," the man said. "I have

many guests this evening. I wouldn't want them disturbed. When they've gone, we'll be back for you."

When they had gone up the cellar steps and through the door, I gave in completely to my terror. For a few minutes, I don't know how many, I jerked and twisted violently, trying to pull my hands free by sheer force. I slammed my shoulder into the support beam. With my boots I throttled it until it vibrated. I worked my tongue against my rough gag. My banshee howls came out as pitiful little squeals. When nothing worked, my knees let go and I slid down the beam, panting and sobbing at the same time.

They were going to kill me. Charlotte and that old man. That had to be Mr. Woo. As soon as they found out what they wanted to know about the money and the papers, they were going to kill me.

Fear is exhausting. Or maybe it was my fear combined with the whack on my head. Closing my eyes, I leaned against the pole. Every part of my body ached. My legs against the damp concrete floor, my arms and shoulders from the strain, my head. And now the pain in my wrists was growing acute.

If only I could relax. I couldn't. Not mentally. But I started doing this exercise I'd used when I was a dancer. Sometimes when it was almost time for our cues and I knew I was going to have to go out on the stage and do something I wasn't sure I could do, I'd start relaxing my body at my toes and work up to my head.

My toes are going to relax, I said to myself. I wiggled them for a second. I rotated my ankles, then thumped my calves against the floor, all the while telling my limbs to relax. I worked my way up to my shoulders, turning my head one way and then the other. Relax. Down my arms I went, loosening my elbows, wriggling my fingers. The pain in my wrists was worse now. What if that man had tightened the belt so much it was going to cut off the circulation? My fingertips were throbbing. Relax, I said, trying to stop my panic before it got the best of me again.

Pressing my hands together, I tried massaging them, one with the other by sliding my fingers under the belt. For a moment both hands throbbed painfully as blood rushed into them. I knew what was happening. Babyface's belt worked not with a buckle but with a roller that reacted to pressure, like the brass fasteners on military belts. Pull on it and it locked into place. Relax the pressure and it loosened.

I stretched my hands against the webbing. The latch caught but seemed just a bit looser. Again I relaxed the pressure and then tightened it. And again. With each try the belt loosened. Not by much, but enough so that after a few minutes I could move my wrists easily.

The feeling was coming back to my hands now. Just a little more, I told myself. Finally, one squeeze of my wrists and the belt hung slack around my fingers. Slipping my hands free, I rubbed them roughly. Then I yanked the tight band off my head, ripped out the hated gag, and gripping the support beam, pulled myself to my feet.

I've never before tried moving in such total darkness. That chain from the light was somewhere close. Feeling carefully in front of me, sliding my feet to keep from tripping, I stretched my hands up and waved blindly through the dark. No chain. I had miscalculated.

I took several steps, becoming more and more disoriented. At last a string brushed across my wrist. Grabbing it, I yanked. A dim light cast the space around me into gray shadows.

I was in a stone cellar, cold as a tomb. At the back of it was a steep wood stairway, the one Babyface and the other man had taken. For me, that offered no way out. I quickly moved to the nearest wall. In the half-dark it took me a moment to find a window. It had been sealed shut with a square of heavy wire mesh. Squeezing my fingers under the mesh, I tugged hard. The mesh didn't budge.

Now what? I covered the rest of the cellar fast. In back, next to the wooden stairs, were three trestle tables, each of them bare except for a strange mechanical device about two feet long by ten inches high. I examined one closely. It had a bin and slot on top, a digital-type reader, and another slot on the side. The slots were a little larger than a dollar bill. Money counting machines, I was willing to bet.

Interesting, but contemplating them wasn't getting me out of there. I eyed the bulkhead across the cellar. The man who had unlocked it from the outside had preceded me down the steps without relocking it. Maybe that padlock was still loose.

Crossing the cellar, I climbed two of the concrete steps and then reached my arms above me and felt the slanted iron door. Taking one more step up, I pressed my arms against it. It held fast. I stepped up twice more, then bent double and pushed against the door with my back. Its hinges gave, but the door held. Someone had locked it on the outside.

I was still on the steps when I heard footsteps overhead. Somebody was outside at the door. There was the click of a lock. Taking a deep breath, I flattened myself against the wall. The hinges creaked and the door opened a few inches.

A long thin triangle of light sliced the basement stairs and shone on the concrete floor to the pole where I'd been tied. On the other side of the door someone breathed softly.

"Miss Indermill?"

Babyface's voice, at a whisper. An instant later the flashlight caught me huddled against the wall. Then the light went out. The door opened wider.

"Come on," Babyface said softly. "Move!"

What was he doing? Could I trust him? I glanced back into the dank cellar. I couldn't afford not to. Rushing up the steps, I looked past him down the dark passage to the street. Standing back, Babyface motioned in the other direction.

"Cut through the alley. Go straight to Captain Lee." Turning, he disappeared toward the front of the house.

I ran until my breaths came in short gasps and my heart pounded so hard it hurt. Through the quiet gloom of the alley, onto Henry Street. There I headed north. There would be enough pedestrian traffic on Canal for me to disappear into it.

I was at the intersection of Rutgers Street a block from Canal when the Trans Am roared up beside me. I started to run the other way. The car slammed into reverse and the passenger door swung open.

"Get in the car, Miss Indermill," Babyface shouted. "I was spotted letting you go. I'm a Treasury agent."

I stepped forward, then hesitated. How could I believe him?

"I'm a Treasury agent," he repeated. "Undercover. I don't have any ID."

Tires squealed down the street. Looking back, I saw Charlotte Smoot's green Cutlass rounding the corner on two wheels.

"Hurry!" Babyface yelled.

I made a split-second decision. He had put Charlotte's coat under my head and let me out of the cellar. I jumped into the Trans Am next to him. We lost the Cutlass a few minutes later when we turned down Bowery toward Police Head-quarters.

CHAPTER 18

◆◆◆◆◆◆◆◆◆◆◆◆◆◆◆

Simultaneous raids on several houses in lower Manhattan, carried out within minutes of the time I got into the Trans Am, closed down the Woo brothers' organization. Or at least caused the organization to make significant changes.

The raids netted, in addition to my blue coat—all I gained from this nightmare—a large amount of cash and the money-counting machines, a cache of firearms, numerous ledgers listing cash turned over to various "smurfs," including Eddie, for laundering, and the numbers of several annuity policies by which dirty money transferred to offshore havens was eventually routed back to the organization.

The raid on the house under the Manhattan Bridge did not net Mr. Woo or Scarface, who slipped past the Treasury agents and disappeared into the night. It did net a hysterical Charlotte Smoot.

Charlotte first told the agents that she was a guest at the house and not connected with the organization in any way. When confronted with the list of deposits I'd gotten out of the computer earlier that day, and those two pages from Eddie's gym bag, she broke down.

While unwilling to admit that her father had dealt in blackmarket goods, Charlotte's earliest memories included her father's friends, the wealthy and charming young Woo brothers, who had extensive connections in the U.S. Years later, when she needed money to buy into Creative Financial, Charlotte looked up Herman Woo.

Translated, the pages in Eddie's gym bag turned out to be an agreement between the Woo brothers and Charlotte. They had made her an interest-free loan of a significant amount in exchange for her expertise, and C.F.'s facilities, in channeling some of their money out of the country. As far as anyone at C.F. knew, W.B. Ent. was a respectable tour office on Bowery Street.

That is, until two things came along to threaten the organization.

First was Gartner's plan to merge with a bank. As Charlotte admitted to me and later to the police, that was what got him killed. Between the waning effect of the liquor, Eddie's rejection, and worry over the possible merger, she was in a frenzy by the time she got home from the Christmas party. Driving to Gartner's apartment, she had tried to convince him not to pursue negotiations with the bank. He refused to reconsider, and she left. Too upset to drive then, Charlotte was sitting in her car trying to pull herself together when Gartner carried an envelope from his house and walked to the corner mailbox. When he returned, she was waiting. She tried to bring the subject up again, but Gartner enraged her by suggesting she had had too much to drink and turning his back to climb his steps. Charlotte picked up the flowerpot and brought it down on his head.

The second kink in the Woo/Smoot network was, of course, Eddie Fong. Having spotted that misfiled entry, he courted Charlotte shamelessly, and Charlotte, with her passion for the Oriental mystique and her desperate need for affection, allowed him into what had been, until then, a quietly successful enterprise. But Eddie just couldn't toe the line.

It was the Treasury agent who told me a lot of this. I feel foolish calling him Babyface, but I can't use his real name. Babyface said that he had been undercover in the organization for about four months, trying to pin down the ways the money was leaving the country, when Eddie showed up on the scene. He knew Mr. Woo didn't trust Eddie and had warned Charlotte about her new lover. But Charlotte—what could she do? She was in love.

About Eddie, nobody was sure. Babyface told me the guys in the Trans Am had spotted Eddie on the street when he left my house that night. He'd taken off running and they lost him. What I think is that Eddie realized that even Charlotte's influence with Mr. Woo wasn't going to get him out of this. You don't steal from organizations like the Woo brothers' and get away with it.

Over the next few days a little information filtered down to me. Sergeant O'Hagan called to tell me that in the middle of that same night that Eddie disappeared, a cabbie in Fort Lee, New Jersey, took a young Chinese guy to Newark Airport.

"A stewardess on a red-eye flight to L.A. remembers flirting with a Chinese guy," O'Hagan grumbled. "She thought he was cute."

"Did you check the passenger list?" I asked.

"Check the passenger list? Sure. No Edwin Fong listed, but you never can tell with a guy like Fong, can you?"

"That's right," I said. "You never can."

Flight to Copenhagen

What do I know about Denmark? Not much. I know about Derek, of course. Not all about him, but I'm going to listen this time. I know about the famous jazz clubs, Hans Christian Andersen's Little Mermaid, the peat bogs, about how King Christian X defied Germany in 1943 and was arrested for it. I know that Tivoli, the famous amusement park, was laid out by an architect who thought that if people were allowed to amuse themselves they would forget to talk politics. I know enough to know I'm going to enjoy this trip.

I resigned to Morton Fike when I went in to clean out my desk. I discovered him huddled over a printout with an obviously enthralled Helen Pilgrim. She was eating up his every syllable. He'll probably make her a manager. If there's ever been a "can do" type, it's Helen.

And Amanda? After my great escape, when I called to tell her she could unlock her apartment door, she told me that what I'd said about Fike had upset her so she'd taken a Valium and fallen promptly asleep. That's why the police never showed up at Charlotte's apartment. Amanda should have stuck with Eddie. What a pair they would have made.

Speaking of Eddie—though I don't know if I should—I got this postcard in the mail yesterday. It's from Manila, a picture of a crowded, neon-lit street at night. Just left of center, in amber letters, is a sign flashing an ad for Double Happiness Beer. On the other side, where there should be a note and signature, there are just seven words: "You're a doll. I owe you one."

400